THE DEATH
OF
THE MANNIKIN

Art Weldy

   www.trafford.com

North America & international
toll-free: 1 888 232 4444 (USA & Canada)
phone: 250 383 6864 ♦ fax: 812 355 4082

Contents

PROLOGUE:
TO "THE DEATH OF A MANNIKIN"

This little book is a gift to my daughter, Susan. If no one else reads it, she will, and will smile at familiar references to one of our favorite places – Atlantic City – and to members of our family who visited and frolicked there for well over a hundred years. Her great grandfather who worked for the "Pennsy" went down to the Shore frequently as early as the 1890's to visit New Jersey relatives. His daughters—Susan's grandmother and great aunt— were professional singers on Radio Station KDKA besides doing secretarial work in Pittsburgh on the side. They began going to Atlantic City in the 1920's — its golden age — and continued to come through the '90's. As a twenty-three year old in the summer of 1928, Susan's grandfather played at the classic Boardwalk Dennis Hotel in an orchestra which included the young Dorsey brothers.

I came to Atlantic City for the first time at nine months of age in 1934, and when Susan's mother and I married, we began a tradition of visiting Atlantic City every other year or so. Carol and I watched the city deteriorate in the 1960's and then revive again with the coming of legalized gambling. A lot of the sites mentioned in the book are fictitious but identifiable to those who know the city from the past, and in the present. Some streets have been "rearranged" to ease the coming and going of the characters, but if you've ever played Monopoly, you'll get the drift.

The two protagonists of the book — Lillian and Tom — are fictitious, but representative of "new age senior citizens." who would have been written off as "old folks" over the age of 70. But today the public begins to recognize that "people of an age"—the Betty

Whites, if you will — have a life and a future and, indeed, much to offer to a younger generation. The book is a dialogue between a man and a woman raised at different social levels and with mixed emotions when it comes to the "divide", for better or worse, between their generation and the "new century generation." But they accept the new rules and enjoy the new technology "toys" and are determined to "hang on."

The book has a detective mystery plot with a surprise ending. The body of a young, redheaded local woman washes up on the beach after a storm. Tom, a retired policeman, and Lillian, strong willed and very wealthy, find themselves falling in love. He's married and she has a "Quaker" conscience and wonders whether they have a "right". The Coates Family of Philadelphia which arrived there before William Penn is mentioned frequently, but after all, they are Susan and my direct descendants.

Lillian and Tom quickly become entangled in the search for the killer. Lillian develops several flawed theories about the murder and the murderer. After everyone "gives up" on the case, a suspect is immediately recognizable as the murderer. It's a *why didn't I think of that* moment. But you must read it for yourself, so let's get on with it.

Chapter One

Lillian: *"I loved the sea from the first moment my father dipped my toes in it."*

It began on a cool, misty morning after a terrible storm during the night brought salt water half way up my street; I left my apartment at the far end of St. James Place at about 6:30am and up on the Boardwalk within ten minutes or so. The air was still damp and salty: the ocean grey and angry, still troubled by the high tide and full moon of the night before. I remember how majestic the waves looked, and because it was Sunday morning I couldn't help thinking about what someone once told me, or did I read it somewhere? "The sea is more beautiful than cathedrals".

As a child who spent many, many summers here on the beach at Atlantic City, I loved the sea from the first moment my father dipped my toes in it, and now I live beside it, seventy-five years later. The city — well, the city has had its ups and downs in all that time. More "downs", I think, but now somewhere in the middle. No, a bit better than the middle. I remember a line from the movie about Atlantic City when Burt Lancaster looked out over the ocean from the Boardwalk and said wistfully to a young lady who had just moved there: "You should have seen the ocean before the war."

Everyone laughed, but I knew exactly what he meant. The ocean back then had a glow about it that was extinguished forever when war and the blackouts began. As a child before the war, I remember women in beautiful summer gowns walking out of the Traymore on the arms of gentlemen in evening clothes. I remember Glenn Miller headlining in the ballroom at the tip end of the Steel Pier. I had my first taste of lobster out at Hackney's while the waves broke just under the wooden floor of the restaurant. My father had money and I guess I saw things at their best. And what a beautiful view it was.

It's a different world now. And how. But we have to live in it. Some of my friends – and they get fewer all the time – still try to live in the old world before 9/11.

I live in the new one. Uneasily at times, and sometimes aghast at the general lack of courtesy and downright barbarity of Century 21. But nothing shocks me anymore. Not coarse language from children nor the near nakedness of young women on the Boardwalk let alone on the beach. And men, too. When I went swimming as a child, both my father and my brother wore tops to their bathing suits. And they weren't allowed on the Boardwalk wearing bathing suits – tops or not . So in some ways it's better now than then. Maybe! I haven't quite decided, but like a barnacle I stick on, and adjust to the tide.

And speaking of barnacles, as soon as I stepped down on the sand that morning, I noticed thousands of them – little black shells – littering the sand at my favorite part of the beach, just in front of the Old Stanley Theatre. It must have been quite a storm during the night. The strong current and high tide must have torn into an entire shoal of them, and now they lay on the beach like waves of coal all the way from the Central Pier up past Bally's to the new City Pier with the fancy shops.

"The tourists will complain about the smell a bit later in the day," I thought.

I wore my good pink summer dress that morning and my old floppy straw hat. I intended to go to early church at St. Andrews's, without the hat of course. But first I had to feed the cats. Yes, I'm one of those kooky old women who carry food down to the beach every morning and feed the feral cats that hang out under the Beach Patrol Headquarters.

I give them a little extra on Sunday mornings. Is that such a crime? And I enjoy watching them—mostly black and white stripes in pretty much the same patterns indicating, I suppose, a great deal of incest and promiscuity. Well for God's sake, they're only cats and not politicians who do the same thing and we pay for it. Cats are delicate and elegant creatures and I've shared my home with one or two of them wherever I've lived, but never tried to humanize them nor give them names. They have their own names, just as they have their own mysterious ways.

The cats who live here under the Beach Patrol Headquarters building are not ordinary domestic types, but free-living feral ones. I feed them early in the morning so tourists won't gape at me and try to figure me out. The storm's kept them inside this morning . . . the tourists, but not the cats. The tourists probably overslept because the electricity went off last night at around ten and stayed off for a couple of hours. Maybe I can feed them in peace and then go up to church. Of course, they'll stare at me in church wearing a pretty summer dress and shoes to service. People go to church wearing less and less. But at least they're in church. The fifteen or so who show up anyway.

Each morning as I step onto the beach I look out to sea and try to identify ships passing by. My husband was in the Navy. He left me a pair of powerful Zeiss binoculars.

He said he got them from a German U Boat captain, and knowing him, I'm sure he did. He was a very persuasive man. They're nearly as old as I am, and they bring the world in close.

On this particular morning, I watched a huge oil tanker riding low in the water as it trailed across the horizon from right to left. Probably on its way to the storage tanks on the Delaware. As it moved out of sight to the far left, my eyes moved down to the tip of the Central Pier. It was damaged badly in the Hurricane of '44, and never completely repaired, but its old wooden pilings still support the far end of the pier which once held amusements and as I recall, an aquarium. That end of the pier was bare concrete now, and closed to the public.

I saw something out there, at the very tip end, but not sure just what, so I adjusted the lenses for a sharper image, and when I saw clearly what it was, I dropped the binoculars on the sand and grabbed my cell phone from my purse.

"Operator, I want to report an emergency. Down here on the beach. My name is Mrs.Lillian Moore, and I'm down here on the beach. Just off St. James Place , near the Central Pier. Right in front of the Atlantic Palace Hotel. The District 5 Beach Patrol Building is on my left just behind me."

"What kind of emergency are you reporting, Mrs. Moore? "

"A drowning."

There was a long pause. "Can you hear me, please?" I yelled.

"Yes, Mrs. Moore, I'm sending an alert to our mobile team", the detached 911 voice replied calmly. "Someone is already on the way, Mrs. Moore. Can you give me some additional details?. Is the person still breathing? I mean, can you give the person CPR?"

"Not very well. She's hung up on the end of the Central Pier. At least I think it's a she!"

"Hanging from Trump's Pier?", she asked hesitantly, using the newer name of something that has stuck out into the ocean and called itself the Steel Pier for a hundred years or more.

"No,' I corrected her.. "The **Central** Pier. Do you know where I mean? Well never mind about that. She's obviously dead, just wrapped around one of the wooden pilings out there, and no way I can reach her."

The 911 voice continued calmly but firmly: "The emergency team is on its way and I'm alerting the Beach Patrol as well. You're sure it's a woman? For my report."

"I think so. From what I can see, she has part of a dress on." I said. "It may be a bit early for the Beach Patrol, especially on a Sunday.

It's only, what, 6:40? At any rate, if anybody needs directions, I'm standing near the District 5 Lifeguard Station.

Straight down from St. James Place.

The 911 voice continued speaking quietly and sensibly. No hysterics. "Someone will be there shortly. Let's keep talking until they arrive. How did you discover the body, Mrs. Moore?"

"I come down to the beach every morning at about this time and I carry some very high powered binoculars . . . my husband was in the Navy . . . . and I can see what appears to be a woman snagged on one of the wooden pilings out there. I can see arms and legs. Poor thing."

"May I have your address, Mrs. Moore?" continued 911 voice politely. "and your phone and email address"

"Yes, of course."

An emergency vehicle appeared just then, speeding through the sand, so I waved them down with a towel. A young man and a tall young lady jumped out and ran toward me. I passed my binoculars to the young woman.

"Look there", I pointed. "Does that look like a female to you?"

"Yes, I think so," she said . "Looks as if she's missing a leg, or else it's folded under her dress. God, what a way to die."

By now, two young lifeguards from the Life Guard Station came running down the sand. The young lady from the emergency team called out to one of them: "Looks like you have to get your ass wet this morning, Chris. Some one's hung up out there."

The lifeguards ran to a boat in front of a beach patrol box, tipped it over, and steered out into the incoming waves. The young man and the lady from the emergency team jumped into the swells and helped push the boat through the first line of large breakers and the boat was soon in open water heading for the tip end of the pier.

"I hope they're careful," I said. "The waves out there can give them a hard knock against one of those wooden pilings."

"Don't worry about Chris and Eddie," the young lady smiled soothingly.

"They've been through this many times before."

"Yes, I know, dear", I said, "I've watched them do it since about 1934!"

She grinned at me.Vacantly.

I kept one eye on the boat with the binoculars while I moved back toward the Boardwalk and opened my large wicket basket. After all, the cats were experiencing what I call a "food emergency alert", moving about nervously as soon as they caught sight of me. Like lions in their den, they expected to be fed. Several of the more friendly ones began to gather near me. None ever took food directly from my hand and I didn't volunteer it that way.

I'm one of the few who appreciate cats around here. Imagine the beach overrun with rats and other vermin without them. A lot of pizza scraps and popcorn falls through the cracks in the Boardwalk after all.

I placed a plate with several varieties of cat food at arm's length in front of me.

They came warily close enough to eat. There would be at least twenty to feed. Normally, these feral cats want nothing to do with gawking tourists who approach them — God forbid — with a piece of hamburger or a morsel of greasy funnel cake.

I guess they recognize that I'm their soul mate, or as close a soul mate as any cat can expect to find. No "*here pretty kitty*" from me. I know them by sight but, as with the cats I've kept in my home, I never assign a name to any of them. I wonder what they call me? Something very comical, I'm sure.

So there I sat on a low bench with my feet in the sand beside one of the planks holding up the Beach Patrol cottage, feeding the cats with one hand and watching the Lifeguard boat with the other, when a voice called down from the Boardwalk above me.

"Hey Lady, are you the one who put the call in about the drowning?"

"Yes, I am". I looked up toward the voice.

"I'm Tom Dillon. I work for the coroner's office. What are you doin' there."

"What's it look like I'm doing," I said. "I'm feeding the cats."

"In your good clothes!"

I answered him a bit sharply: "Mr. Dillon, it **IS** Sunday and I'm on my way to church after I take care of these animals."

"Well", he said "I just meant that sitting on a sandy beach in your good shoes and a nice clean dress amongst all that cat poo . . . it isn't healthy."

I gave him a cool look: "Neither is that corpse floating out there. Isn't that who you're supposed to interview, and not me?" I didn't mean to embarrass him. Cops take a lot of abuse and he was obviously trying to be kind to this dotty old lady sitting in the sand.

"Look," he said, "I don't mean any disrespect. Nothing like that. But you know we have lots of . . . funny folks around here."

"Well I'm not one of them, thank God." I answered with a full, angry stare into his face. "Not funny at all. And not some seventy-five year old kook."

I put the plates down and said more respectfully, "Now why don't we go down together to where those two people from "emergency" are standing and see what's going on."

He apologized again. "Sorry lady. I'm sorry. I didn't mean anything. Really! I'm seventy-five myself."

"And you look every day of it," I said with a laugh. But of course, he didn't look anymore than I did. In fact, he looked pretty fit for a man his age. He smiled back:

"I got old doin'my job, ma'm. Just by doin' my job."

I wonder why 75 year olds are regarded by younger people as so many fossils.

Don't they know that many of us have full rich lives and clear minds. Yes indeed, the man on the Boardwalk looked good to me. I still have "appetites", and I don't mean for ice cream and fudge – although I enjoy them as much now as I did when I was seven..

Believe me, life is not over at 75, or beyond, unless you want it to be. When I dwell on "growing old" I think about Betty White and Raquel Welch and Bill Shatner, and a lot of other vital people leading productive lives and enjoying it. As a matter of fact, Larry King was born on the same day in the same year as me, and I think he's on his fifth wife at this point in life. So excuse me if I confess that I began to flirt with the man on the Boardwalk. Age 75 in the 21st Century "ain't what it used to be" in the 20$^{th.}$ I prefer to think of it as "a short stretch from middle age."

"I'll meet you at those steps over there," I said as I rose up from the bench and brushed the sand away with my hand. "I want to see what they've found out there. By the way, my name is Lillian Moore. For your report."

"Nice to meet you, Mrs. Moore," He said cheerfully. "Nice morning, isn't it?" He touched the tip of his cap with his thumb and forefinger. Nobody under sixty does that anymore and it's such a nice courteous gesture. These days the kids and even some of the adults give each other "the finger" and it's not because they want to be polite. Well I have to admit that when someone cuts me off in traffic I feel like doing it myself. But I don't.

We walked down to the water's edge and watched as the boat pulled away from the Pier and headed toward shore. I put my binoculars up to my eyes.

"My God", I said ,"Talk about disrespect! They're laughing. What are they laughing about?"

Chapter Two

Dillon: *"Not murder," I said," but possible suicide"*

I got word about a drowning early Sunday morning on my cell phone. I really enjoy my job as a county coroner's investigator, but not at daybreak. Not until I have my coffee. Well what the hell. I haven't been sleeping so well lately anyway and 6:00am is as good as anytime to get up and going. **If** you have the strength to get up and going at age 75. Lucky for me, I come from a long line of tough Irish Micks . . . the Dillons from Pittsburgh.

This job isn't a real job. By that I mean it's a favor. I've been working temporarily—just a couple of weeks — for a friend, the county coroner down here. He's more than a friend. He grew up practically next door to me in Pittsburgh. His Dad went to college with me at Pitt in the fifties. Now his boy, Bill Jr., is doin' real well down here in New Jersey and . . . gosh . . . I call him a boy but he's already in his early forties.

I have my social security and I draw a pension from the Pittsburgh Police Department after thirty-five years on the force, and I've been living in AC for the last couple of weeks. There's not much money layin' around in law enforcement either here or in the city or the county, so I volunteer my time with Bill, who, like I said, is a really smart young fellow and goin' places in politics someday. He gives me a few bucks here and there to make it worthwhile, and he knows I'd do it for nothing just to help him out and to keep busy.

My job is to make the initial investigation homicides here in the county—and specifically in Atlantic City proper —and then turn it over to the coroner. After thirty-five years of seeing every possible kind of homicide, murder or suicide in my days on the Pittsburgh force, I have a kind of — what would you call it — a sixth sense of what happened at a crime scene. Anyway, my guess is as good as anybody else's and based on my experience it's better than most. As I tell my drinking buddies here, it keeps me out of trouble! Or it gets me into trouble. However you want to look at it.

I have a little apartment on Chelsea Avenue down near the Auditorium, so I was able to get to the beach off Kentucky just a couple of minutes after the alarm came in. Some old lady on the Beach made a call to 911 this morning and they automatically hit my cell phone number as well as a couple of others. I guess the Beach Patrol was included as well.

I got right over to Kentucky, and looking over the steps leading down to the beach in front of the Atlantic Palace there was this older woman in a nice clean pink dress sittin' on a bench under the Beach Patrol building in the sand and feeding the cats. I took her for an odd-ball but the more she talked I realized that she had all of her senses about her, and moreso. Pretty sharp at that, with a tongue to match. But I kind of sweet talked her and walked her down the beach where the Beach Patrol boat was returning through the surf.

She got upset when she honed in with her binoculars and realized that the two young fellows in the rescue boat were laughing like hell as they rowed ashore.

And no wonder!

All their rescue efforts amounted to bringing a *dummy* to shore. I mean a real honest-to-God mannikin like you see in a store window. Its legs were floppin' out over the side of the boat, and I have to say I started laughing like hell when I recognized that it was somebody's dress dummy and not somebody's Mother.

It was then that I discovered that Mrs. Moore had a sense of humor, because she was laughing, too. She even called out to the two young guys pulling the boat up on the beach: "Why's a pretty red-haired girl like that taking a ride with you two lugs?"

Honest to God, it was funny all around. Especially when the youngest lifeguard— probably just out of high school —carried "her" out of the boat just like a new bride. To make it even funnier, she had long, flaming red hair and an odd kind of pretty face with a painted pout on her lips as if she resented such rough treatment.

He put her down on the beach, gently, just like you'd do with a real person. "She lost her dress," he said apologetically. With that the two other young fellows "got funny" and started to arrange her arms this way and that. The young lady with them laughed right along with them. She even placed the "dummy hands" in an embarrassing position.

Well it was embarrassing to me and Ms. Moore. I could tell from her face. But she didn't say anything . . . just turned and looked at me as if to say: "Kids nowadays have no sense of modesty . . . none whatsoever."

After a bit of fooling around with the mannikin's arms and legs, I stepped in and told them that although it was a bit unusual, I would have to make an investigation of the "body." Of course this just broke them up even more. The young lady said with a big grin: "Should I turn my head?", and that brought another howl from all four of them.

Mrs. Moore leaned over the mannikin and started her own investigation. "What do you think, Dillon," she said with a straight face:"Was it murder?"

Well of course this cracked them up again. And it was damned funny, I have to admit. "Not murder", I ventured, "but possible suicide!" I think the young lady wet her pants on that. She just leaned on the boat and laughed her head off.

Mrs. Moore got a bit more serious. "What's this word printed on her cheek, and I don't mean her face cheek."

That brought the house down. Me included. The three boys were holding their heads, they were laughing so much, and the young lady actually fell down on the sand.

It was really funny. But I guess you had to be there.

"The word is "Pengo," Mrs. Moore said solemnly, as she looked at it closely.

"Pengo", she repeated.

I asked her :"What the hell is Pengo?"

The kids laughed even harder. "Don't you get it," the young lady said, with tears streaming down her cheeks. "Pengo is an Internet Game character. Or used to be when we were kids."

"So?"

"The Internet Pengo is a penguin, and it has flaming red hair . . . just like the dummy. And it lives in Antarctica." All four of them looked at us with this last remark and impishly awaited our total bewilderment. Which was not long in coming.

Adolescent humor escapes me and I guess it escapes Mrs. Moore as well. And the kids just kept laughing like hell. One of the lifeguards explained that it had to do with an internet game all the kids used to play **long ago** . . . when they were in high school.

"You don't hear much about it any more," the younger lifeguard said solemnly.

"A red headed penguin?", Mrs. Moore uttered sharply with a frown on her face.

"What's that all about?"

"Never mind", said the girl. "It's too hard to explain. But some college kids up on the Boardwalk right now must be having a helluva good time laughing at how hard Beach Patrol had to work this morning to rescue Miss Pengo. I doubt that high school kids of today know any more about her than you older folks do. It's like when Warhol talked about five minutes of fame!"

"It was *fifteen* minutes," Mr. Moore corrected her. "My friend in New York and I had a delightful lunch with him not long before he passed away. My friend bought one of his smaller pieces and wishes now that she'd bought more."

"I guess we can wrap it up," said the older lifeguard. "But how do we report this?"

I stepped in and told him to report it as "*debris*" rather than "something which appeared to be a human body from a distance." Otherwise, I said, somebody will want to make a big deal out of it. Just treat it on your report as if it were a piece of driftwood, which of course it is.

"Good idea" said the young lady. "We'll do the same, and just say that someone with bad eyesight made a bad call on what they thought they saw this morning."

"Make sure you say 'some old person'," said Mrs. Moore rather sarcastically.

"That's a good idea," said the young lady brightly. "It makes it more believable."

"Now what do we do with the dummy?," asked the younger lifeguard. "We just can't leave her lying here . . . naked."

"Well it's your fault," said the older lifeguard. "You're the one who pulled her dress off and dropped it in the ocean."

More laughter. Even Mrs. Moore had to take her handkerchief out on that one.

"I tell you what," said the older guard, "The damn thing looks so real! Let's take her up to the Beach Patrol Building and sit her on the toilet. That'll give Mack a real shocker when he comes in later this morning. "They all agreed that "Mack" would flip when he saw that. More adolescent humor.

Mrs. Moore looked over the dummy one last time with a professional eye and said she used to be a buyer for Wanamaker's but never saw a manikin quite like this one.

She moved her hand through the hair. "This is real human hair", she said, "Not fake, and sewn into the 'scalp'. The body and legs are articulated correctly, and it has the feel of real skin rather than plastic." She gave it a final look. "It's sculpted differently than the mannikins I worked with at the store. Miss Pengo has boyish hips and is rather flat chested. This is an old dress dummy, probably from the Twenties."

I laughed and said to her: "Mrs.Moore, I'm supposed to be the investigator here.

But I can assure you that I'm putting none of your comments on *my* report. It's just a piece of debris. I'm telling you that if we say anything "human" about this dummy we'll never hear the end of it." Then I added: "Now how about some coffee and donuts? I haven't had anything to eat this morning and my head always hurts if I don't eat breakfast right away." The young people were already hauling the mannikin off in high spirits to the Beach Patrol Building.

She answered politely: "I'm partial to having breakfast at the Traymore, but since it hasn't existed for forty years or more, maybe we can compromise on the Wedgewood Room at Resorts?"

"You hit me at a bad time, Mrs. Moore, " I said. "I'm not exactly dressed for the Wedgewood Room, but there's a donut shop right up there on the Boardwalk and I'm sure we can find a helluva nice place to watch the sun rise at one of their outdoor tables."

"I accept your invitation," she said sweetly. "And by the way, can you please leave off the profanity. I hear it everywhere now days and it doesn't shock me anymore –since I know all the words anyway – but too much of it annoys me. How about it?"

"Agreed, Mrs. Moore, if I can call you 'Lillian', I said with a grin. "Of course you can, *'Tom' "*, she emphasized with a very broad smile.

Chapter Three

Lillian: *"I was beginning to like Tom. I was beginning to like him a whole lot, and I wondered if maybe I was just a little too old for that?*

Well what do you know? Tom called me for a date on Sunday evening. I haven't had a date since . . . I suppose 1958 or so . . . when Rodger came by and swept me off my feet. So now it's 2009, and I wonder how to approach this new ripple in the rising tide of my life.

He was rather tongue-tied when he called, making some small talk first about our morning at the beach. Then he told me that he'd keep in touch with me about the rescue of Miss Pengo. He figured it was just a college prank. It was August, after all, and just about the time of year when boys are doing their last fling before school starts again.

"They haven't gotten any smarter than when I was a freshman at Pitt in '51," he said.

"Not much of a prank," I said, "when you consider they were putting the lifeguards in danger. Or scaring to death some poor seventy-five year old lady down on the beach feeding her cats."

I don't think you scare that easily, Lillian," he said, in a tone that I was sure would soon lead him to pop the question about a *"date."* I could read it in his voice. I wasn't too old to recognize the drift of the conversation.

"By the way," he began rather off handedly," I was wondering if you had any plans for dinner tomorrow evening. Nothing special, you know. Just trying to make up for being a bit . . . a bit . . ."

"A bit disrespectful when you first saw me feeding the cats?"

"Well I was pretty much of an ignoramus going at you like that."

"No, of course I'm not angry", I reassured him. "I was just pulling your chain, Tom. Do you remember that expression? Now let me review my very busy schedule for the week and see if I can fit you in. Ah yes, there's a window of opportunity open on Monday evening. That's tomorrow night," I said as coyly as I could.

"Cool," he said, with evident relief. Just like a 21st Century sixteen year old would have said it.

"What do you mean, **cool**? " I said. "That's not what you would have said in 1950!"

He laughed. "You're absolutely right. I probably would have said something much more stupid than that and then hung up the phone in total disbelief that such a beautiful girl would agree to go out with me. And then I would have thrown myself on my bed and punched my pillow yelling: "I did it. I did it!""

We both laughed, and as the memory of a first date popped into my head I answered: "I would have been wondering about what I'd wear and what I'd do if you got fresh. After all, I hardly know you."

"I can guarantee you that we'll have a 1950 type date," he said. "You know what I mean"

"I hope I do," I answered.

We agreed that he'd pick me up at 7:00pm at my apartment: "On St James Place, side entrance of the 'Los Campesinos Restaurant'." I knew he could hardly miss the place. It's a narrow old Victorian building with twenty or more different colors of paint and odd architectural angles that make the building seem to lean out over the sidewalk. I live on the second floor, up a narrow, spiraling staircase. I love it!

Monday passed slowly as I dithered about how to act when he arrived. What if we couldn't keep the conversation going between us. How awkward would that be? The thought which kept reoccurring was that I really didn't know this man. Not a thing about him! Except that if he were a policeman, he couldn't be an ax murderer. What silly thoughts at age sixteen or at seventy-five.

When he came to the door that evening he seemed surprised that I lived in a restaurant, or at least upstairs of one.

"It's an arrangement I have with the Sanmartino family," I said. "They have a security system and I act as a kind of backup 'night watchman', although I'm not quite sure what I'd do if someone tried to break in my front door. Yes, I **do** know. I'll lock my bedroom door and call 911. Or perhaps I'll pull out the little revolver that I keep in my nightstand and shoot right through the door. I'm registered by the way. Rodger, my late husband, would have done it that way, but that was a different day and age. I suppose 911 is the better way to go, though not quite an immediate remedy..

Tom and I talked about how the neighborhood around St. James Place wasn't so much "bad" as it was empty. So much of the Atlantic City we both knew has been torndown and turned into parking lots for the casinos. He and his family used to come down to the beach nearly every summer. He knew the area well and agreed with me. .

My restaurant/apartment faces the old Flanders Hotel. Just a shell now. At one time it was a charming little place with a solarium on the roof and some of the best food in the city. The duck was as good as anything in Paris.

One stayed at the Flanders on "the American Plan" which meant that the cost of your accommodations included a full breakfast, luncheon buffet and dinner. If you went "deep sea fishing" and brought home some of your "catch", the hotel chef would prepare it for your supper. All the "good" hotels in Atlantic City, including the elegant Traymore where my family stayed, offered the same courtesy. I wonder if anyone goes "deep sea fishing" anymore?

The neighborhood has changed, and now I live in a prairie of parking lots. All around me. They tore down the Sands Hotel on the other side of Kentucky Avenue and cleared the ground for a bigger, fancier casino with an "entertainment center' – whatever that was supposed to be. But all that was planned before the Recession. And now, with money tight and the ground cleared, it's just an empty sand lot.

St. James Place, and Kentucky Avenue once throbbed with life: restaurants; jazz bars, small hotels and boarding houses, and more jazz bars. Music floated down the street most of the night. One of the clubs with black entertainment had a special "sunrise" show at 6:00am each morning and people lined up around the block to get in. Big name entertainment. And now it's empty. As empty as the steppes of Siberia.

I showed Tom through my apartment – a long, narrow space— but elegant in its own way. It's about sixty feet long, and fifteen feet wide with no partitions. Believe me it was a challenge to furnish. Thank God I worked for a time in the fifties at Wannamaker's in the furnishings department. They taught me a lot about design and "ambience."

I started our "tour" at the tiny reception area at the top of the stairs leading up from the restaurant. There's a long space of bookshelves on both sides of the walls, with hard wood floors and some pretty oriental rugs and ottomans and little brass tables here and there leading to a small living room. Rodger and I bought most of the stuff in Istanbul back in the sixties. There's a skylight running down the full length of that part of the building. So I get plenty of light for my potted plants, and I have plenty of them. The living room is a tiny space, like a jewel box. Lots of pictures on the wall; a lovely marble mantelpiece. Comfortable chairs with satin cushions from India.

My bedroom is all the way to the back, with French doors leading out to a very small veranda where I creep out in the morning in my jammies and have coffee on my deck, watching the sun rise over the ocean. Tom wondered what my view will be like when they start work again on the new casino. I told him that one of the benefits of my "advanced" age is that, with luck, I probably won't live long enough to see it built.

"But doesn't it smell?," said Tom as we walked back down the steps and through the restaurant.

"It's a good smell," I said, "if you like real authentic Mexican food. And I do.

The restaurant is just as long and narrow as my apartment. I can't imagine what kind of business occupied it before the Sanmartinos bought it in the 70's. I think it might have been a shoe store. But at any rate, they used their imagination and placed little enclosed booths on one side of the room, each with the name of a city in Mexico: Acapulco; Guadalajara; Tampico, Puerto Vallarta. The thatched roofs over each of them are a bit kitchy, but so what! I told Tom that I love having dinner in Puerto Vallarta every Thursday evening. He laughed at that. He laughs a lot.

"But I'll bet you'd rather have dinner in the Nereus Room at the Traymore," said Tom. "Wasn't that the name of the fancy night club there? And if it were still standing, I'd take you there tonight."

"What a thrill", I said. "The Traymore! I wonder if they'll let me in the Nereus Room with this woolen sweater? Probably not for dinner, but maybe for breakfast, just coming in off the Boardwalk after a long walk on the beach. Yes, that would be so elegant. Breakfast at the Traymore. Poor Traymore. Gone with the wind. Just like the movie. But they do have a fantastic breakfast buffet which is very much like the old Traymore's up at the Sheraton across from the

Convention Center. I ate there once and a couple came to brunch in their pajamas and robes. Imagine that at the Traymore!"

As we reached the sidewalk, Tom said: "I don't dwell on the past too much. I just run to keep up with the present. Do you have an email address by the way?"

"Yes, of course" I said, "and what about you?"

"Wouldn't be without it. Greatest thing since sliced bread," Tom said. "In fact I don't even have a land line phone anymore. I never thought that would be an option. But my cell phone works for me and the email comes off my laptop, or I can use one of the computers at the police station. Of course I'm not into twittering or flexing, or whatever the hell the kids do. But I'm looking into it. Excuse the profanity," he laughed, "I was a cop for thirty-five years and it's hard to stop."

"I had a sailor for a husband, "I said, "And I made **him** stop, or at least tone it down indoors,." I laughed. Then I continued with my view of 21st Century communications. "It's texting I refuse to do," I said, "because I understand that you can only use 150 characters. I may be wrong about the number but it's not much more than that: my problem is that I'm the only person in the world anymore who sends grammatically correct email messages with full page attachments. I love to write letters but no one answers them anymore. So email has to do, and I make the most of it."

"Me, too," he agreed and then said "I thought we'd take the jitney out to Mama Mia's. Is that all right with you, Lillian?' I told him it was fine with me and that I eat there myself quite often. Best Italian food in town. And I know the chef.

It started to rain a bit, so we walked up St. James to the corner under one umbrella. Pretty good start for a first date.

"Funny we haven't met before," said Tom, holding up two fingers to signal a jitney hurtling down Pacific Avenue.

"I guess we've been moving along on different paths," I said. "You're from Pittsburgh and I'm from Philadelphia, and we just happen to wind up together in Atlantic City where we both spent a lot of time as kids and learned to love the place."

Tom and I talked about the two cities we were born in: Philly in the east and Pittsburgh to the west. You'd think the two cities would be pretty much the same since they're both in the same state, but nothing could be further from the truth. Tom tells me he went to a big city school in the Lawrenceville area of Pittsburgh, a rough edged area of town. I went to a small private school for girls in Berwyn on the Main Line. The only thing that ties Berwyn to Lawrenceville is the fact that Amtrak runs in a somewhat circuitous line from one to the other through the mountains. And then there's the Steeler-Eagles thing. Oh yes, I follow professional football. I'm an Eagle's fan, but cheer for the Steelers, except when they play Philly.

As for Atlantic City, if you didn't know it, jitneys are the best transportation.

They're little white bus things, holding about ten people, but without springs. Privately owned and operated.

It was a bumpy ride out to Mama Mia's but Tom is such good company with funny stories about an Italian Restaurant in the Bloomfield section of Pittsburgh where the waitress is a gal named Rita who always mixes up the orders. When she gets rattled she holds her hands up to her head and says: "Tuttee patz.. Mee cabo jee-da jee-da" which Tom says means: ***Everybody's crazy and makes my head go round and round.'*** He says he used to say it to Italians who worked on the force with him, and they laughed and laughed about his pronunciation.

I was beginning to like Tom. I was beginning to like him a lot, and I wondered if maybe I was just a bit too old for that? And by the way, Mama Mia's mussels with marinara sauce ***are to die for***.

Chapter Four

Dillon: *"I don't know a lot about Bryn Mawr. I just know that no guy I knew ever dated someone from there, or even from Philadelphia"*

I really had a great evening with Lillian. Her apartment is something to look at.

Long and narrow, like a bowling alley with one lane. But she has it fixed real nice. Lots of pictures and things that she picked up all over the world. She's been everywhere:

China, India, Australia, you name it. And of course, all the major cities in Europe like London, Paris, Vienna . . . even Moscow.

Her husband, Rodger, was a Commander in the Navy according to what she said, and worked in Naval Intelligence in posts all over the place. A lot of secret stuff that he didn't talk about, or at least which *she* doesn't talk about. Apparently he comes from a good family in Philadelphia. After all, his middle name was Biddle.

He's gone now. She said he always wanted to go with a "quick drop." Well that's what he did back in '93. Heart attack. No hangin' around for him. And that's just the way I want to go, when I go. At 75 I think about it a lot. But what the hell, we all have to go one way or another, so why dwell on it.

Now Lillian, she always takes the humorous point of view. She says she has her obit ready and waiting. Wouldn't trust anyone else writin' it up. She pulled it out of her purse during dinner, and we laughed about it as she read it to me:

"MOORE, Lillian Coates "Born November 19,1933 to Elmer N. and Olive Coates. She grew up in Philadelphia where she attended the Friends (Quaker) School in Eldon , PA. Matriculated at Bryn Mawr College, a double major in Fine Arts and in English."

'That's what got me the job at Wanamaker's," she said in an aside, as she straightened her glasses and read further.

"She was a life member of the Episcopal Church. Married the late Rodger Biddle Moore on November 21, 1959. She loved animals and Japanese flower arranging and traveled the world from Antarctica to Siberia. She encouraged the love of travel in two beloved nieces, Nicole and Nathalie, and took them on her final road bike trip to Bhutan in the Spring of 2006."

"Now who's gonna know where Bhutan is?" I interrupted.

"Some of my sorority sisters at Bryn Mawr — at least those who're left — will be asking that same question" she said. "At least I hope they do."

She continued with a smile: "She has lived in Atlantic City as near to the Boardwalk as possible for the past ten years since the passing of her beloved husband, Commander Rodger Moore of the United States Navy. There will be no viewing. Her ashes will be strewn in the Atlantic Ocean on (date to be determined). Donations may be made to Friends Meeting House on Arch Street in Philadelphia, St. Andrew's Episcopal Church in Atlantic City, or to the Philadelphia Zoo."

"That's it?" I said.

"That's all I have to say," she said, putting her glasses down. "My nieces know all about what to do when I pass. They'll take care of things for me. Anyway, I left them a book called 'When I Depart' which covers all the things they need to know. You have to be prepared at our age, you know. Don't want to leave other people worrying about details. My obit says it all. Oh, and one thing more", she said as she tucked the paper back into her purse." I told my nieces that for the obit I want them to use the picture of me wearing my big floppy straw hat."

"The one I saw you wearing on the beach?"

"That's the one. Ugly as sin, isn't it? But very comfortable."

I have to say that Lillian is a very special person. Just just when I think I have her figured out, she tells me something I never expected to hear. I can understand the Philadelphia Zoo part – one of her ancestors lived on the property way back in the late 1600's, but what's this road bike trip in Bhutan all about? That's way over in Asia somewhere. I think in the Himalayans. She would have been 72 or 3 at the time.

Now if I were to write my obit – and I have no intention of doing so in advance – well, it might just say that I was born eight months sooner than Lillian Moore. Ha!

I attended Arsenal High School – when it *was* a high school – in the Lawrenceville section of Pittsburgh.

I came from a good Catholic family, with two sisters and a brother. Went to Korea right out of high school and when I came back, attended the University of Pittsburgh. Joined the Pittsburgh Police Force and stayed with them on active duty for thirty-five years. Retired from the Force in 1998. Saw the best of life and the worst. End of Obit.

Then I told Lillian the rest of the story.

The best of life, I explained, was the time spent with my wife, Evelyn. Until she got sick. She has Alzheimer's and living now at the Home of the Good Samaritan for the last nine years. She doesn't know me anymore. She doesn't know anybody. You should have seen her in high school. Prettiest girl around. A cheerleader. It's too bad we didn't have kids. But, in a way, maybe it's better we didn't. She just goes on living and dying, and part of me is dying with her when I see her the way she is now and remember the way she was then..

I visited her every day after she went into the Home. Last month my sister, Mary Catherine, who still lives in the old homestead, told me that I had to take a break or I'd go crazy. She said I should take off for at least six weeks. So I came down to Atlantic City where my family used to come almost every summer. An old Army buddy, Bill, is the father of Bill, Jr. who's now the County Coroner down here. Their family grew up practically next door to us in Pittsburgh. Bill Jr. invited me to do some part time work for him while I'm here investigating homicides, suicides, whatever. Something I know plenty about. It's been real interesting. But I think I should start thinking about going home. It's not right leaving my sister to look after Evelyn without my being there.

I told Lillian the whole story so there wouldn't be any misunderstandings, and I told her frankly that it feels good to be out, after such a long time, with a nice lady. She understands completely. No questions asked.

Lillian is one fine person even if she likes to wear funny hats and feed the cats down at the Beach Patrol. Sometimes I think she's very, very lonely. And then at other times she seems more than able to take care of herself and keep herself busy, mostly with artsy stuff, but a lot of charity work, too. I don't want to get too attached to her inasmuch as I'll be leaving for home soon. But it feels so good being with a lady again. And she's quite a lady. I can't imagine what she sees in me. If she *does* see anything.

Well, what am I saying? Who says she wants to get attached to me anyway? In lots of ways, she's out of my class. And yet, she's so easy to be with. She's just herself.

No pretences about her .Even though she went to Bryn Mawr. Or maybe *because* she went there.

I don't know a lot about Bryn Mawr. I just know that no guy I ever knew ever dated someone from there, or even from Philadelphia. I have to laugh to myself. I guess it's that Steeler-Eagles thing.

By the way, Mama Mia's mussels are really great, but the marinara sauce is just a bit too rich for me. Or maybe it was the Chianti. Or maybe it's because my stomach is 75 years old. I think I'll sleep in tomorrow and, maybe, call Lillian to see what she's doing for lunch. But maybe she had enough of me this evening. My life is full of maybe's.

We'll see what happens tomorrow.

Chapter Five

Lillian: *"I find it curious that a girl who worked in a donut shop on the Boardwalk wears expensive clothes and ultra-expensive Italian-made shoes"*

Tom called at 8:00 this morning. I just came in after feeding the cats and having a bit of breakfast at Johnny Rocket's on the Boardwalk. I knew he enjoyed our dinner date, but was he that "smitten" enough to call me so soon?

"Guess what?" he began. "We had another drowning this morning. But this time it was for real."

"Where did it happen?" I asked. "I was down at the beach at 6:30 or so and didn't see anything unusual going on."

"It happened just a little while ago. They found her way down on the Beach near the Tropicana. It was a young girl. And she had reddish hair. Does that start any bells ringing?"

"You mean Miss Pengo? It may be just a coincidence," I said. "There are a lot of red-headed girls around nowadays and most were born with brown hair."

"I know, Lillian, but there's just something about this one that I feel in my gut.

The dummy's more than a coincidence, maybe. They have the girl at the Atlantic City Hospital. In the morgue. I have to get down there right away." He sounded very stressed. "It always affects me like this when I have to deal with young people", he said quietly.

"Listen, Tom," I said. "Would you like me to meet you there?"

"I was hoping you'd say that," he answered, "But do you think you can take it?

With men, I can give bodies a look over and pretty much figure out what happened to them and, depending upon the circumstances, sometimes *why* it happened. With most older women, too. But with young people it takes more time to figure out the 'why", and you might be able to fill in some details that I'd miss."

I put my phone in my purse and was out of the apartment and down at the hospital in minutes. After all, I can see it from my balcony. I met Tom in the lobby and we checked in with a policeman who knew him from previous visits during the past weeks.

"This one's a sad case," the cop said to Tom. "Just a kid and real pretty, or at least she used to be. A shame. A damned shame. The forensic people are waiting for you before they start their work. They took some prints and a blood sample, and some other things, but they don't want to go too far 'til you look in on it."

We walked into the examining room toward a large steel table with a glaring light overhead. Tom asked me again if I could take it, and I told him I'd seen far worse. My husband, Rodger and I were in Saigon for several months in the sixties, and I volunteered as a nurse's aide at the Military Hospital near the end of the war. Some of what I saw was unmentionable.

The examining room was antiseptic and impersonal. And there she lay on a slab, not more than a child, very cold with an odd blue color, and naked. "Sad. Sad, "said the cop, walking away from us as we moved closer to the body.

I stood back while Tom walked over to her and made some notes: some bruises but no tattoos. No track marks on her arms or legs. Which means she probably wasn't involved in gangs or drug activity. Her head lay at an odd angle, and even I could see that she might have a broken neck. No rings or jewelry. I looked over her clothing neatly folded on a chair nearby. Good quality stuff. The skirt and blouse were expensive. The shoes *really* expensive, the kind that wrapped tightly around the ankles in a kind of Grecian style. And a row of semi-precious stones along the sides.

The nurse standing next to me said in a whisper: "She works at a donut shop on the Boardwalk and she probably got those things at the Outlets." To explain: there is an Outlets shopping area right in the heart of the city. This was a place where boarding houses and bars were cramped together for almost a hundred years between Atlantic Avenue and the railroad station. Now that's all changed. You can buy a Brooks Brothers suit, or Bass shoes, or Armani there. It's almost as diversified as anything on Miami Beach or Worth Avenue in Palm Beach.

Anyway, I wondered if this girl was poor, and maybe she was and simply had good taste. But the shoes told me something more. They were Italian-made and not available in the Outlets. She wouldn't have been able to buy anything that stylish or that expensive in AC. Probably got them in Philadelphia. Strange that she had no jewelry. Not even a ring or a watch.

Tom offered his professional opinion that she was dead before she went into the water — probably a day or so prior to washing up on the beach. Actually, she was not in the water very long at all. Later he told me that if she'd been in the water anymore than a few hours in the daylight hours, her eyes would have been gone. The gulls go for the soft parts of a floating body. She was probably dumped in the water an hour or two before dawn when the tide was highest. But she was definitely dead for some time before that.

He looked carefully at her fingers – short and stubby, but well manicured. Even her toes. Whoever she was, she took good care of herself Tom did some additional tests, then stepped back and directed his words to the cop: "I have to think it's a homicide. Certainly not a suicide. She was killed somewhere and then hidden away for a while. Then, for some reason, the person responsible dropped her in the ocean late last night or, like I said, maybe early this morning. The tide was up at around four in the morning. And she floated around for a while and then washed up on the beach."

"You can never tell where the current will take a body," he said. "Here in Atlantic City, it might take it out to sea and then bring it back again, or take it out so far that it'll never come back again. Sometimes they come back very near to the same place they were dumped. You can never tell. In Pittsburgh where the river currents can be very strong we sometimes found bodies twenty or thirty miles downstream from the Point. But the ocean is erratic, depending on tides , currents and riptides. And a drowning death is one of the most difficult to pin down so far as time of death, cause of death, and all the rest."

Tom touched her neck gently. "The trauma to her neck indicates to me that no weapon was used. No gunshot wounds or cuts to indicate weapons. She was very petite. The murderer wouldn't have had to be a very big guy if he caught her by surprise and knew what he was doing. The neck snaps very easily. Like in a quick wrestling move. No violence. No struggle. No bits of skin under her nails. From what I can see there was no sexual molestation, but the autopsy will have to verify that."

"It looks as if it could have been an accidental homicide," he continued." But as far as police are concerned, every drowning is a potential murder. Maybe it was an accident, but why would someone hide her away for a day or so before throwing her in the ocean?"

I asked Tom how he knew she was "hidden away" for a while. He explained that when someone's heart stops beating, the blood pools in the lowest spot on the body and appears as a large bruise around that spot. In her case there was a very large bruise across her stomach. He said that it meant she was lying on her stomach for some time. The condition of her lungs indicated that she was dead before she went into the water.

Asphyxiated, and not drowned. Rigor mortis remains for about two days, he said, depending upon temperature and other things. "You can read my report to the coroner. It explains all this stuff in more detail," he said.

Tom went through her clothes on the chair. "The killer didn't take her wallet."

Tom directed his words to the policeman. "It was zippered in her jacket. Her money and her credit cards are still there" He flipped through them. "He even left her driver's license. Like he didn't care whether we could identify her or not. Or . . . perhaps he didn't feel right about searching her body or taking any of her things. Or maybe he was just in a hurry. The missing jewelry might have something to do with the motive. Every woman wears jewelry, or does she? But all in all I suspect he wasn't trying to rob her."

The cop, Tom, and I left the room and walked to the garage where an attendant from the coroner's office had already arrived to take the girl away for further examination. Tom knew him well after weeks of working with him. "Tell your boss I'll get my notes to him by email within the next hour or so."

"And by the way," he turned to the cop: "Her driver's license gives a local address – Baltic Avenue".

The cop told us that a girl had been reported missing from up there for two days.

Her mother had made several calls and was frantic about it. "She worked at the donut shop across from that tourist museum on the Boardwalk," he said "What do they call it? 'The Panorama of Crime'?"

I looked at Tom. "Do you suppose there's a link there? Or maybe I'm just caught up in the theatrics of the name and location."

"There's nothing very theatrical about 99% of crimes committed", Tom said.

"Crime, and particularly murder, isn't like what you see on tv. Mostly just grim and ugly. The people who murder are usually stupid. Otherwise they wouldn't do it. Nobody confesses at the end of the story as they do on those detective shows. Sometimes the police never find out what really happened, or why it happened. Every murderer pleads "not guilty" and even when he's sentenced he doesn't put all the dots together to make sense of it. And why am I saying 'he?' There's lots of 'she's' involved as well. And they're just as dumb and lethal."

"In this girl's case, we have to wonder why the murderer carried her body around for awhile?," he continued. "Couldn't seem to make up his mind: whether to turn himself in or dispose of the body. That tells me that the homicide was probably an accident rather than premeditated. If it had been a drug "hit", the body would never have been deposited in the ocean where it could re-surface, You have no idea how many "creative" ideas the drug lords have when it comes to getting rid of bodies. They learned a lot about it during Prohibition. We had an old fellow in Pittsburgh – long before my time – who specialized in dropping bodies with "concrete boots" into the Ohio River. That's old technology.

Nobody would try it now. There are better ways. That's why I know that the murderer of the girl from Baltic Avenue was an amateur."

We went back to Tom's apartment and worked together on his computer, filling out the initial investigative report.

"Want to add anything before I send this along? " asked Tom.

I told him that, as a woman, I find it curious that a girl who lives on Baltic Avenue and works at a donut shop on the Boardwalk wears expensive clothes and ultra-expensive Italian-made shoes. Maybe the Outlets explains the clothes, but not the shoes."

"Probably drugs are involved somewhere," Tom surmised. "In all the homicides I've investigated in the past couple of weeks, at least 80% have been involved with drugs.

Same was true in Pittsburgh. Except for the domestic quarrel here and there, like the one over in Wilkinsburg near Frick Park last year where a woman chopped her husband up with a meat axe because he ignored her, or so she said."

"Probably deserved it", I said with a faint smile on my face.

Tom walked to the window. "You know, Lillian," he said, "Atlantic City gets a bad rap. It's a pretty safe city when all's said and done. You can walk on the Boardwalk at any hour of the night knowing that the casinos are all lit up and open and that cameras inside and out are keeping tabs on everyone in view. And God help anyone who tries to intimidate a woman, or steal a wallet. Gamblers, professional ones, keep a tight watch on their ship. If you know what I mean. They don't want petty crime to ruin the good thing they have going for them. In fact, you're a lot safer here at night than you are over in Philly or even New York. "

I had to admit that I'd never been threatened or even approached on the Boardwalk let alone in any of the casinos. Now of course there are parts in every city that I wouldn't venture into after dark. But I've never been afraid in AC. Maybe because I know it so well. The streets I walk behind the Boardwalk at night aren't threatening, just empty.

"I'll have to stick with this report until the Coroner replies to my email message, " said Tom. "Maybe we can get together later for dinner and I'll let you in on everything I know." I told him that I'd be ready at whatever time he chose.

As a woman, I wondered who the girl lived with and whether she had a child.

There's always a human side. I lost my little girl many years ago and still think about her everyday. But I don't want ever to talk about it. I told Tom that my husband never talked about the war unless he was with his buddies, of course. And then they proceeded to sink the Princeton over and over again.

"Wasn't that one of *our* ships?" said Tom, scrunching up his face in surprise.

"That's just the point", I said. "But please, Tom, please don't make me repeat the story. I must have heard it a thousand times. Look it up in your history book. World War II, Pacific Theater, and you'll see that Commander Moore was there."

I asked Tom if he needed me any further. He took my hand and thanked me for being with him this afternoon. I left his apartment and walked down to the Garden Pier where there was a display of Japanese flower arrangements. When I see them I keep it to myself that the arrangements are "almost" Japanese flower arrangements, but very nice. Not quite the perfection of exquisite arrangements I've seen in Kyoto or Nara. But very nice. Thinking about Japan, I remember how much we hated the Japanese during the war. And now . . . I also couldn't stop thinking about the girl on the slab and about **what Tom would have to tell me this evening.**

Chapter Six

Dillon: *"For a moment I had forgotten about my wife. Like she was already dead. I quickly picked up another candle, said a prayer especially for her, and lit it."*

I wanted to get the taste of the morgue and the crime out of my mind, so I offered to take Lillian to some nice place, maybe out on the pike to Smithville Village or over at Bellagio's. But she said she wanted to go to Kornfeld's if it was okay by me. Kornfeld's is just a deli, more or less, but they have good food. If you like Jewish food. And I do. And it's just down the street from where Lillian lives.

"Why Kornfeld's," I asked, "when I would have taken you anywhere?"

"The atmosphere," she said with a wicked smile. "The atmosphere."

Talk about atmosphere, the place is swimming in it: the overpowering smell of hot pastrami, stuffed cabbage and Hungarian goulash. Waitresses move around at breakneck speed carrying trays and yelling "hot stuff" as they bend like toe dancers over the tables. Mr. Kornfeld sits behind the cash register with a face as sour as one of his bilious green kosher pickles. Mrs. Kornfeld, a big boned lady with a high decibel voice, serves as hostess as well as inspector general. Occasionally she'll glance at one of the trays the waitresses carry by and yell out (apparently to the kitchen staff who are already deafened from the general din): *"Tell them not so much sour cream on the blintzes!"*

When we arrived the whole place was already in full motion with customers coming and going; waitresses shuffling from kitchen to tables and back; Mrs. Kornfeld barking orders which were occasionally directed to Mr. Kornfeld who sat stolidly at his register with a dyspeptic look on his face, generated either by the overpowering smell of the food, or the sound of his wife's shrill commands.

"Isn't it wonderful!" said Lillian, as we waited in a crowd that stretched out the door.

When Mrs. Kornfeld spotted Lillian she came right over and pulled us out of line, leading us to a table in a quiet corner of the restaurant. "Same as usual" she asked?.

Lillian said "yes". "And the same for him," she said, pointing to me. Lilllian nodded.

"Good choice," said Mrs. Kornfeld and added: "You're a smart man!" as she hustled away from us back through the pandemonium to the waiting crowd.

"What did we order?" I asked. "Stuffed kishka," smiled Lillian, "and you're going to love it."

Lillian explained that it was goose neck with wonderful herb stuffing, but assured me it would be delicious. I told her I knew I'd like it, considering her excellent taste.

"Anyway", I said, "I guess I've had worse!"

"Faint praise, "she replied with a grin.

Mrs. Kornfeld stormed back through the crowded tables carrying a small dish of chicken liver paste — Lillian called it pate'— and toast, as well as a bottle of dark red wine, and I mean dark. It was the color of ink. Lillian said it was a Hungarian specialty called Ox Blood. Once again she assured me that I'd like it, but I didn't. Kind of bitter at first taste, but maybe better as you drink more of it.

"Rodger and I drank this for the first time in Budapest way back when, "she smiled. "Quite an aftertaste, don't you think?"

Lillian said that once she asked Mrs.Kornfeld why they had a German name when, from all indications, they were Hungarian. She said that Mrs. Kornfeld just laughed and said that Kornfeld was her Mother-in-Law's maiden name. They changed to that name when they escaped from Hungary in 1956 and came to the United States. They realized that when they opened their little restaurant, no one would be able to pronounce, let alone spell, their real name: ***Szilagyi.***

I didn't really like the taste or aftertaste of the "Ox Blood" but I lied. I told Lillian that I liked everything that she liked. That's why we got along so well together. Despite the chaos around us, the little corner we were squashed into was surprisingly – what do I want to say—intimate. I mean, we could talk on the quiet.

I broke the silence and told her that the murdered girl lived with her Mother up on Baltic Avenue and there was a little girl, about three years old. The cops broke the news to her sometime around noon, and she took it real bad. Real bad.

"I've been thinking of that girl all day," Lillian said. "And I know how a Mother feels when they tell her that her child is dead. Oh I just feel so bad for her."

I told Lillian that we were never lucky enough to have kids, Evelyn and me. But I felt bad for the girl as well. That's about the crappiest job a cop can have: knocking on the door of a stranger and telling them that one of their family members is dead. Once I made a terrible mistake and knocked on a door to tell a woman that her husband was killed in an automobile accident. I told the woman who answered that I had very bad news about her husband, and she screamed and said it was her brother, and that I had to go next door and give the same message to her sister-in-law. What a mess that was.

Normally, you want to get in and out quick. You know better than to get personally involved in any way. But it's really tough when it involves kids killed in a car accident, for example, or one like today who might have been murdered. .

I explained to Lillian that I talked to a cop who stopped by my apartment later this afternoon and told me the girl's name was Rachel Egron Bauer. Actually, she wasn't a girl. She was twenty-six, but looked a lot younger. No police record. Not even a parking ticket. She lived with her Mother, a Mrs. Ruth Egron, who was taking care of Rachel's little girl. Rachel's husband walked out on her about two years ago. Hasn't been back since. He's up in New York City somewhere living like a bum, from what Mrs. Egron knows. She's a widow and takes care of the kid while Rachel works in the donut shop at the Kentucky Avenue corner of the Boardwalk.

Apparently, up until recently, Rachel used to work at Bally's as an accountant.

But she left last year sometime. Don't know why. The casino said she was a good employee. No trouble whatsoever. In fact, they hated to see her go and would take her back if she re-applied. .

Lillian asked if I thought it would be all right for her to stop by and see Mrs. Egron tomorrow. She said she could give her a telephone call in the morning and tell her she was sent by the police as a kind of social worker to see if she had any questions or needs. She thought that maybe she could get some additional information, or maybe just help to console her, as one mother to another.

She told me that she thought the AC police would be willing to trust her on this one. After all, she was on the Board of the Police Widows Association.

I told her I was sure they would, but that I'd check with the Chief first thing in the morning. "I'm pretty sure they'll call her in for a talk sooner or later anyway," I said, "and maybe you could prepare her for it. It's pretty intense, you know, with a couple of cops from homicide grilling her for an hour or so."

We finished dinner and left the atmosphere of hot paprika in the restaurant for the cool breeze on Pacific Avenue. There's a big Catholic church across from Kornfeld's called: St. Nicholas of Tolentine. Been there forever. My family and I used to go to mass there every Sunday we spent at the Shore. My mother more often. Like every morning at 6:00 am. Mass. I try to go once in a while when I'm in Atlantic City for old time's sake and for my mother's sake.

I stopped for a moment and looked over at the church, where 8:00 pm Mass was leaving out. "Do you want to go in?" Lillian said.

"Do you mind?"

"Of course not. I'll sit quietly in the back."

We walked through the doorway into the vestibule and I dipped my fingers in the holy water font, then went up to the altar and genuflected. I sat in the first pew and prayed for a minute and then walked over to where the votive candles were burning. I lit one for my Mother. Then I thought about it for a moment, and lit another for the girl we found in the ocean this morning. I wondered where her soul was resting tonight?

My God, for a moment I had forgotten about my wife. Like she was already dead.

I quickly picked up another candle, said a prayer especially for her, and lit it. I felt guilty. Maybe I needed to go to Confession. Hadn't done that for years. Maybe I ought to start again.

Lillian was praying, too, in her own way, in the pew with her head down and her eyes tight shut. When she finished, we walked back out on Pacific Avenue without saying very much, and then up on to the Boardwalk. The ocean was calm as glass, with the waves making just a ripple as they reached the shore. The beach extended a long way out from the Boardwalk. It was low tide, and the night was full of stars. Somehow there always seemed like a lot more of them in the sky in Atlantic City than in Pittsburgh!

We were standing right across from the old Warner Theatre—or at least the facade of what used to be the theatre. They preserved it and built around it. But the thing I remembered most was the ceiling of that theatre that must have had a thousand stars on it. All lit from behind. I tried to count them when I went there as a kid, but there were way too many.

I asked Lillie – that's what I call her now – if she remembered the ceiling. She said that of course she did. And she even remembered the first "grown up" movie she saw there, called "All This and Heaven Too." She forgot who was in it – maybe Charles Boyer — but she loved it.

Then Lillian took a deep breath of the salt air as we leaned over the railing looking out to sea. "You should have seen it before the war," she laughed.

"I did, Lillie", I said. "Do you see where we're standing," I pointed. "This is the spot where my father used to take a family photo every year we came down here. Always on a Sunday afternoon when we were all dressed up and coming from Mass. Right here in front of the old Warner Theatre, and posed at an angle where you could see the Million Dollar Pier in the background. A whole generation of Dillons are on those pictures. You can watch all of us growing up as you look through them in the family album. Now," I said, "all of them are gone. Evelyn and I used to stand here, in this same spot, and have our picture taken every year since we were married. Now when I look at those pictures, I can see her fading away year by year. I can see it in her eyes."

"When I was a little girl, " said Lillian, "we walked on the Boardwalk for an hour or so in our very best Sunday clothes after coming from church, and there was a man from the Traymore who took professional photos. The Traymore was just over there." she pointed behind her. "He'd pose us in front of the big glass doors that led into the hotel, or up on the Sundeck. Then on Monday morning we'd look over the pictures which were pinned to a bulletin board in the lobby and we'd decide which ones we wanted."

"That must have been some hotel in its day", I said.

The memory of it made Lillian smile. " The best part, the very best part, was early in the morning—just at sunrise— when they brought horses and a few ponies down on the beach and Dad and I would ride just at the water's edge with some of the other guests. The horses seemed to like it as much as we did. Well as a kid, you can imagine what a thrill it was.

But most mornings we'd rent bicycles. My Dad and I shared a double bike and had a great time shooting down the Boardwalk at breakneck speed in the cool of the morning. We'd always stop for a cup of hot chocolate at a little restaurant on the corner of the Central Pier. And my father never failed to tell me the story of how his sister Millie, my aunt, was learning to ride a bike, way back in the late thirties, and how she lost control and headed for a stained glass window in one of the auction houses along the Boardwalk which luckily for her, and the window, she missed. What a character she was.

I told Lillian that my biggest thrill as a kid was on Saturday mornings, down at the end of the Million Dollar Pier. At about 7:00 or 8:00 am, they'd bring up a net that they'd put out the night before. When that thing came up, there was a load of jumping, wriggling fish like you never saw: baby sharks and blowfish and sea bass. All kinds of strange creatures. That was my thrill of the day.

"I remember that, too," said Lillian. "I guess it didn't take much to amuse us in those days."

"Well the thing of it was that things like that were free", I reminded her. "It didn't cost a nickel, and a lot of the folks watching didn't even have a nickel."

We just stood looking at the ocean without saying anything. Then Lillian broke the silence ."How is she doing? Evelyn, I mean. Any better or worse?"

I told her that my sister, Mary Catherine, called me the other day and told me that Evelyn was getting weaker. Not responding.

Sleeping more. Not eating at all. My sister is an angel. She thinks it's just a matter of time, but she wants me to stay here a little longer.

Until the weather changes. She says the worst is still ahead and that I need to prepare myself and get my strength back before I face that.

I didn't tell Lillie that I had some real problems before I came done here a couple of weeks ago. Depression and some heart murmur thing. So I'll stay a while, but as soon as this murder thing is cleared up, I'll get my stuff together and go back to Pittsburgh.

Who am I kidding. I'm living like a real person for the first time in ten years, and I'm liking it. And in my heart, I don't really want to go back.

I took Lillian's hand."I wish it could be different. You have no idea how happy these last few days have been. I've been . . . . ."

She put her fingers to my lips. "Don't say anything more. Just take every day as it comes. Like this evening. Let's walk down the Boardwalk as far as we can."

"Maybe I can make it to the Hilton, "I said, "but that's about it"

"Actually," laughed Lillian, "I was thinking of going as far as Lucy the Elephant. I haven't seen her for over sixty years. My father used to say she was a hotel at one time, but that was hard for me to believe. After all, as I told you, we always stayed at the Traymore. That was the only hotel I knew in Atlantic City. I remember that there was a little window in Lucy's backside, just under her tail. My father said that his father knew a man who once stayed there. Let's go down and see her, Tom. Let's go see Lucy."

"I'll give it my best," I laughed, knowing full well that they moved Lucy many years ago all the way down to Ventnor, miles away. But I meant it when I told her *I'd give it my best.*

Chapter Seven

Lillian: *"The color on the Monopoly board for Baltic is purple, which means it's a very low rent district".*

Arrangements were made through the police department, and the next morning I was on my way to see Ruth Egron., Rachel's Mother.

I walked up through the Outlets to Baltic Avenue and followed the numbers to her apartment house. I never spent much time on Baltic. That part of town was always out of the way and badly worn down, even in good times. Lots of aimless people on the street.

Most people who aren't familiar with Atlantic City at all recognize Baltic Avenue from the Monopoly Board. I think the color on the board for Baltic is purple, which means it's a very low rent district. That about sums it up. But in the past few years, the city has cleaned up the area and added some new housing. Maybe they should have changed the name of the street as well.

Tom says it's that way with Pittsburgh. People who don't know any better, and probably have never been there, still think of it as the "smokey city". I have to admit that it was just that way when I was growing up. I remember visiting an old aunt there in the East End of town and I was shocked, as a little girl, to see soot coming down with the snow one January evening. By morning, the snow was dotted with black spots which by noon had turned to gray slush. Even the little sparrows were gray rather than their natural brown color.

I've been back many times since and happy to say that Pittsburgh is quite beautiful now. I mean it. The smoke is gone, and the rivers are clean. Maybe you saw some of it during the International G20 Meeting held there a while back.

I approached Mrs.Egron's apartment with some hesitation. I suddenly felt like the worst kind of intruder. But in all honesty, I really did want to console her and help her if I could. The idea of getting some additional information for Tom was secondary to my visit. I knew what it was like to lose a child, and my heart ached for her. That was my prime reason for coming, murder or not.

I don't know what I expected when I rang the bell, but to my surprise she was a rather youngish looking woman, somewhat shy, but very welcoming under the circumstances. I could see grief in her large blue eyes. I know all about sleepless nights and endless tears and, yes, about questioning God. And I knew she was going through all of it, just as I had.

"Please sit down," she said, as I introduced myself. "I just made some fresh coffee. Would you like some?"

"Yes, of course. But I want to make it clear from the start" I said, "that I didn't come here to question you. Just to talk with you about Rachel, woman to woman. I lost my own daughter some years ago and I know that nothing I can say — or anyone can say — really makes a difference at this point.. Nothing could console me. I used to make up her room every morning and put out her clothes and toys. I did that for five years, until my husband put an end to it. He told me very bluntly that it was time to stop. And I did, and I began to live again. But a part of me never healed, Mrs. Egron, and I don't expect it will ever heal for you, either."

She put her handkerchief up to her eyes. "She was the best girl in the world. She never did a bad thing in her life. After my husband died, she looked out after me. Helped me pay my bills and showed me how to write a check. Drove me everywhere I needed to go. I never learned to drive. Still don't. If it weren't for little Melanie, I don't think I could go on. I **wouldn't want** to go on."

"Where is Melanie now, Mrs. Egron," I asked.

"Call me Ruth, please" she said. "Melanie's with the neighbor. I didn't want her to be involved with the police, but if I had known it was someone like you I wouldn't have sent her away. She's just across the hall."

"And her father?"

"They probably never should have married. She was so young, but he seemed like a nice fellow at the start. Kind of boyish. Maybe a bit 'uncommitted', if you know what I mean. But aren't most young people today? It's a wonder any of them get married at all.

He just wanted to live with her. But she wouldn't have it, and so they were married, and of course the baby came shortly after. She had a little trouble with the delivery. Then the hospital bills began coming in, and he walked out. Just left one day after a long talk with Rachel and a kiss on Melanie's forehead. We got a postcard from New York City. He said he was sorry he caused her so much trouble. And that was it. Haven't heard from him since."

His name is Gary Bauer, but Rachel took back her maiden name after he left and said she'd have Melanie's name legally changed to Egron before she starts school.

She just wanted no further contact with Gary. She was very stubborn about things like that.

"Do you think he might have had something to do with her death? I mean, could he have come back and perhaps they had an argument?" I asked.

"No," said Ruth. "I called his parents, and they told me that they knew he was somewhere in New York City trying to find a job. They didn't know any other details. They get a card once in a while, but that's about all. He says he still loves Rachel."

"They liked Rachel, too ," she said, "and after all, they are Melanie's grand- parents. They were terribly shocked to hear about Rachel, but they're out in Iowa, and both of them up in years. So what can they do? They had Gary late in life, they said. I couldn't help thinking that maybe they shouldn't have had him at all. But it's not their fault. And neither of them are doing well. I suppose they love him just as much as I loved Rachel."

She began to cry again, sobbing deeply now.

"Is there anything I can do for you, Ruth. Anything at all. That's really why I came to see you."

"I'm just confused, that's all," she sobbed. "Everything seems to be closing in."

"Anything at all?" I repeated.

"Not really," she said. "Rachel had things fixed for me, even though I'm sure she didn't expect to die before me. Anyway, she invested some of her money when times were good back in the nineties, and it's been a Godsend to me."

I had to ask the question which had been bothering me from the start. "I don't want to be personal, Ruth," I said '"but knowing that she was apparently making good money at Bally's, with even some to spare for investments, have you any idea why she left her job at the casino to work at a donut shop? There seems to be a clue in there somewhere. It doesn't make sense unless there was something bad happening with her at Bally's. Perhaps someone was threatening her?"

"I wondered about that myself," said Ruth. "But they really liked her a lot at Bally's and she made good wages. They were surprised when she left, and wanted her to stay. They called here several times to see if she'd change her mind. I live on the annuity checks she arranged, plus my husband's Social Security. Without the annuities , I wouldn't be able to make a go of it at all. But financially, I can't complain. I'm doing fine."

"But that's what I mean about Rachel," she continued. "She was a good girl, always looking out after people, and especially after me, since she knew I didn't know anything about finance or income tax, or any of that. My husband always took care of it, and when he died, Rachel stepped in and handled it. She told me that she was even putting away some money to make sure Melanie got a good education. That child meant everything to her. Everything."

"She had beautiful taste in clothes," I said.

Ruth agreed, and said that she was such a tiny girl that she had to buy some of her things in the junior department. But when she went over to shop in Philadelphia about once a week, there were several stores that catered to smaller sizes. " She loved shoes. She had a closet full of them. But no interest in jewelry. She said she'd spend that on Melanie's future. I suppose I'll give Goodwill a call." Her tears began again.

No doubt Rachel was a wonderful and very thoughtful daughter. And smart. And very pretty. But some of the things that Ruth told me began to trouble me. She wasn't aware of where her daughter was getting enough money to arrange annuities, and she didn't ask. In fact, she had no idea how much money was involved.

Ruth told me that she herself had been a waitress for most of **her** life, and worked a couple of years after she got married. Then she became a housewife. Simple as that.

She always knew that Rachel was "smart with figures" and wasn't surprised , or perhaps not aware, of how much money it took to set up a decent annuity. And didn't she talk about annuities in the plural? More than one annuity. And besides all that, apparently there was money going into an educational fund. The expensive clothes and shoes were another matter.

All this talk about clothes got me thinking on another plain. Why didn't we find a jacket or a sweater among her things at the hospital. It was a cool evening. Did she wear one, or did she leave it somewhere, or did someone take it from her? Or was it lost in the water? And when I think of the atmosphere at that bar, I wonder why someone her age would wear an expensive skirt and blouse rather than jeans? Was she planning to meet someone "special" there? Did she have any particular person in mind? Oh well, back to Ruth.

I began with some financial advice. "I think you need to know exactly what you own and what kinds of funds Rachel's money is invested in. There've been a lot of problems in the money market since she made those investments. Do you have any passbooks or electronic records?"

Rachel looked perplexed. "I just know the name of her investment firm. I couldn't find any passbooks or papers. And her computer is a mystery to me. I know she had a password, or something like that. But I have no idea what that's all about. The police picked the computer up anyway and want to take a look at it."

I told her that it was just a formality that the police took the computer. In fact they were required to check it since a homicide was involved. In the meantime I asked her if she'd trust me in telling me the name of her investment firm.

"It's in Philadelphia, "she said. "She went over there almost every week, and sometimes she had me sign papers. I have something here. She picked up an envelope from her most recent annuity check. "It's a company called "Emory, Drexel and Coates".

Rachel said it was one of the oldest and most reliable firms in Philadelphia."

Yes, indeed, I could attest to that. My distant cousin, Jake Coates, is a partner in the firm. And I believe if one went back far enough they'd find that my great-great-great grandfather, Isaac Coates – and Jake's as well— had a hand in founding the company. Or perhaps it was Isaac's father, Moses Coates, who was a Quaker, but by no means resigned to poverty. As a matter of fact, he owned several lots in the center of Philadelphia back in the 1680's when William Penn laid it out. He also owned a farm 'outside of town' on the land where the Philadelphia Zoo stands. I wonder what **that** real estate is worth in today's market?"

"Ruth," I said, " I know some folks at that company and I'm sure they'd be willing to review all of your accounts with you. I don't want to get personal or intrude into your business, but if you'd like I can give them a call and we can go over there together. I won't sit in on your financial business, but I'd be more than happy to introduce you to at least one of the partners and see that he explains your accounts very thoroughly. Would you like me to do that?"

Ruth was more than eager to have me handle things for her, and we agreed that if I could arrange it we'd take the train over to Philly in the morning. We talked a bit more, and then I said I'd have to leave.

"Not before you meet Melanie," she said, as we stepped out the door from her apartment. She knocked on the door across the way, and her neighbor, a large, pleasant- looking black woman, held Melanie in her arms.

"She's been so-o-o—good", the woman said. "And she ate all her lunch." Melanie threw out her arms and with a big smile leaned forward as far as she could to kiss Ruth.

Her neighbor and I looked at each other without a word, but with the same thoughts passing between us.

Ruth, took her into her arms eagerly. She had tears in her eyes. "Call me later today," she said, "if you can arrange things. And thanks for coming".

I walked away quickly because I knew I'd break down myself if I stayed any longer. A lot of thoughts about my own little one came back to me in a blur. "It will never go away," I said to myself. ***"Never!"***

Chapter Eight

Dillon: *"Lillian will be surprised to know where our next 'date' will take her"*

I had a little light supper with Lillian and then left at about ten because I was on an unofficial assignment from the police department to check out the Rendezvous Club on Kentucky Avenue I say a "light" supper because she's really not equipped to have a "heavy one." By that I mean I couldn't even locate the kitchen in her apartment until she moved a beautiful Japanese screen in one corner of her living area and introduced me to the smallest kitchen I've ever seen. It's only about six feet long and three feet wide, and the sink takes a good part of it. She told me it's modeled after the kind of kitchen they have on submarines where they serve the whole crew from a space not much larger.

Let me try to describe it. She has a crockpot; a built-in-the-wall microwave; a food blender; an electric can opener; and one of those little round cooking appliances that heat from top and bottom like a waffle iron. You see them advertised on tv all the time.

There are cabinets above and below the sink containing all the food, dishware, and tea towels she needs. Under the sink she has the smallest fridge I've ever seen. She tells me that since she buys fresh produce every day she doesn't need much food storage space.

She pretends she's not much of a cook and that the small kitchen is a good reason to eat out. Which she loves to do. No wonder she's acquainted with every chef in every restaurant in the city!

But I must say that the meal she served me was terrific: big chunks of nice Jersey melon wrapped in Italian dried ham and mushrooms stuffed with fresh crabmeat. And that was just starters. She said she thought she should feed a hungry man like me a hearty seafood meal, and she came up with lobster chowder and home made biscuits. The green salad with balsamic dressing came after dinner, just like the Italians do it. We finished up with cheese – Brie and Camembert. The moldy, oozy kind. I thought I wouldn't like it, but I did! There was a fine white wine with the meal, but I don't remember the name of it. It was the best "small meal" I ever ate. She must have been kidding when she said she couldn't cook.

As for my trip to the Rendezvous Club, it's the first solid lead we've had.

Apparently, this was the last place Rachel Egron was seen before she was murdered. The word "murder" comes to me more quickly to me than "accident."

The police had already checked it out, but they wanted me to go in "undercover, so to speak," just to see what more I might pick up. I've only been to the Club once since I came down to AC this summer. Tried it and didn't like it, but I've passed it at least a hundred times since.

It's kind of a night club. Big barn of a building, with a flat roof. Stucco front, right behind a Boardwalk attraction called "Panorama of Crime". Anyway, the club started out as a hotel many, many years ago, but the 1944 hurricane tore the top two floors off and it's been a restaurant, speakeasy, bar, nightclub – whatever you want to call it – over the years that followed. There's talk at the police station that drugs are passed there. It's a young crowd. I wouldn't be surprised.

Believe it or not, it was a top entertainment hang-out in the thirties and early forties. All of Kentucky Avenue had jazz joints and hot spots where big names used to come and perform. I think I told you that once before. Anyway, by now its glory days are over and it's well worn down with an iffy clientele.

My Dad used to tell me that when it was a hotel, and when the "Panorama of Crime" as it's known now, was called the old Globe

Theater , there was a door between the theatre and the hotel so the girls wouldn't have to go outside after the shows.

Very considerate. I have to think that it might have served other purposes as well, but that's all in the past and long forgotten. The Globe started out as Vaudeville, but regressed to Burlesque.

Burlesque was the mildest kind of porno compared with what any kid can find on the Internet today. My mother used to tell me with a sly laugh that many years ago she and her sister always wanted to sneak into the Globe to see what all the fuss was about.

Their father — my grandfather – who played there in a little orchestra when it was Vaudeville promised to take them in when they were twenty-one, but there was hell to pay when my grandmother found out. Imagine two good Catholic girls being exposed to "a spectacle" when they were hardly out of their teens. Times certainly have changed since then, haven't they!

There was also a rumor that there is a trap door in the basement of the Globe which takes you right down onto the sand under the Boardwalk. The story is that bootleg booze used to be brought in that way for the speakeasy next door, a.k.a. the Rendezvous Club today. How it worked and whether it's really there, I don't know. A good story, but maybe just a story. No one alive at that time in the late twenties is around to say aye, yes, or no. The police told me that the one of the properties is owned by Istavan Nagy, and the other by Nagy S. Istavan. Maybe they're cousins, or maybe someone in the city just mixed up the names when he made out the deed. Curious.

Anyway, I stopped by the Rendezvous around 10:00pm — just about the time that Rachel Egron was spotted there a couple of days ago. I sat at the bar looking over the action, which wasn't very much. Just a couple of kids with plugged-in instruments playing songs they wrote at the highest pitched decibels they could reach. Honest to God, I didn't know where one song ended and the other began. But they were earnest in their work, and everybody else in the joint seemed to know who they were and what they were playing. And they were enjoying it. So much for being 75 in Year 2009, and being musically illiterate.

I made some small talk with the bartender, a very young bartender, who had a book on specialty drinks at the ready on the table behind him. Not that he needed it. His repertoire was pretty much limited to several brands of bottled beer (which he could handle) and an occasional martini or Manhattan and maybe some vodka drinks, which were easy enough.

"It's pretty quiet in here tonight," I said, picking out some cashew pieces from the mixed nuts on a plate in front of me.

He told me it was like that almost every night. "I don't know how the boss keeps it going," he said. "I'm not sure what kind of crowd he wants to cater to, but so far he hasn't discovered it."

The bar was in a dead sound spot which allowed for conversation while the band played on and on. We had a long talk about his studies at the local community college, and what he thought about life in general. Not very deep conversational material, but it kept him interested as long as I asked him about *his* life and *his* ambitions. A nice kid all in all. I'm not making fun of him. He works hard for his money.

After a while I brought Rachel Egron into the conversation. I didn't mention her by name, just said that I understood the neighborhood girl who was murdered earlier in the week worked in the donut shop right across the street, and wasn't it too bad the way she died.

The bartender volunteered that he'd been interviewed by the police and told them she was a regular at the club, but not a drinker.

"What do you mean by that?" I asked.

"Well", he said, "I mean she came in after the shop closed across the street and sat here at the bar but only drank ginger ale with a shot of cola in it. That made it look like hard liquor, but it wasn't. I talked to her a lot," he said, "and she was a real nice kid.

Always left a nice tip even with a cheap drink like that. Such a little girl, he added, and nicely dressed for this place. When she came here – or any bar , I suppose – she said she never wore jeans because they were sure to 'card' her. I think she was in her early twenties. But she looked much younger."

I asked him whether she ever had anyone join her and he said that a lot of guys w**anted** to, and that she'd sit and talk with some of them for a while, but mostly she came for the music. That's all she came for. And he added that when the band was playing it was hard enough to make yourself heard over the noise, let alone carry on a conversation.

"You never saw her go home with anyone?"

"Not once," he said. "not a single time. I told you, she came for the music and always at around 10:00pm after the first show started. She usually stayed until about 11:00 or maybe a bit later, and then she was out of here. When this one particular band was playing — they call themselves *The Restless* — she came every night. They're regulars, but sometimes we have "spot" bands as well. When Restless played, she was here maybe once or twice a week.

I ordered another beer and asked the bartender if he was on duty the night she was murdered.

"Nobody knows exactly how she died," he corrected me. "I can only say that the last time I saw her here there was a big storm brewing. Raining like hell. The tide was up, and the ocean was real high that night. Some of it even came inside on the floor here," he said, pointing to a dark patch behind the bar. "It was about hub deep out at the bottom of Kentucky Avenue. It was salt water, not sewer water, and you could see that the beach was already covered up and you could hear the water sloshing around under the floor here, so you know it was already under the Boardwalk. This is a low spot, here at the bottom of Kentucky."

"People started to scatter," he continued,. "That's when she must have gone out with the rest of them. Pretty soon all the customers, including the band were out the door, so I started closing up. Fast! Lucky for me, because all the lights went out in this part of town just at that time. I think I saw her leaving earlier, but there were too many things happening all at the same time for me to notice. I took a last look around, as well as I could see in the dark with only the emergency lights on, and locked the door behind me. I guess she died sometime later. Maybe she slipped in the water and got carried out with the waves, or maybe someone in a car picked her up. I don't know. I ran like hell through the water up to the Boardwalk and down to the fudge store where my friend was waiting to take me home. I was soaked to the skin. "

I thought about all that the bartender had told me and still couldn't get a lead on it.

I knew she didn't arrive home that night. Maybe someone *did* pick her up in a car. Maybe a taxi. Anyway, somewhere along the line she just disappeared. It can happen quicker than you think. I remember a kid in Pittsburgh who waved to his mother as he walked toward the school bus and when she looked around again he was gone. She thought he was on the bus. But he wasn't. Disappeared just like that.

I paid my tab and got up off the stool to leave.

"Now there's a suspicious character," said the bartender, pointing to a big hulk of a guy who had suddenly appeared at the other end of the bar. "He's really creepy. Just kind of appears and disappears. Has a couple of straight vodkas. Silver bullets, he calls them. Never talks to anybody. In fact I'm not sure he speaks English that well. Must be some kind of Russian, or something. He just drops into a barstool and points at the vodka and grunts. Me and the other bartender have never spoken too much with him."

The bartender moved a wet rag over the top of the bar "Like I said, he's kind of a creepy guy. And he never tips. Never. No social graces at all", he laughed.

I asked where he came from, and the bartender said he worked next door at the "Panorama of Crime" on the Boardwalk

"I guess he's some kind of security guard," the bartender said. "Anyway, they have him dressed up in a costume. Like a Cossack, I guess. From what I heard he's been there since the place opened, and before that in another similar kind of attraction up the Boardwalk a ways."

As I sipped my drink I remembered the Globe as it was when I was a kid. Now it was renovated with a new name: "The "Panorama of Crime", or whatever they call it. Like I said, it was a burlesque theatre through the war years and into the late forties. But times and fashions change, and it sat empty for a couple of years. There was a pizza shop in the front part of the building for a couple of years, but the back stayed empty. Then a souvenir shop took the place of the pizza parlor, and it lasted a year or so When Atlantic City began to revitalize and Boardwalk property around here became attractive and valuable again, a big movie company from the West Coast came in and refurbished the entire building. Turned it into a tourist attraction and gave it a new name: "Panorama of Crime". They have plenty of room in there, and they tell me that they've reproduced places where major crimes occurred in the past. Like for instance, they have a short street made up to look like London at the time when Jack the Ripper did his dirty work. Fog and all. The audience stands in the middle, and they show one of those 360 degree wrap-around films—if you know what I mean—and then some real actors come rushing in as if they stepped out of the movie. Parts of it are in 3-D. Totally realistic, they tell me. But tickets are expensive. Not like the Ski-Ball and the Penny Arcade and the Funhouse that used to be in this stretch of the Boardwalk..

They also have a basement scene of the police station where Lee Harvey Oswald was shot. They reproduce the action with blank bullets. Damndest thing. They don't spare the artificial gore. But that's what kids want now days. The gorier the better. I guess it's pretty popular and I'm not surprised that a big bozo like the guy who just came in is working there. He looks the part, as we used to say on the Force.

I looked him over carefully. Then I moved from my stool and leaning on the stool next to him, I reached across for the peanuts in the plate in front of him. "Sorry," I said, "I didn't mean to bump your arm. Just wanted to get some peanuts."

"I suppose you want to talk to me," he said softly, and in plain English, looking straight into my eyes. "You're a policeman, aren't you?" So much for my "cover." I was just a bit thrown off, but I said in all honestly: "No I'm not a cop. Just doin' some work for them on the case of that missing girl from across the street."

"I have nothing to hide," he said. "I knew her and I liked to sit and talk with her once in a while. She was a nice lady. Nice to talk to. I told them that already. There's not much more to tell," he said. "A lot of people are afraid to talk to *me.* They think I'm some kind of brute, I guess, because I'm so big." He made a fist – a large fist—to prove his point. " I don't know what they think. Sometimes they ask me if I'm a Russian Cossack. Look," he said, curling his fist, "I was born here. My father was, too. My grandfather was born in Hungary, but he came over after the First World War. He owns this place."

I asked him directly: "Is he Istavan Nagy or Nagy Istavan."

The "Cossack" laughed. "It's a Hungarian name, and in Hungary they always place the last name before the first name. Here in America, of course, we put the first name ahead of the last one. My grandfather just happened to buy both properties at different times, and since he had a great sense of humor, I think he did it just to confuse the Recorder of Deeds. Or maybe he had other reasons. Anyway" he said extending his hand, "I am not a *Cossack.* I'm an American of Hungarian descent and damn proud of it. My name is Imre Nagy."

I shook his hand and told him that I was glad to know something about Hungarians that I hadn't known before. Then I told him it was natural that the police should start looking here in the club because this was the last place anybody saw the girl before she was murdered. I noticed that he kept looking around a bit nervously as we spoke.

"I don't think she was murdered," he said, tossing the rest of his vodka down. "I think it was an accident. It was a bad night. Pitch black outside. Anything could have happened."

I told him that the police hadn't made a final report on the matter, and perhaps there was an accident. Or maybe suicide.

"Not suicide," he said with conviction. "She was a nice lady. She wouldn't have done that. She wouldn't have done that," he repeated.

I couldn't have agreed with him more. I've investigated enough suicides in my time to know that there's always something very unstable in those people's backgrounds. They usually don't have much to lose. In fact they have something to gain in most cases: *recognition,* in many cases, in situations where they've been totally ignored up until then. I sensed there was nothing to be gained by Rachel by taking her life, considering her little girl, not to mention her Mother. Suicide wouldn't have helped them in the slightest way. Only make it worse. No, I don't think she would have taken that path.

"I don't like people saying I'm a Cossack – a goddam Russian," he said, banging his fist on the bar and ordering up another vodka.

He pointed to his forehead. "See where the North Koreans carved up my head."

He pointed to a deep depression in his skull. "Look, I'm an American and fought for my country and got a metal plate in my head for it. I still get headaches and black-outs from it. I fought for my country and I only dress up like a foreigner next door because it fits the action.

He paused to pick up his drink, then took a long slug and spit out the words:

"They call me 'Igor', but they make that up. I never give my real name. I'd like to yell out sometime: I'm not Igor the Russian. I'm Imre, an American and proud to be one! But I keep my mouth shut, and collect my pay every week. "

I told him there was no shame in playing a role as he was doing. It was only an act and everybody knew it. At least anybody with any sense knew that, and who cares about the rest.

I suddenly felt rather sorry for the guy. The crease in his head was very deep and extended back behind his ear. He was obviously in pain a lot of the time.

I suppose the vodka helped ease the pain, and I didn't begrudge his drinking. God knows, my Grandpap liked his beer and came home just a bit woozy more than once.

Like I told you, he was an entertainer — played the guitar — and who can pass up a drink when one of the customers is buying it and pushing it in your face?

I never held anything against drunks in all the years I was on the Force. Only when they **drove** drunk Most of the time they were just trying to shut out something bad in their lives. Like Imre. I never had much trouble with drunks because I knew it would wear off after a night in the sling. With druggies – well, that's another thing.

Drugs! That's something else. After dope entered the scene big time in the sixties and seventies, you couldn't control those guys. They could inflict terrible injuries, but they never felt it themselves. When I started off as a cop, you could tap a guy on the leg and put him down without too much force and no major injury.

But these guys on dope today! You could hit them with a truck and they wouldn't feel anything and they'd still be able to hurt anyone trying to control them. Dope is what changed it all. And to make it worse, we have people taking home movies as three cops try to bring down one screaming dopehead. Hell, it ***takes*** three men sometimes. They ought to try it themselves.

Imre put down a ten dollar bill to cover his tab. "Look", he said to me, "I'm really tired right now, just coming off the show. Why don't you come over to see me at the exhibition tomorrow. I have some free tickets here". He rustled through his pockets.

"Come to the exhibit and I'll try to think of anything more that might be of help to you.

Why don't you come tomorrow at about 2:00. That's always a slow time," he said as he got up to leave.

"Well thanks. Maybe I'll just do that," I said, stuffing the tickets in my wallet.

"And remember. The name is Imre" he said. "Imre Nagy: a good American name, and a good Hungarian one as well, if you know your history at all. When you read the history of the Hungarian Revolution in 1956, you'll find it there."

I raised my glass of beer in salute. "Thanks, Imre. You just might see me tomorrow."

I left the club and walked outside into the cool, salty air. "Lillian will be surprised to know where our next 'date' will take us." ***I smiled to myself thinking about it.***

Chapter Nine

Lillian*: "I meant it when I said I'd look after Ruth. She's as innocent as a lamb."*

My long-time-no-see-distant-cousin, Jake Coates, called me and told me to bring Mrs. Egron right over on the next train. There was a lot he had to tell us. So I took a cab up to Baltic Avenue and hustled Ruth over to Amtrak, and we were at the 30th Street Station in Philly about an hour and forty-five minutes later.

Jake's Office is not far away on Rittenhouse Square. We had a happy "reunion" as I greeted him with*: "How art thou, Jacob."* He laughed because I had once shown him some ancient letters written by our mutual ancestor, Moses Coates, sometime in the late 1600s. Moses was a real live, honest-to-God Quaker who addressed his brother, Isaac, in the traditional form.

The letters were amusing because Grandad-many-times-over-Coates was trying to decide whether he should purchase more lots on Broad Street or on Market. His farm was on the edge of the city — in the "Northern Liberties" as they called it then — and he wanted to move closer. As it turned out, he moved to Arch Street, bought an additional two lots on Market, and donated his farm to the city for an "animal park"

As I've said to myself so often: just imagine what that property would be worth today! Well, Jake would know better than me because some members from his side of the family still retain the Market Street properties right up to the present day.

I reminded him that Fairmount Avenue was once called Coates Street and asked him whether he might consider reclaiming the

Zoo for me. I'm not quite sure whether the present day Philadelphia Museum might also have been within the boundaries of the Coates farm and perhaps some of the property where those boathouses along the Schuylkill are located. At any rate, as far as *my* side of the family is concerned, we went westward from Philadelphia and founded Coatesville, Pennsylvania. Not many millionaires out there, but lots of good people and of course, lots of horses and cows.

"I've always wondered why *your* side of the family has such an affinity to animals," Jake laughed. "Are you still feeding the cats down on the Boardwalk?"

"You'll find me there every morning at about 6:15", I said as sweetly as I could.

"Why don't you take off that high hat, step down from Society Hill, and come over and visit me sometime."

"I fully intend to do so," Jake replied, jokingly wiping his forehead, "whenever the business load gets a bit lighter."

"Aw, you always say that, Jake, but you never do."

I suddenly realized that we were there for Ruth, and not for reunion. I introduced her, and Jake asked us to step over to the sofa in a corner of the room. Coffee and sweet rolls suddenly appeared. "I asked Mr. Balcer to join us," said Jake. "He's your daughter's financial advisor, and both he and I are extremely sorry for the circumstances of this visit today. Your daughter was a fine young woman, and a valued customer. Our deepest sympathy."

Mr. Balcer, a trim young man in his mid-thirties, entered the room holding a thick folder with papers and settled into a chair next to Ruth. "This is a terrible moment for all of us," he said, "But I think you'll be consoled in some small sense to know that she took great care to assure your well-being for the rest of your life, and certainly the future of your granddaughter." He took some files from the folder and spread them on the coffee table.

I turned to Ruth. "Look, I won't sit in on the financial details. That's your business and there's no need for you to share it with me."

Ruth took my hand. "Please stay, Lillian." she said. "I don't know anything about finances. Rachel took care of all that. I know that you know a lot more about these things than I do. Please stay. I trust you."

Mr. Balcer picked up some forms, passed them to Ruth, and explained that these were two annuities that her daughter had arranged for her some months before. "You're getting monthly checks from these, am I correct?" She nodded.

"She had that money in CD's," he explained, "but when the rates dropped so significantly she decided to move them into annuities. That means that the income from these products will continue to come to you throughout your life. And when you pass away, your granddaughter will continue to receive the money for a reasonably long time afterwards.

"Rachel has me sign the checks and deposit them every month in my personal account at the bank in Atlantic City," Ruth said quietly. "That's all right, isn't it?"

"Of course, "Mr. Balcer continued. "Just keep on doing that. The annuities are in your name and your grandchild's together. As the checks come in each. month just continue to do what you've been doing." He repeated: "Sign them with your name and deposit them in your bank. Or, if you want them directly deposited, of course, we can arrange it if that would make things easier for you."

"No," she said. "I'd rather get the checks and take them to the bank myself, if it's okay." She looked at me: "Don't you think that's what I ought to do, Lillian?" "Whatever makes you comfortable," I answered, and glancing at Mr. Balcer, I added: "Let's continue things just as they are for the time being."

"Of course," he said. "And now there's the matter of the educational fund for little . . . Melanie, isn't it? I think you'll be surprised to know that a very considerable fund has been invested in a product which, if not disturbed, will assure that she can attend any college she wishes when the time comes in, what, fourteen or fifteen years from now?

"Even Bryn Mawr?", she asked.

"It will be Bryn Mawr if I have anything to say about it, " I interjected. "I'm on the committee that interviews new applicants and I'm sure I can twist a few arms and open a few doors for her. However, she'll have to have the grades. Connections alone won't get her into a school like that. You understand, Ruth, that she has to work hard to get an invitation to apply."

Ruth smiled. "There'll be no problem in working hard if she's anything like her mother. Rachel already figured out her entry year at Bryn Mawr. It will be in September of 2023, and she'll graduate with the Class of 2027!"

"Oh dear," I said with a smile. "When you pin down the actual dates, I'm afraid she may need an interviewer other than me. I'll be in my nineties at that point. But don't worry, I'll put a little notice in my bequeath that they won't be able to ignore."

We all laughed at that, and I wondered just how much was in the educational investment product that had been opened for her. Plenty! I thought.

Mr. Balcer continued. "Then there is the matter of her personal accounts. She had three. All of them, Mrs. Egron, list your name first, and her name as an "and". Do you understand what I mean. It means that you have complete access to the money in these accounts. You can draw checks on them at any time. In essence, the money in them is all yours now, but you have the option of adding the child's name as well." He showed her balance for each account.

"I had no idea that so much money was involved," she said with astonishment,

"And , yes, of course I want Melanie's name added."

"I understand she was an employee for a time at one of the large gambling casinos", noted Mr. Balcer.

"She *was*", I ventured, and looking directly at both Jake and Mr. Balcer I said:

"She's been working in a donut shop on the Boardwalk for the past year or so."

"Does she work there, or does she own it?" asked Mr. Balcer in a very surprised tone. "Well I'm not sure," I said, somewhat surprised myself. "Does she own it, Ruth?

Or more likely, is she the franchise operator?"

Ruth began to sob. She took her handkerchief from her purse and dabbed her eyes. "She was always thinking of me," she said. "She always said I'd be taken care of but I wasn't sure what she mean until just now. Oh my poor baby." She broke down completely.

To me it meant that either she didn't know, or she didn't want to answer. Mr. Balcer caught my eye and said quickly: "Don't trouble yourself with that, Mrs. Egron, We can check into all of that for you."

I touched Ruth's hand and said gently: "Would you like to use the washroom?

Mr. Coates has a private one here in his office. Why don't you go in there, have a good cry, and put a cold towel on your face. Then we'll go have some lunch. Mr. Coates won't mind."

"Of course not, " said Jake, taking her by the arm and leading her to the restroom.

"Take as much time as you need."

After she'd gone into the restroom, Jake looked at me and said in his professional tone: "It's drug money. It has to be. How else could she accumulate so much money in such a short time. After all, she just graduated from high school in Year2000. And besides all that, do you have any idea how large a franchise fee she has to pay for a location at a corner on one of the most heavily traversed parts of the Boardwalk?

Mr. Balcer nodded in agreement. "At first I thought she was just a well-to-do socialite type. She always wore expensive clothes, and she was smart as a whip when it came to financial matters. She came in fairly regularly. About once a week. Always beautifully manicured. Very much a lady."

Jake came right to the point. "A donut shop, or something like it, is one of the best vehicles for either accepting dope, or money. A casino job just wouldn't do. Too many people looking over her shoulder. Especially over croupiers' shoulders. They don't want conversations with the clientele. They want total concentration. That's not to say that she couldn't have been involved with the drug trade in one way or another. But certainly not with the casino management being involved in any way."

"We'll have to find out who does her income tax," Mr. Balcer explained further. "There might be some problems on what she claims as income. But that can come later."

Jake continued. "Drugs are death so far as the gambling industry is concerned. They don't want anyone even *suggesting* any involvement in the drug trade, especially when they pride themselves in running a clean game under the close and careful eyes – and they are plural — of the State Gambling Commission. And they sure as hell don't want druggies on the payroll or on the premises."

"And what's more," he added, "They know that folks who need drugs are not going to spend their money on the slots or at the tables."

"You're absolutely right, " added Mr. Balcer. "In Ms. Egron's case, it would be difficult to account for the amount of money involved in her transactions over the past ten years without considering drugs. Of course we have to admit that times were very good when she began investing with us. And she was very careful to cut her losses so far as stocks and bonds are concerned. I can give you figures. And of course we can't discount the fact that the money might have been gambling winnings. Not at Bally's, of course.

They don't allow employees to gamble at their own tables. Perhaps that's why she left."

Jake looked over the documents and said: "Everything is in her Mother's name.

As I recall, Mr. Balcer, I think Melanie asked for this as she was setting up the accounts – am I correct? And didn't she tell us that her father died several years before. So we might wonder whether *he* was involved in drugs and stashed the money at home until he died, and she invested it? She might have carried it to us in small portions over the years."

Jake came to the point. "Let's not alarm Mrs Egron. Let the police handle the case, and we'll watch where it goes. Meanwhile, it's business as usual here at 'the store.'

The accounts will continue to draw interest and the checks will continue to go out ".

"These things sometimes take years to sort out," he continued. "It could be that she'll outlive litigation, in any case, if it comes to that. The courts can get badly scrambled up on matters like this, and some lawyers drag it out as long as they can. That seems to be the American Way," he sighed.

"I think we all agree that Ruth has not been involved in any of this", I said. "She's an innocent in every respect. A typical mid-Twentieth Century woman who always depended on her husband, and now on her daughter, to make decisions for her.

"So unlike you, Lil", laughed Jake.

"Yes, and thank God for that," I answered, not too demurely.

"By the way, " he continued, "Are you going to the Cotillion this year?"

"I'm a bit too old for Cotillions in Philadelphia or anywhere else, Jake. As you well know, the Coates family had already lived in the city about a hundred years before the first Cotillion was ever held. So what was the point of "introducing *us* to society"?

We *are* society, for God's sake. So I'll probably just look out at the stars moving over the ocean above my little apartment that evening. And by the way, when are you and Jean coming over to visit me?"

"We'll come the day after the Cotillion just to tell you who was there . . . and who wasn't," laughed Jake

"As if I care, " I said.

Jake smiled wickedly at me. "Well at least your place shouldn't be too hard to find. Jean tells me that it's over a Mexican Restaurant. And by the way, Jean gave me all the details of your furnishings, and, of course, your extensive kitchen facilities.

"Yes, I showed her everything,." I smiled back. "And Jean said she was enchanted by it."

"The Restaurant or your apartment or your kitchen?" he laughed.

"All three", I said, "And Jean especially loved having lunch with me in Puerto Vallarta."

Jake looked puzzled, but kept smiling anyway.

Mr. Balcer carefully returned the documents to his binder. "I wouldn't put Mrs.Egron completely out of the drug picture, "he said. "You have no idea how many widows tell me that they had no idea what kind of business their husbands were involved in. Then they settle accounts after the death of their spouses and happily enjoy the winter in Boca or take a private jet to Vail at Christmastime without another thought."

"You're probably right, Mr Balcer," I said. "But in this instance I think she is exactly what she seems to be. At any rate, I'll keep my eyes open and keep you informed as to what I think is going on."

Ruth re-appeared from the restroom, and thanked all of us for our help and for our patience with her. "When I think that little Melanie may be going to Bryn Mawr someday, or maybe the University of Pennsylvania, I don't know. It's just too much for me to imagine."

"Come with me, Ruth", I said, "and let's leave these two fellows working hard today to make more money for us to spend. You see, I have some accounts here as well."

Ruth sighed: "If you feel that my money is safe here, then I guess I have nothing to worry about, since your money's here as well."

"The little I have," I answered, and Jake laughed heartily at that.

We left Rittenhouse Square and I was planning to take Ruth for crepes in a little French restaurant just around the corner. Then I realized that she needed "some air" as so my mother used to say. I could tell she was intimidated by the financial talk which was well over her head. Obviously Rachel was still very much on her mind, and why wouldn't it be, so I suggested we take a long walk down to the Reading Terminal Market where I knew she'd feel more comfortable surrounded by all the sounds and smells of that delightful place.

She told me that she'd never been there before. She was just a Jersey girl, she said, and didn't get to Philadelphia very often. I was happy to introduce her to one of the city's oldest and most popular attractions. It's not just a market, of course, but a meeting place and an eating place, and a lot more than that.

My mother first took me there in the thirties and I was enchanted from the beginning. People tell me that it was a rather "dirty" place back then, and unsanitary.

People actually reached into barrels and pulled out the pickles of their choice, green and glistening. But what did I know? It just smelled so good, and the fresh peach ice cream was fantastic, and I loved the home made pretzels offered by pretty Amish girls wearing their long dresses and white lacey bonnets. No, I never cared for scrapple. But the home made fudge and cupcakes were to die for. Mother always bought "specialty vegetables" when she was there, like mushrooms, ginger root, parsnips and okra, and she especially liked all the varieties of meats and cheese that were on display. My Dad liked the scrapple and especially the pork rolls which are uniquely Philadelphian. I never heard of them anywhere else, except in Atlantic City which, of course, is a gastronomical extension of Philly and supplies a lot of its seafood and produce.

Ruth and I strolled through the aisles, stopping at the flower market and of course the fish market where she bought a very nice piece of flounder which she said she'd make for dinner and share with her neighbor, the nice black lady who watched Melanie while we were away. I bought some special coffee beans from New Guinea —who can believe that — which they roasted and ground while we were standing there. All in all, a very delightful afternoon. We took SEPTA to the 30th Street Station and then home to Atlantic City.

I meant it when I said I'd look after Ruth. I'm convinced she's innocent as a lamb. ***And I couldn't wait to hear from Tom about his "adventures" as an "Under-cover" man at the Rendezvous Club.***

Chapter Ten

Dillon: *"A few psychopaths are able to tell any story with a straight face, but they often incriminate themselves by being too smart."*

I called Lillian at her apartment on my cell phone and asked if she was ready for a *really* exciting experience, and could she be downstairs within the next fifteen minutes or so.

She said "yes" to both, and I met her in front of the Mexican Restaurant at Noon. "Maybe we ought to get something to eat first," I suggested, "before going to the attraction on the Boardwalk."

"That all depends on what the attraction is," she said. "Just what have you got in mind, Dillon?"

I took her arm and we walked down St. James Place toward the Boardwalk. "We're going to the 'Panorama of Crime' this afternoon." I said. "I got two free tickets from Imre."

I told her about the fact that he was of Hungarian extraction — but an all-American Vietnam Vet— and on the staff as a security guard at the "Panorama of Crime" exhibit on the Boardwalk. I explained that he was in the Rendezvous Club the night Rachel was murdered and that I met him on my undercover trip to the place last night. Fine undercover man I am. Everybody knew I was a cop before I opened my mouth. Including Imre.

"Well now I *am* interested," said Lillian. "There was an exhibit remotely similar to that on the Boardwalk years ago. Do you remember it? On the Million Dollar Pier, to be exact., but tucked away in one of the mustier corners. They had a bunch of oddity displays. I guess that's what you'd call them. One gorier than the other. As I recall, there was something called the den of Chinese horrors with some fake heads impaled on spears. And another tableau showing a wolf attacking a sleigh with a Russian peasant cracking a whip over its head and a Russian lady lying in the snow in front of him. I always wondered if the wolf got the lady. It scared me to death when I was a child."

I told her that I vaguely remembered those same displays on the Pier, and my Dad telling me that they were originally exhibited much earlier in the old Fun House which stood on the spot where they built the Auditorium in the late twenties. Now that's going back before you and I were born. Apparently, the displays were moved across the street to the Million Dollar Pier when they didn't know what else to do with them. I told her that maybe some of them even found there way into this "Panorama of Crime" attraction.

Lillian laughed at that. "Young people today wouldn't pay a nickel to look at something like that today. It's much too tame compared to what they see on television or in those chainsaw movies. They'd be bored to death. Back in older times they left things to our imaginations. Now it has to be right out in front, in full color, and in three dimensions"

"Funny you should say that," I said. "Imre told me that the best part of the 'Panorama' is the 3-D presentations in some of the displays. Real Hollywood stuff."

"I can't wait", Lillian huffed.

"We have arrived! " I said, as we walked up the ramp to the entrance of the Panorama building. It was hard to miss. The raucous blare of hip hop music flowed out of the entrance to mesmerize and draw in the younger crowd.

The front of the building—which, as I told you, used to be the old Globe Theatre—was now completely renovated, or should I said, "bedeviled". It was painted a weird off-shade of purple with black and gray trim around the windows. It had a black plastic kind of mansard roof with pictures of ominous looking characters painted on all the window shades. All in bad taste, of course. I passed it many times during the week and was always amazed at its god-awful vulgarity. Even the old Globe was kind of chaste in comparison.

Lillian called it fake Victorian gothic nonsense. I had to agree and to wonder what all this goth and vampire stuff is about now days? I'm amazed how many young people dress goth today, with long straight hair and ghoulish makeup to match. Eye liners and mascara. Boys and girls alike. You'd think they'd realize how ugly it makes them look. But maybe that's what they want.

Lillian says they want recognition more than **anything** , and that's why they thrive on shocking "normal" people who stare at their "unnormal" personas," as she puts it. She feels sorry for them but she knows they'd deny their need for attention to anyone who would tell them that in plain words. Mostly they expect stares or curses, and they act more outrageously to encourage disgust when people ignore them. It's as though they want to submerge – maybe **murder** is a better word – their real personalities. This whole thing about connecting suicide with the need for "recognition" fascinates me. I'd write an article about it if I was smart enough about grammar and things. I think Lillian must have taken a course in psychology in college. She's good at figuring things like that out. And this vampire thing? Every movie and tv show seems to glory in gore, if you know what I mean. Blood dripping. Fangs.The whole bit. And all of it in three-D.

We gave the ticket lady our passes and suddenly passed from bright sunshine into a foggy, black velvet-draped reception area where a small group of us gathered to await our *"step into hell"* as the young lady with a microphone told us cheerfully. Yes, I mean foggy. It was seeping up from the floor.

The young lady explained that we'd see scenes from the greatest crimes of this, and past centuries. ***"Actual reproductions of crime, accompanied by visual embellishments,"*** she intoned, ***"as well as appropriate screams and gunshots in some cases. But not to*** *be frightened,"* she added with a smile. *"It's all in fun."* Lillian groaned audibly at that.

She continued her spiel: *"All of our presentations are based entirely on actual events, and we present them to you in a surround-a-rama dimension that fills the room, front, back and to the side, with sound and action, as you stand at the center, absorbing it all in three dimensions."*

I turned my head toward Lilli. I could tell at a glance that she could hardly wait for the show to begin . . . and end.

"If you feel faint," the young lady continued *,"just close your eyes and keep your hands on the rail in front of you."*

"Remember that, Dillon, "Lillian said in a whisper with a poke to my ribs. "I don't want you keeling over on me."

It began shortly as the lights dimmed and we were ushered into a small circular area with a setting inspired by the basement at Police Headquarters in Dallas. When it was fully dark, we found ourselves surrounded by a wrap-around screen with 360 degrees of action. Did I mention that we also wore 3-D glasses. Lee Harvey Oswald was on the screen being led slowly through a crowd of onlookers directly toward us. A commentator described the background of the President's assassination and the capture of Oswald, the murderer. Now he was being led to . . . suddenly, the film went blank, and live actors appeared, very animated and realistic, and just as suddenly there was a sharp **BANG!!**

As the shot rang out, the Oswald character crumpled into the arms of two policemen while he looked directly at us. You could almost feel the pain of the bullet entering his chest while police and news people swirled around him. I'm telling you, I looked directly into his bulging eyes as he clutched his chest and blood oozed out, and all the while, falling toward us in 3-D. We actually flinched to get out of the way and wondered how the hell they did it? Then the scene went completely dark and we stood in shock, amidst the screams and sounds of utter confusion for a minute or two, wondering what was next.

A guard in a Dallas policeman's uniform opened an exit door, gathered us together, and moved us quickly into the next exhibit. The same sequence of dimming and darkening began.

Suddenly, we had been transported to a rutted road in Louisiana. That's what the commentator told us, and sure enough we were surrounded by bayou back country to the right and left and behind us. We could almost smell the heat and hear the buzz of the mosquitoes and dragon flies that flew directly toward us. ***Flinch again***! Suddenly, an old time Ford V8 came rattling down the road and pulled over in a grassy spot across from us. There were two actor figures inside the car, and their heads turned toward us. The commentator, hidden to us, began a short synopsis of the escapades of the Barrow Gang and its crime spree in the early 1930's.

Just as his low, mellow voice almost lulled us to sleep, shattering blasts from not one, but at least **FOUR** machine guns split the air from behind us. Some of the audience screamed, and no wonder! So did I! There was a pall of smoke, plus moans, and frantic yells in all directions. Then it all cleared and Floyd and Bonnie slowly oozed out through the half-opened door of the car, directly toward us. Bullet holes and gore everywhere. They managed somehow to appear romantic, but I knew the real story from an old cop who actually was there. He told me that Bonnie and Clyde were just kids and probably the most inept robbers who ever stumbled into crime. Clyde never made it through Fifth Grade.Dumb as a post.

It was over as quickly as the real thing. An appropriately dressed G-Man escorted us to the next exit. I told Lillian that the thing that surprised me most was that I thought it happened in Texas. But apparently it was in Louisiana, and as we left the Bayou State, we entered an execution chamber at Sing Sing, New York.

The Rosenbergs were about to be electrocuted for treason. "Charming", said Lillian under her breath." I'll bet half these people don't even remember the case."

As if to answer her, the commentator complemented the film with a very brief history of the trial, concentrating on the history of death by electrocution in the United States since the invention of the "chair".

We watched guards bring the two of them, Ethel and Julius Rosenberg, a husband and wife team, into the death chamber. As the seconds audibly ticked away, they fastened them into their respective electric chairs. A loud switch was pulled; the electric lights glowed eerily on and off above us and around us while the "hot seat" sparked and sputtered realistically. The producers of "Panorama" didn't spare the jerking, smoking, and agony of the condemned; all in 3-D of course. I wonder how many times those actors went to the "hot seat" each day? Lillian thought it was the most depressing "fun" thing she ever witnessed. I whispered to her that in real life, Ethel Rosenberg didn't die immediately but required three jolts.

Lillian thanked me somewhat sarcastically for that bit of insight she could only expect to hear from a retired policeman . . . and wondered how much more her stomach could take.

We happily left New York, and entered a sinister little side street in London where Jack the Ripper plied his trade. It seemed almost cheerful in comparison.

Lillian thought the artificial fog was quite charming and the reproduction of the street corner in Whitechapel faithful to what she remembered from the real spot she visited some years previously. "They have midnight tours of the district," she said, "And people line up in droves to participate in them. Mostly American tourists, and all of it quite exciting in an understated British sort of way."

I told Lillian that I could never understand why people in every country are so anxious to experience the macabre. In Pittsburgh we actually had folks come regularly to the morgue up on Ross Street to see who was fished from the river each night.

And then, just as suddenly and silently as the Ripper, Imre appeared at our side. .

He smiled benignly as he put his hand on my back and shoved us gently but firmly away from the rest of the crowd, all the while touching the brim of his fur Cossack hat with his other hand in a rather old-fashioned way to Lillian. "Have you had enough?" he laughed. "It's obnoxious, isn't it?"

"Quite enough," said Lillian. "I shudder to think what came next."

"I hope you weren't frightened," he said to Lillian. He repeated what I had just said: "It's all in poor taste, isn't it? People are fascinated with death and misery. They should have been with me in Viet Nam. There was enough death there for a lifetime."

I quickly introduced Lillian to him as he moved us courteously toward a small reception room, and we settled back in some easy chairs. "There are a few more tableaus", he said. "You can go back whenever you wish, but I thought you'd had enough and probably wanted to get to the business of asking me all the questions you raised last night. I remember it all more clearly now," he said. "In the evening when it gets dark, I don't think so well. I'll be happy to tell you all I know," he continued. "I have nothing to hide."

"Nobody said you did," I hastened to add. "I'm just here to get any additional helpful information which the police might have missed. They told me that they had given you the Miranda spiel and that you didn't have to say another word to me if you didn't want to."

Imre said he wanted to tell everything he knew. There was no question of him holding back anything. He was as anxious as us to solve the mystery of what happened to Rachel.

I began with the essentials." It would be helpful, I said, "if you could tell me once again the names of everybody who was in the Rendezvous toward the end of the evening.

The police mentioned that you recognized two brothers named Nolan, as well as the kids in the band and the bartender, and of course, Rachel. Was that all?

"I told the police that I thought it was a very poor crowd around that time," Imre began. "The band was playing for itself more than for the audience. As you know, the wind was blowing pretty hard and you could feel a storm coming. Everyone else had left or was thinking of leaving. Marty, the young bartender who you already met, was at the bar, as well as two men at the middle of the bar. Two brothers, both named Nolan. The oldest is Jack, and the younger one, Matt. I don't like either one of them, but I like Matt the least. He is a very disagreeable man, very sarcastic, and always hurting in what he says. I went to high school with him here in Atlantic City in the late sixties. His brother is about ten years older than us.

The Nolan family lived in Atlantic City," he continued. "Then they moved up to Newark. Matt lives up there now, and so does Jack, but Jack also has a summer home in Stone Harbor up the beach a ways. He's extremely rich from what I hear."

Imre poured each of us a glass of water from a pitcher which Lillian immediately recognized as a piece of very rare and beautiful crystal. She ran her hand over the designs and asked Igor if he knew the origin.

"You have a very discerning eye," he said. "This pitcher and the glasses are from the Russian Imperial household. My uncle told me that the Tsar and his family drank lemonade from them on the Imperial Yacht."

"Lemonade?" questioned Lillian, as she grasped the delicate glass between her fingers and brought it closer to her eyes. It's better suited for champagne."

"Yes, lemonade," said Igor, "for the children's use at High Tea. The Empress Alexandra was raised in Germany, but with British customs. Her grandmother, after all, was Queen Victoria. Anyway, you may have it as a souvenir. I don't have any guests and a lot of stuff just sits around here gathering dust. My grandfather and his son, my Uncle Istvan, were great collectors of things. Collectors, yes, but they never seemed to get rid of anything. It's time for me to begin ridding myself of a lot of their old rubbish."

Lillian made gestures of not wanting to accept it, but he insisted and drew out a purple velvet cloth from a small wooden cabinet to wrap it. "Look," he said, as he held the crystal glass up to the light. "Each glass has an engraved initial for each of the children. This one has an "A", which means it was used by Anastasia, the youngest daughter. There is an "A" plus a little crown on another glass. That was used by Alexis , the little boy who was the heir apparent. But I think you will like Anastasia's better because they made a movie about her, didn't they? Now each time you show it to a friend you can tell them the little story that goes with it. They were all murdered, you know. By the Reds."

Lillian said she would have to go on the Internet when she got home to find out more about the Russian Imperial Family, although she was already very familiar with Anastasia because of the film, but she wasn't aware of the Empress Alexandra's connection with Queen Victoria. She asked Imre if he used the internet to get additional information on the crimes which were depicted in the Panorama productions.

Imre bristled. "I don't know anything about the computer. In fact, I don't even want to be in the same room with a computer. Why would I need people emailing me or putting me in their —what do they call it – their facebook?"

Lillian was enchanted, of course, with the crystal and the story, and she said she didn't want to break up the collection, but Igor insisted. When she asked where in the world he got the set, Imre told us that it was part of his grandfather's imported oddities from

Europe just after he arrived here following World War I. He dealt in many things," he explained, "and sold much of it in the auction houses along the Boardwalk. And he made enough money to buy this building," he said, "and the hotel behind it, as well as other properties."

Then he commenced to tell us more about the Nolans.

"The Nolans hardly ever step into a place like the Rendezvous Club", he began. " I've seen them here only once or twice since they moved away. What they were doing there that night? I have no idea. *That Matt fellow!*" He almost cursed the name. "He used to bully me in school. I was a slow learner. He called me a "retard." As soon as he saw me that night sitting here at the bar, in my uniform, he began to make fun of me, and asked me if I had signed up with the Cossacks. I asked him why the hell he wasn't with me in Viet Nam and he shut up quick enough. His brother, Matt, gave him a punch in the arm. His brother also told him to shut up. They both hide secrets. I can tell. But maybe you've heard about them already. I know the police have."

His forehead furrowed as he concentrated on my question.

"Oh yes, there were also two young men sitting together at a table who I've seen from time to time. I think one of them is named Swanson. He's in the merchant marine, and the other, I'm not sure about. I think they're gay. Anyway, they left at least half an hour before the rest of us did. I told the cops about them.

"Yes, you did," I said. "The police said they were very forthcoming witnesses and so were you. They like that. They also told me that Matt Nolan has a long rap sheet, including assaults on young women, and drug charges as well. He's just a person of interest right now, but becoming a prime suspect."

"There were more people in the Club earlier in the evening, of course, before the weather threatened. When I first got there, I remember one well-dressed man particularly 59 who came in looking for something or someone. He walked around the bar and around the chairs looking. But I never saw him before, and he left just as quickly as he came in."

Imre then voluntarily began his narrative of events that evening. "It was about 10:30 when the storm knocked the lights out at this end of the Boardwalk," he began.

"The band was putting away its instruments and just finishing up when everything went black. Rachel was just leaving the club when the storm hit. The rain came down in sheets. I saw her walking toward the door, quite alone, as she was accustomed to do. The emergency lights came on, but they were no more than just a dim red glow. Within five minutes, everybody was gone, including Rachel, the band, the Nolans, and Marty, the bartender."

"I had it much easier," he continued, "because, you see, I didn't have to go outside. I carry a flashlight and I have a room on the second floor of the Panorama building, above the exhibits . . . just over London scene. There's a door in the back of the pantry of the Rendezvous Club, just next to the men's room, which connects to the Panorama building which was, at one time, an old theatre. Nothing sinister about it. The door's been there since the club was a hotel. It's locked and never used anymore except by me. Many of the customers comment on how I suddenly appear and then disappear. I enjoy the adventure of scaring the hell out of them sometimes," he laughed, "just as they're coming out of the Men's Room. Marty the bartender knows all about it."

I told Imre he'd be surprised to know that both Lillian and I had heard rumors about a door like that from different people at different times in the past, but of course we didn't expect it to still be in use. And no one except people our age remembers what these buildings *once* were, only what they are now.

Imre responded by telling us that it's easy to understand the arrangement when you know that both these buildings are owned by his uncle Istvan and by his father before him . . . my grandfather. Imre explained again that his grandfather came here as a young man right after World War I with his two son, Istvan, and Imre's father, Josef.

"Both my grandfather and Uncle Istvan did quite well in the importing business – mostly luxury items from Central Europe", he said. "My mother and father were killed in an automobile accident when I was quite young. Uncle Istvan has been taking care of me ever since."

Imre was not embarrassed to say that his Grandfather and, yes, Uncle Istvan, even though he was just a young man, made a lot of his money in illicit liquor. It was Prohibition at that time, and as Europeans they couldn't understand why the government would forbid a man from having a beer, or a good Tokay, at dinner. "Yes, he was a bootlegger, as they called it", Igor continued. "But he became perfectly legal in 1933. Well, they made fun of him, too, because he spoke with a slight accent and came from Hungary. They called him a 'Hunky.' but he became wealthy with property. He bought most of it with the money he and Grandfather made from liquor."

"When my father died," Imre continued, "Uncle Istvan looked after me and my Mother, too. So I guess I'm a Hunky, too, in a way, but without the property. Although I suppose I'll inherit it when my uncle dies. He's 91. Quite an old man now. But his mind is still clear, Thank God."

Imre went on with his story :"Why do I live in such a gloomy place? Because my uncle continues to look out for me. He was my father's oldest brother, but my father has been gone for many years now. All the rest of the family is gone, too, and at his age, Uncle Istvan soon will be, too. When I returned from Viet Nam , I was in bad shape, you see. Both physically and mentally. I had this metal thing in my head, and there were other things on my body that were damaged. You might not believe it, but I was quite a good athlete in high school."

His face darkened. "I was a prisoner of the Viet Cong for almost a year. They kept me in a cage. Luckily one of our patrols found me when they shot up the place. Do you wonder why I hear voices talk to me sometimes? All the guys in my unit were killed, and I was spared. My uncle arranged for a little apartment right above us, above the London exhibit, and it's in the contract with the Hollywood people that I have a permanent job as long as the Exhibit runs."

He continued bitterly:"I am so ugly, that I fit well here, don't I. Like the Hunchback of Notre Dame, don't you think?" he said with a wry smile."And the people began calling me Igor. So Igor it is when I'm on the job here. But Imre is my name, and it's a good Hungarian name, and American as well. As American as any Irishmen like the Nolans.

He continued without pause: "I have very little in life, Mr. Dillon. Not even a complete body! I walk up past the New Jersey Korean War monument on Park Place next to Bally's and I read the names with stars on them. Most of those boys died long before Viet Nam. And they were just boys. Nineteen, most of them And worst of all, now I see other young boys going to Afghanistan. My life has never been complete since being in a cage in Viet Nam, and I will never let myself be put in one again, Never!"

Lillian rose from her chair and spoke softly: "Excuse me, Imre, is there a powder room nearby?" I could feel her discomfort as the full picture of this troubled man became clearer.

"Yes, of course," said Imre, rising from his chair. "Just outside the door and directly to the right. May I show you the way?."

"No, I'm sure I'll find it," she said, moving quickly from the room "So Imre, " I said, "Did you see any contact between the Novaks and Rachel during the evening?

"Not really," he said, looking down at the floor. "No, I'm sure she stayed at her table near the bar and they stayed in the middle. I'm certain that's what Matt will say as well. But what happened when the lights went out and they all scattered for the door, I can't say. She could have found a cab out there, or maybe they offered to take her home in *their* car. I just can't say one way or another. The water was already covering the beach and over the curb on Kentucky Avenue. There was a full moon that night with a high tide and a huge storm coming in from the northeast."

I reached out and shook his hand. "I want to thank you for telling me what you know, and of course for spending some time with me talking about Rachel. I know it must be hard for you."

"It is very hard," he said. "Rachel was always kind to me; always had a good word for me. I don't think she had bad things to say about anybody. She just minded her business and did what she could to keep her mother and her little girl. She surely loved both of them and especially the little girl. She told me once that she was taking care to see that her daughter would go to one of those high class schools over on the Main Line. Too bad she'll never see it happen."

Lillian appeared at the door, and I stepped past Imre and told him that I'd make my report to the police and hoped they wouldn't have to bother him again. He took us to an exit that avoided the crowds, and we left through a door, concealed from the outside, that opened out to a parking lot which had been the site of what used to be Woolworth's 5 and 10.

We both took a deep breath of fresh salt air. The gulls hovered around as they always did at that particular spot at New York Avenue and the Boardwalk. Lillian thought that it might have been the lingering smell of about seventy years worth of roasted peanut remains at what had been the entrance to Woolworth's.

"Here's where the Kazoo Man stood," I said. We both remembered this cheerful little man in a white suit selling kazoos by the kazillions just inside the store, but mostly out on the Boardwalk itself. He played all the current tunes, and of course the old standards about moons in June and four leaf clovers. He left sometime in the sixties. Some said he moved to Florida with the millions he made from selling kazoos. Others said he simply died. Some mysteries are never solved.

Lillian said, sadly: "That poor man, Imre, at the Panorama is very troubled, and very nervous. He talked very calmly, but did you notice how his fingers were twitching, especially when he talked about people who made fun of him, and about being caged in Viet Nam. I didn't want to take the glass, but he seemed so eager to please me by giving it to me. And it is quite elegant."

I told Lillian that I talked to hundreds of suspects in hundreds of different crimes in my time. There were some who were congenital liars. You could tell it from the first words out of their mouth. And then there were some who were totally innocent, and you could read that, too, in their faces and in the tone of their voice. A few psychopaths were able to tell *any* story with a straight face but they often incriminated themselves by being "too smart"; by giving more information that they needed to; and especially by trying to "*solve*" the crime by themselves before us dumb cops could figure it out. The psycho-path needs recognition as well, you see.

"And which group does Imre fit into," asked Lillian.

"I don't know, "I said. "I just don't know. The war did a lot of damage to him. He said he was a slow learner when he was a kid, but he sure didn't sound like it, did he? All I know is that he's angry. And no wonder. Angry people do bad things. Sometimes. I wonder how he would have turned out if there hadn't been a Viet Nam?"

"So do millions of people," said Lillian. "And look" she said, "You don't have to be so formal by calling me Lillian. Lillie will do. It's what my father used to call me. And *I loved him very much.*"

Chapter Eleven

Lillian: ***"Do you understand that you're tearing a piece of my heart away?"***

While Tom and I waited for the Atlantic City Police Department's full report on the Rachel Egron case, we continued to do some investigating on our own, but there weren't many trails to follow. We talked to Marty the bartender again, but his story remained the same. We even looked up the band that played that night and found them in a little hole of a club in Vineland late one evening. There's nothing any of them could tell us that they hadn't already told the police. When the lights went out, they said, their instruments went out. And they just wanted to get the hell out of there before the storm broke.

In the days that followed, the case was officially classified as a homicide by the ACPD and the search for a murderer has already begun, with Matt Nolan pegged as more than just "a person of interest". Only the motive remains a mystery.

Matt told the police that he and his brother left the Rendezvous Club together. He said they drove up to Jack's summer home in Stone Harbor and stayed there most of the night because of the rainstorm and the fact that the roads north to Newark were blocked. Of course, Matt's alibi was not highly regarded by the ACPD which booked him so often in the past for a number of petty crimes, and some violent ones as well involving young women.

His brother, Jack, has been good at getting him off, up to now. There's enough circumstantial evidence to believe that Jack was involved in the Egron murder. Both he and Matt are deep in the drug trade. And apparently, so was Rachel.

Nobody actually saw them step out of the door at the Rendezvous with, or without Rachel. But then again, nobody could verify their alibi for the rest of the evening. Jack's wife said that he came home alone to Newark early in the wee hours of the morning. If he had called her, she said, she would have told him to stay at the house in Stone Harbor until later in the day.

"So why didn't he call her," the police asked Jack? There would have been a record of the call which might have backed up his alibi. Jack said it simply didn't occur to him. He was often out late at night, he said, and he didn't want to wake her.

I telephone Ruth Egron every evening and manage to stop by for a few minutes or so almost every day.. It doesn't have as much to do with solving the case as it's simply to see that both she and little Melanie are still in good shape. Ruth has become my friend and I know she counts on me a great deal to check her legal and banking affairs and make sure all her bills are paid. She has little need to worry. Rachel left her very comfortably fixed.

Like Tom, and cousin Jake at the investment firm, I realized that all of Rachel's money could not have come from her job at the casino or from her donut franchise. I wonder if Ruth ever thought about that? But she takes on a totally blank look when it comes to how Rachel accumulated so much cash in such a relatively short time. She assumes that she made good investments when times were good in the '90's. But the accounting doesn't add up to me or anyone else. It just isn't possible. And drugs or very successful gambling are the only two viable means of accumulating cash so quickly. I push her on finding Rachel's tax returns but she claims she can't find them.

I've grown to love little Melanie. She quickly became the child that I had lost. Her grandmother and I take her for long walks on the beach, gathering shells just as I did when I was a child. We made wreaths out of them, and I glued some of them on a pair of her little sandals. She loved them. I glued some pieces of sea glass on a little mirror that I gave her, and it's become became one of her prize possessions.

I'm introducing her to all the attractions of this exciting city by the sea . . . not as faded as some magazines often depict it. We play ski-ball until my arms ached, and win tickets that are promptly redeemed by the attendant for "beauteous" (her word) prizes that line the wall behind the cash register ranging from hair combs to stuffed animals. All of them are precious to her. We enjoyed playing "goofy golf" on the charming little greens on the Boardwalk near the Kennedy monument just across from the Auditorium. For a four-year old, she hits a hard but erratic ball. Often, it careens off the green and soars almost to the beach.

Of course, Tom is included in our fun time. We allow Ruth to have some badly needed "time-off" and we're only too happy to have the little one to ourselves. Tom and his wife didn't have children, but he dotes on his two nephews, taking them as often as possible to football and hockey games in Pittsburgh. They're all devoted Steeler fans, of course. Being with Melanie brings out his softer side. He carries her gently into the ocean, and dips her toes in the water, just as my father had done to me —so gently —so many years before.

The Atlantic can be very cold most of the time. Not too cold for adults to swim, but a bit frigid for one of tender years, But it was late August, and the water was nearly perfect on several days, and Melanie got the full advantage of being taught to paddle, and then swim, by a man who was gentle, but tough enough to stand up against the heaviest waves.

I watched from the beach and enveloped her with hugs and kisses when Tom brought her back to me. I pulled a warm towel around her and held her close to my breast. When the ice-cream man came by across the sand, I bought her one of those chocolate ice cream bars that "hit the spot" on an especially warm day. What a lot of happy memories it brought back.

I have to say that for a seventy-five year old man, Tom still looks pretty good in a bathing suit. Of course he always worked out when he was at home, and managed to eat the right kinds of foods. And he never smoked. He says that when you're a cop, you have to be in as good shape as the criminals you pursue. I won't say he looks like Brad Pitt, but all in all, not so bad. At least that's the opinion of a seventy-five year old woman who's in pretty good shape herself. Or so she thinks.

One afternoon we took Melanie sailing with us. Somewhere along the line, Tom learned how to tack as well as handle the wheel and the rudder, and all the rest. Of course, I learned to sail as a ten year old, and my husband and I did some serious sailing while he was stationed in Hawaii. When I showed some surprise at Tom's sailing skills, he reminded me that he came from a city with three rivers and 500 or so bridges – a lot more than Venice, he bragged..

We drove to Smithville Village one day which is just up the highway from Atlantic City, and a charming place with buildings dating back to Jersey's colonial past. Melanie was especially enchanted by the Christmas Store which smells of cranberry candles all year round and holds a treasure of ornaments from all over the world. Although the temperature was in the high 80's as we enjoyed some pleasant late summer weather, she had to have a few ornaments for her tree, and we were happy to oblige.

She sometimes asks the funniest little questions. For example, she always wants to know how old we were, and I give her misleading answers which she accepts, but not without skepticism. Once she asked how long we were married. When we told her we weren't married, she asked the very logical: ***"Why not?"***

We changed the subject.

There's a famous little pet cemetery on a side road back from Smithville Village, and it intrigued me as a child. I wondered if she were too young to understand the significance of a cemetery for little dogs and cats and other critters, and I decided that it was time to introduce the subject in a gentle way, just as my Mother did for me back when I was her age. We walked through the tiny gravestones and paused at some very expensive monuments . . . many with photos encased in the granite.

The names on the stones are humorous, but touching. "Spot" and "Boots" and even "Peaches". She asked me the inevitable question: "Why do we have to die?" And I answered just as my Mother had answered me: "We don't really die, but just pass through a gate into a garden where all our loved ones and family members and animal friends are waiting for us. The garden is called Heaven. Your mommy's already there and waiting to see you again."

"I can hardly wait," she said innocently, and added that she wondered why her mother had to leave just now? I smiled and said God made that decision and not us, and that's why we have to go to Sunday School and Church to find out more about it.

Our last stop that happy Sunday afternoon was a drive down about two miles south of Atlantic City where we introduced Melanie to Lucy the Elephant. Lucy has been a point of interest to visitors coming to the Shore for well over 120 years. She's made of wood and tin sheeting and stands about six stories high. Apparently she was built as a gimmick to promote beach real estate in the 1880's. That was back in Victorian Days when curiosity-type architecture was a delight to the eyes.

They say that at one time Lucy contained a number of small hotel rooms and a bar inside her "belly". Tom says his grandfather knew a man who once rented a room with a large window just under the tail of the creature. I suppose it might have been true. The window obviously is still there, in exactly the correct anatomical position. On the other end of her interior space, one can look through Lucy's two large glass window eyes and view the beach from on high.

She's painted a light sea foam gray, with a large multicolored "howdah" on her back. It serves as an observation deck and adds an exotic Indian touch. Melanie was entranced, and of course we had to climb the winding spiral staircase which went up one of her thick wooden legs. And then we had to buy a souvenir "Lucy" at an outside stand close to her trunk. I couldn't help remembering when I saw Lucy for the first time about seventy years before. How thrilled I was to tell my little friends in Philadelphia all about her at my fifth birthday party.

That gave me an idea! Melanie would soon be five, and it was time she started Kindergarten. There is a wonderful school right in Atlantic City founded by the Quakers a long time ago while New Jersey was still one of the colonies. It's called "Friends' School" and equal in prestige to any of the upscale private schools throughout the Northeast that provide credentials for entrance to the Ivy League. Or to Bryn Mawr, for that matter.

The teachers are very sensitive to the needs of their children, and classes are small and intimate. Better than that, it's only a few blocks from my apartment, and not much further to Baltic Avenue. Once again, one of the Coates' Quaker relatives had a small hand in founding it in Atlantic City on the pattern set by the original school in Philadelphia. Several generations of cousins, somewhat removed, passed through Friends' Schools and did very well for themselves. I knew I could pull the strings that opened doors for a poor girl from Baltic Avenue. And I could hardly wait to tell Ruth my plans when I brought Melanie back to her apartment that evening.

Ruth met us at her door with a look of despair. I could see immediately that she was troubled and I asked what the problem was. She told me that she had just come home from a short trip up to Trenton. Her niece lived there with her two little boys. She wasn't married and didn't plan to be. But she was behind in her rent and obviously couldn't work because she didn't know what to do with the boys, one of whom was two and the other just four years old. Two children in diapers is a problem for rich or poor.

"She was a mess," Ruth lamented. "A big seven-room house, and all of it in disarray. Lots of unwashed dishes piled up in the sink. The children crying bloody murder. Newspapers and magazines all over the place. Not a place to sit down. Not a single place that wasn't covered with some sort of rubbish or another. She started crying as soon as I walked in the door. No job. No money. What was she going to do?

"She's my only niece," said Ruth plaintively. "Her mother — my sister — died of cancer a few months ago. She used to sit with the babies while my niece worked as a waitress. But now she's gone and everything has gone to hell, and she has nobody else in the world except me."

Ruth cuddled Melanie as she spoke, but the child got restless and held her hands out to me. "Lillie take me?" she asked in her childish voice.

Ruth's eyes met mine, and I understood in a moment. We both realized without saying it that the child was growing towards me and away from her, and unconsciously I was promoting it. I wanted her to be the little one I lost, and I had tremendous resources to do just that with my money, mobility; and, oh yes, a man to help. I gently took Melanie in my arms and sat her back in Ruth's lap.

"Of course you have to go, Ruth," I said, trying to hold back both my tears and my fears for the child. I knew without asking that Ruth had already made up her mind and that she would choose to go up to Trenton rather than stay in Atlantic City for more than one reason.

"She lives in my sister's house, just on the edge of the city,." said Ruth. "There's lots of room there, and a big yard for the kids to play in. And not too far from a school. And transportation to downtown. Of course there's lots of work for me to do, putting the house back in order. And I'm not sure whether I'm ready to care for three children. But you know, Lillian, it will take my mind off things. It will be good for me. If I stay here I think I'll go crazy, thinking of Rachel all of the time and hoping she'll step through the door at suppertime. I still have all her clothes. I need to get rid of things and start all over again. You understand, don't you?"

I wanted to say: "Do *you* understand that you're tearing a piece of my heart away?"

She couldn't know all the plans I had for Melanie's future. And she couldn't visualize that placing her in that particular environment in Trenton would stunt her and close doors that were opening for her. Is that being elitist? You're damned right it is, because I have already gauged the world that's coming and I know that by the time she's a young woman she'll need all the education and all the contacts and all the little " social entrance slips" necessary to "make it" in Year 2024 and beyond.

But I held my tongue. I would have gotten down on my knees and begged, but I held my tongue. I was not "family" after all. I couldn't play God with her life, much as I knew I could make a better life for her than the one for which she was bound.

I suppose I thought I could bring some "poetry" into her life. I had some pieces of sea glass in my purse that I found on the beach that morning. She loves these little jewels, as she calls them. I explained, as I handed them to her, that when we have rough seas at night, we have the best chance of finding new pieces in the morning. Sea glass is smooth and frosted, not jagged at all. It enters the ocean as chards of broken bottles, windshield fragments, pieces of old fruit jars or medicine bottles. Colors range from brown and green to cobalt blue, bright yellow and wine red. My pieces were white and a very pale aqua-marine, as beautiful as jade. .

I explained to her that after the glass has been tumbled around and scoured by sand and salt water for a very long time, it metamorphoses into a thing of beauty and mystery. Like an ugly caterpillar turning into a beautiful butterfly.

And what stories I wanted to make up for her.

What princess sipped from the deep blue goblet, or what naughty sailor boy threw his root beer bottle in the alley? And where have all these pieces been hiding all these years as the sea worked its magic on them, changing them from trash to treasure? Perhaps among the mermaids. I thought we might even design a real piece of jewelry from the luminous fragments.

It was not to be, and it would be the second time in my life that my little girl was taken away from me. There wouldn't be a third, I promised myself.

Ruth put the child to bed, and I kissed her gently as I tucked in the blanket. I left the sea glass in a saucer by her bed. Then I left quickly. Made a clean break of it. Much easier for both Ruth and myself. And I walked home, all the way from Baltic Avenue, crying every step of the way. When I reached my apartment I washed up, put on my nightgown, and sat up reading Emily Dickinson by the window for an hour or more; **then closed the book and went to bed.**

Chapter Twelve

Dillon: *"We never kidded each other about my marriage"*

I got a hurry-up telephone call from my sister, Mary Catherine, this morning and headed to the Turnpike and home to Pittsburgh right away.

Evelyn isn't doing well, and Mary Catherine tells me that she called for the priest to come and give her the "anointing." They don't call it the "last rites" anymore because I guess it scares people too much. The way I look at it, it means the same thing no matter what you call it. Why do they need to change everything in the church now days? When I was a kid it was different. Nothing changed and everybody knew where they stood with God. The only thing that's certain is that it will never turn back to the way it was. It'll never be the church I knew.

I stopped at the Good Samaritan Home on Penn Avenue as soon as I reached the city at about 3:00pm. I sat with Evelyn for over an hour. Mary Catherine had just left. The nurse said that she seemed to be near death in the morning but that after receiving the anointing she seemed to take a turn for the better. I knew that Mary Catherine, good Catholic that she was, would consider that a small miracle had occurred. But as I sat there, watching and waiting, there seemed to be no improvement from the last time I saw her. Her eyes were closed and she lay in a fetal position. It was hard to tell whether she was breathing or not. Hard to tell whether she was alive or dead. But the doctor who came by and checked her pulse and heart beat said her vital signs had greatly improved since he saw her earlier in the day.

Art Weldy

When I arrived home at Mary Catherine's – our old house on Carnegie Street – she began apologizing.

"No sooner than they gave her the last rites," she began, "Evelyn started to come around. All her signs started looking better.Even her color came back. Of course she's still in that same kind of stupor where she can't talk, and she has her eyes closed all the time. Anyway, I thought she was gone early this morning when I called you, Tommie. But she's doing better now. What more can I say, except to say I'm sorry I had to bring you all the way from Atlantic City."

"It's okay, " I said."I should have checked in with you by now anyway. It's been a week or more, hasn't it? I've been busy and I don't mean to leave you with all my problems."

"Oh Tommy," she said, softly smoothing my hair with her hand, the way she used to do when I was a teenager getting ready to go to school in the morning. When Mother died, she was just seventeen, but she raised me and my kid brother and sister. Now I'm 75 and she's ten years older, and both the "kids" passed away in the last two years.

"Tommy," she said, "I wish I hadn't called. You've spent every day of the last nine years taking care of her, and now that you have a few weeks to yourself, I had to call you back. You know I don't mind going up to the Home to see her. It's just up 63rd street. And there's nothing you can do for her. She sleeps nearly all the time. She really left us a long ago, Tommy."

"For better or worse," I said. I almost felt guilty saying it, knowing that I was . . . well . . . interested . . . in Lillian, and having a wonderful time with her while poor Evelyn just lay there. "Is she in pain," I wondered? Mary Catherine said: "No. No pain. Definitely not."

"But how do we know?"

"I can tell from her face," Mary Catherine assured me. "She's perfectly at rest. and I only wonder why God hasn't let her slip away. I thought she did yesterday, and again this morning. But Father Jim says God has his reasons. That has to be enough."

I know my sister is devout. I know that she would never think of praying for Evelyn to die, but the thought crosses **both** our minds without either one of us saying it out loud. I know my sister so well that I almost always know what she's thinking. And in my heart I know she's "thinking the unthinkable." I suppose she'll have to go to confession for it. It isn't that simple for me especially now that Lillian has come into my life — which makes it a helluva lot more difficult for me in so many ways.

I decided to tell Mary Catherine about Lillian. I began by telling her that there wasn't anything shameful about our relationship at all. We both knew where we stood. We never kidded each other about my marriage. We're both 75 years old, for God's sake. But the trouble is that the rest of the world doesn't look at it the way we do.

My grandfather was 75 when he died back in 1944, but he was an old man at that time. He dressed old, always with a vest and a tie. He acted old. He looked old. And he **was** old, in that day and age. Everyone was amazed when he took a train trip, all the way to Florida mind you, just a few months before he died, to see his grandson, my cousin, who was in Air Force training.

But times have changed. Now days, 85 year olds fly from Pittsburgh directly to Paris to spend the week and come back without thinking a thing about it. I know an "old fellow" who's 90 and just back from a tour of China. He always wanted to do it, he says, and better now than never. China! Imagine!

Mary Catherine gave me her *"don't worry, things are okay with me, even though I'm 85"* look.

"Does she make you happy? "she asked. "If she makes you happy then that's all that matters. Once I would have cared what the neighbors said," she laughed. "But now I don't even know who half my neighbors are. Oh, the Michaelsons still live up on the corner, and the Cavanaughs are still down the street, but they're all getting older. Nobody sits out on the front stoop and passes the time anymore. They're all inside in the summer-time with their air-conditioners going full blast. Some of the neighbors I wouldn't have anything to do with anyway," she huffed. "A couple down there, "she pointed. "They have two little kids and let them run wild and nobody seems to care. Nobody cares whether they're married or not, either, and the language they use! You wouldn't believe it. And them next door," she said with a frown. "I can smell the marijuana through the walls. I just say 'hello' to them, but that's all."

"Why don't you move, Mary Catherine?" I say very cautiously to her. "Get out of here and move over to the High Rise up on 54rd Street? I hear the rooms are nice, and that there are plenty of people your age.And Bingo every Thursday night," I laugh.

"Me? In a Home?", she replies incredulously, as though it were the most preposterous idea in the world. "They'll carry me out of here. This is my *home.* I don't need nobody looking after me. And I don't want to be with people 'my age'. God forbid! I'd have Evelyn home here with me right now if I was able to handle all her medicines and the oxygen." she says."But I wouldn't be able to move her and clean the bed. You know what I mean."

"Of course I know what you mean", I reply. "That's why she's in the Home. We know it's the best we can do for her, the way she is."

Mary Catherine took my hands in hers. "You've had such a hard time for almost ten years now. You were just getting yourself back in order down there at the Shore.You would have had a nervous breakdown going to the Home every day, and sometimes twice, and just sitting there without a word. And now I call you back," she said. "But listen. There are a couple more weeks of good weather left. After you have dinner with me tonight and get a good rest, I'll cook you breakfast tomorrow morning and send you back to Atlantic City. Stay there at least until the end of September, and maybe even into

October. You can play it by ear. You know you can be back here in six or seven hours if you need to."

I told her that I felt as if I were loading everything on her back, and after all, I am the husband and you're only a sister-in-law. But she wouldn't hear of it. "What else do I have to do at my age," she laughed. "Listen," let's have a good talk over supper, and you can tell me how the hell *you* got to be 75. Jesus, Mary and Joseph ," she gave me one of her Irish smiles, turning to the stove, "I never thought you'd pass me in age someday."

We had a good talk during supper. Some of it about death, but not as morbid as you might think. She just wanted to make sure that I knew that there's a grave for both of us over at old St. Patrick's Cemetery.

"We'll be laying next to each other with all the rest of the Micks," I laughed. "The whole family," she agreed. "The whole bunch of them Dillons."

"Evelyn has a place over at St. Augustine's across the river as you know," I added. "In their family plot. I've arranged it with the funeral director over there in Millvale. It's paid for in advance. "

She shook her head for a moment as she passed the mashed potatoes to me. "I don't know whether that's such a good idea, Tommy. I heard of some old people getting ripped off doing that. Paying in advance, I mean."

I assured her that I knew the funeral director very well and that he deposited funds like that into a controlled account which nobody, not even him, can touch until the "client" passes on.

She continued to shake her head. "And what if *he* dies first?" she asked. "Oh no, I've got my money in a special bank account, and you know your name's on it as well as mine. I have all the particulars upstairs in the tin box under my bed. When anything happens, you just go get the tin box and everything's there." she assured me. "Do you remember how Mother kept everything important in that same tin box?"

"Yes, I do. And I only learned in later years that the tin box was my grandfather's old lunch pail when he worked on the Pennsy years before. By the size of it, he must have had quite an appetite. Sorry I never got to know him. I never heard him play his guitar."

"He was quite a man. Quite a man," said Mary Catherine, pushing the coleslaw toward me. "Eat up, and maybe you'll grow up to be like him," she laughed.

After dinner we just sat and talked. Mary Catherine never tired of telling funny stories about old timers in our family. And I never tired of listening to them, punctuated with her only profanity — **"Jesus, Mary and Joseph "**— which she would begin her sentences with when she had some sensational or unusual story to tell.

"Do you remember when you were just a kid, Tommie, what you did to Mr.Dugan he came to visit his sister, Katie, at No. 410 down on the corner.?"

Of course I had told the story a hundred times before, but I started it once again.

"How could I forget it?" I said. "He chased me and Mike Riley for a block or more, and we damn well deserved it."

We laughed at it all over again, as though it was the first time she heard it. She egged me on with each detail.

"Well you know," I began: "Mr. Dugan– Paddie Dugan, as they used to call him – came over to visit his sister Katey about once a month. He lived way over in Castle Shannon and probably had to take two streetcars to get here."

"Oh yes, " Mary Catherine agreed. "He'd have to change in town and then take the 77 to get out this way. I can still see him — how he was all dressed up and with that black derby. I don't think anyone in Pittsburgh still wore a derby hat at that time. But he did."

"He must have been up in years, don't you think?"

"Well," guessed Mary Catherine, "I suppose he was about 70. But an **old** 70 if you know what I mean. It was around 1940 or so. Before the War. There was snow on the ground. Probably he was going to his sister Kate's for Thanksgiving Dinner. She told me once that he came over from the old country when he was just a young man and never lost the brogue."

"Oh I don't know," I said. "I bet he could speak English just as good as we did, but the brogue and the derby hat made him feel more Irish, so he talked that way, don't you think?".

Mary Catherine moved the story on. "And you two, little Mike and you, were sitting up in that old apple tree that stood on the corner of Carnegie and Butler."

"We were, indeed" I laughed. "It snowed pretty hard that morning and kind of smoggy from the mill — Heppenstalls— down by the river. But you can imagine, we still could see him coming from a mile away."

"Well who wouldn't have seen him with that old-fashioned hat," she laughed .

I picked up the story. "Mike jumped down out of the tree and made a snowball, and then climbed back up and sat next to me on the big branch. I knew what he had in mind but I didn't believe he'd actually do it. In fact, I even egged him on.

"Just watch this," Mike said back to me." "Bet you won't ," I said, looking at the snowball in his glove. "Bet I will," he said, gritting his teeth and clenching the snowball in his glove.

We waited until Mr. Dugan was just below us, and then passed by. I thought for sure that Mike had chickened out. But in a split second, I knew he hadn't.

"Wham!" The snowball hit Paddie's hat and knocked it off to one side, making the poor man look funnier than ever .He looked behind himself and then up to us, bold as brass, sitting in the tree.

"You little sons of bitches," he said, spitting out the words. And then he said some other words that I could hardly believe were coming out of his mouth. He reached up toward our branch with the tip of his folded umbrella . . . . with the sharp tip!"

"Too bad he didn't poke you both in the behind," Mary Catherine laughed, as she always did at that part of the story.

"But his umbrella slipped and knocked his hat all the way off. It was round, as you know, and the wind caught it, and it started rolling down the steep side of the street. And him after it. Running like hell. If only you could have seen it".

Mary Catherine laughed so hard that she pulled out her handkerchief to dab her eyes. "I didn't see it, oh but I heard about it, all right. I was just 17 at the time and the next day Paddie's oldest granddaughter, Colleen, caught me in Stringer's Store down on the Avenue. She gave me all kind of hell about Mr. Dugan having a bad heart and him having to run for it like that." Both Mary Catherine and I laughed at this, and shouldn't have, but couldn't help it. The picture was so clear. .

Mary Catherine continued: "His granddaughter said he could have keeled over right there on Carnegie Street and you two boys would have been held for murder. I asked her how she knew it was my brother and she said it was because you and the Riley kid were the worst kids in the neighborhood and always getting into trouble. Jesus, Mary and Joseph that made me mad. I told her I would never talk to her again. And I never did. Not even when I saw her on the streetcar or in church or anywhere else. We Dillons always remember a slight to the family and always hold a grudge long after we should have dropped it.

"Those were the days, "I said. They seem so wonderful looking back, but I'm sure there were just as many bad times as good."

"The thing of it is, Tommy", she said, leaning over and kissing my forehead. "We can always remember the happy times, and it's just as well we forget the bad ones. Just as well."

Very early in the morning, after breakfast, I got my things together and kissed Mary Catherine goodbye. She put her hand gently on my arm and said with a cautious tone, "One thing we didn't talk about. This Lillian. Is she Catholic?" "No," I said without further comment. Her forehead furrowed a bit, but she took me by the arm and walked me to the car.

"Not to worry, "I said. "No matter what happens, we have no plans to ever marry again. Neither one of us. Besides, it hasn't come to anything like that." She smiled and blew a kiss as the car pulled out from the curb, headed east.

At about 7:00am I called Lillie on my cell phone at a pit stop on the Turnpike. No answer! "Oh hell," I said. "She's probably down with those damned cats." I laughed at myself when I thought about it. ***They were damned lucky cats.***

Chapter Thirteen

Lillian: *"Life is full of new beginnings"*

I left a call on Tom's answering machine. "Call me anytime when you get home," I said. "It's about Imre. Hope you had a good trip"

He called me later that afternoon as soon as he arrived home and got my message. I told him to get ready for some really bad news.

"Imre hung himself!", I said straight out. "They found him when they opened up the Panorama this morning. Apparently he did it sometime last night on a light post in the London setting. He had a note pinned to his jacket. It was on the 6:00 o'clock news, of course. The police haven't released anything about what the note said. Your friend at the police station asked that you call him s.a.p."

Tom told me later that you often hear about someone getting a pain in their stomach when they're told bad news. "Well I felt pain for sure," he said. "I had to sit down hard on the chair before it sunk in, and I kept asking myself: *"My God, why would he need to do that?"*

Of course, Tom went right down to the police station as soon as he got off the phone to get the facts from Lieutenant Crosby and make his examination of the body. Tom called me from his cell phone about two hours later and gave me the whole story, or at least as much as the police knew at this point. After he filed his report with the Coroner I met him in the park just in front of the Claridge and we walked down onto the beach just as the sun set.

"The note was written in pencil," Tom said, "and pinned to his uniform, and it said simply — here, I wrote it down for you – "*Sorry for all the bother. The voices have been talking to me again. I'm all screwed up. But at least I won't be put in a cage again. Now you know that I didn't kill her. I think Nolan killed her.*"

That was all he wrote," Tom said. "Jesus, what a shame."

As we walked along the beach without speaking, I kept thinking about Imre's words. After all, I was an English Major and had a minor in Psychology. "You can read his message in one of three or four different ways," I said, breaking the silence..

"I mean you can read it with the emphasis on *"I"* and it would come out as:"You know that *I* didn't kill her," meaning obviously that someone, like Nolan, did. Or what if he were trying to say: "At least you know that I didn't *kill* her." Meaning that it could have been an accident and although she was dead, and although he was there when it happened, he didn't cause it. He might have added the words about Novak just to create some additional suspicion. Or he could have meant: "*Now* you know that I didn't kill her", meaning that something about the circumstances of his suicide would convince us that he wasn't a murderer, and that somebody else was – like Nolan.. Or he might have just reminded us that before we met him we thought he was some kind of freak in a Cossack costume, but after having met him we realized he wasn't a strange or evil man at all, and we knew better that than even to imagine that he might have murdered her. Take your pick", I said. .

Tom shook his head in dismay. "It's all so ironic", he said. "Crosby told me that he called Imre yesterday afternoon merely to ask him to come down to the station next day to answer some additional questions. But as it turns out, the questions he wanted to ask him dealt solely with the two Nolans who were in the bar that night. They're the persons of interest, and Brother Matt is the prime suspect. It had nothing to do with Imre.

Tom explained that the ACPD already has evidence about Matt bring involved in moving dope around for some time. "And get this", he said, "Rachel was definitely a 'bag lady'. In other words, she carried the money from the deals in her little backpack. They suspect that sometimes she did it with the little girl in her arms. She picked up the money from the dealers and passed it on to the 'big guys,' and the Rendezvous Club was one of her many transfer points of choice. Her donut store on the Boardwalk was much more convenient during daylight hours."

According to Tom, the police checked out their sources, put two and two together, and now are pretty sure Matt Nolan was planning that evening to turn his money over to her for 'transport' to the big guys in Philadelphia, or at least to someone in Philadelphia who'd pass it further along the circuitous route that leads to the *really* big guys. Apparently her usual pattern was to stash it in her apartment for a day or two, and then make one of her weekly runs to Philly, probably with her little girl in tow. A perfect get-up and not bound to arouse suspicion. She looked like such a kid herself that it was easy to move around without much notice.

"Lillie," Tom explained, "You'd be amazed by the amount of trust there is among contact people in these operations who pass along dope and money to each other. They know damned well that if someone gets out of line, they get wiped out, and quickly. They have a variety of complicated transfer points and techniques, because when it gets eventually to the really big shots, it has to reach them as inconspicuously as possible. Obviouslly , they don't want a straight line between themselves and the transactions.

Not when the really big guys are well known in the music world or in politics.

"There are a couple of good places to make connections and pass on the goods," he continued,"whether it's dope or money. A big railroad station like 30th Street in Philly used to be one of the best, but it's closely watched now. A big exhibit hall like the one here in Atlantic City or the new one in Philadelphia is another, and probably the *best* if there's a show going on that attracts ten or twenty thousand people."

Tom explained that the Russians used trade show locations like that in New York, Chicago, LA – you name it — for years during the cold war. They weren't exchanging dope, so far as we know, but information, documents, money, secrets! A baseball park used to be a good spot, but they started to check bags, and that's not a good thing for traffic of this kind."

I told Tom that this explained what Ruth had told me. She said Rachel made a trip to Philadelphia at least once a week, and sometimes twice. But she said Rachel *never* took the little girl with her. *Never.* Ruth thought it was for shopping, and in fact, when Rachel came back home she always had something for the baby and even a few little things for herself and for Ruth. That's where she bought her pretty shoes," I added.

Tom said that her dope dealing explained a lot of things about Rachel. Especially the number of separate money accounts she had in Philly. She made a lot of cash and she had to put it in safe places.

So it was drugs all the while, just as I thought almost from the beginning. It seemed so plain now. All the pieces fit together. Of course we might never know why Matt killed her. Was some money missing or did he make a proposition that she refused? We'd probably *never* know, unless Matt comes up with a full confession. But at this point in time, Matt doesn't have any intention of doing any such thing. Tom said that he pleaded complete innocence. Matt said that he didn't see Rachel leave the bar, and that he and his brother headed straight out the door and into his car heading for Stone Harbor because of the storm. Rachel just disappeared in the space of a couple of minutes, according to his story.

Matt insists that he and his brother drove directly to Jack's beach house that night – just as he said from the start — and that they stayed there most of the night until the storm passed.. That was all there was to it. His brother Jack backs him up all the way.

As far as using Rachel as a transfer for dope or money, Matt swears he didn't have either on him that night. He knew from street talk that Rachel was a carrier, but he never did any business with her. She was really "small potatoes." They just happened to be in the same bar on the same night. Or so he said. And of course, his brother Jack sub-stantiates his story..

The police have Matt's record all nicely pieced together, and it's a long one, extending back many years. They found another assault charge against him in Asbury Park earlier in the summer that involved a girl he manhandled. That girl was also involved in the drug trade and there was a hint that she'd been beaten up for "holding back" some money in a trade. Matt denies that he had any part in it and the girl has suddenly changed her story —accusing another man from New York who she says only *looks* like Matt. A case of mistaken identity. All charges were conveniently dropped. But the suspicion remains.

As I said, the apparent confirmation that Rachel was in the drug trade didn't come as a complete surprise to me. Cousin Jake at the Investment Company had already begun making his own investigation and has kept me in touch with his suspicions. The only thing I can't forgive is that Rachel might have used her little girl as a feint as she made her rounds. It breaks my heart, and if it turns out to be true I'm sure it will break Ruth's as well when she hears about it. I know I'll have to pass that damned Rendezvous Club almost every day and imagine Rachel sitting on that table near the bar doing what she was doing.

Of course I was troubled by Imre's suicide. If he knew that *he* didn't do it, and suspected Matt, why would he kill himself? He obviously knew something that we didn't and probably never will. As I reflect on his death and his state of mind, I have to think that he'd have done it anyway sooner or later at some point in his life. He was obviously stressed when we met him and carrying a "monkey on his back" after his experiences in Viet Nam.

I've read a great deal about servicemen — and women — who can endure the worst kinds of atrocities while they're in harm's way in a war zone, and then find themselves in a state of shock and bewilderment when they arrive safely back home.

My husband told me that no one he knew who served in action during the Second World War really wanted to talk about it in public. Sometimes he could share a story or two with a buddy over a beer, but he knew, for example, that no one on the home front could possibly envision what he saw on Iwo or Okinawa.

Then curiously, he said, when these old service guys pass the age of sixty or so, they start to have recalls in their sleep, or in times of stress. One old sergeant he knew scared the hell out of his wife as he moved along into his eighties and started jumping out of bed at night because he thought the Japs were tossing grenades at him – which they very well did on Guadalcanal back in '42.

He never told her that he lay under a pile of dead marines for two days, completely unconscious while the battle raged around him. Do we wonder why he had bad dreams? Do we wonder what Imre experienced in Viet Nam, and particularly what they did to him in his "cage." God help them all.

Well at least Imre is at peace now. No more voices talking to him. There's nothing more we can do for him now unless it's to confirm his innocence and punish the criminal if that's possible.

I asked about funeral arrangements. I felt we owed him something. The police told us that his uncle was taking care of everything. They also told us that they had some reports indicating that his uncle himself was also participating in the "trade." Did that implicate Imre as well? They weren't free to tell us at this point.

Tom and I went to dinner that evening at Abe's Seafood Restaurant on Atlantic Avenue. It just missed the total "community-tear-down" that leveled that particular blighted neighborhood in order to create "The Outlets". Abe's was never blighted itself, mind you. It's just one of the best, most genuine seafood eateries in the city.

Its oyster bar is thriving, even after 90 years or so of constant operation. Of course, old Abe, the founder, died long ago, but his two grandsons, now well into their seventies, continue the operation. I used to go there with my mother and father back in the late thirties, and it was considered old even then.

At Abe's they feature all kinds of "festivals" throughout the year, celebrating the shad run; the beginning of oyster season in September (the first "r" month since summer); soft shelled crab season; and a lot more. And they hang a turtle shell on a hook outside the door every Friday to announce the best turtle soup in the Atlantic City. Maybe in the world.

I know both "Kremer boys" who operate Abe's now, and I dread the day when they announce their retirement. They threaten to do just that each time I go there.

Frank, the elder brother, talked with us at our table when we settled in for dinner.

"Honestly, Lillie, I don't know how much longer we can keep it going", he said. "You know my brother picks up the produce in Philly every morning around 5:00 am. He brings it here and works on cleaning and fixing up the seafood until noon. Then I take over until the supper hour. The prices on everything are going up. And neither one of us is getting any younger. I figure we can make it for another year or so, and then 'hang it on a hook,' as Dad used to say. But then again, if we stop working, what will we do with ourselves?"

It's too bad that a lot of the aimless persons twenty or thirty years younger strolling the Boardwalk and waiting for their welfare checks in the sunshine don't have the same feelings as Frank. But then again, none of them inherited a restaurant either.

Frank brought us a complimentary bottle of Riesling and I told him to serve us what he thought was best on the menu that night. He didn't disappoint with the Crab Imperial. How I dread to think that sooner or later, Abe's will close. It will certainly leave a big empty spot in my life, and in my stomach as well. But at my age you have to get used to it – these closings and goodbyes. You just have to move on. *"Life is full of new beginnings,"* as someone more famous than I once said.

Chapter Fourteen

Dillon: ***"When peanuts were a dime a bag, and a big bag at that."***

Despite the news about Imre's death and all the anxiety it brings, it's good to be back in Atlantic City. Pittsburgh is my home. Well it used to be. Mary Catherine is all that holds me there now, except for Evelyn of course. And when Mary Catherine is gone . . . ? But Lillian is *here*, and that's where I want to be. No doubt it's a mortal sin to think that way while Evelyn is lying there in The Good Samaritan Home, four hundred miles away.

I just don't want to think about it. I have to live! If there's any chance she'll come out of the coma, I'll be back in Pittsburgh in a minute. I still love her.

When I got back from Abe's I noticed the red "message" signal on my phone. My call back alerted to me to the fact that it was coming from Jack Nolan. I had no doubt it would be "interesting" considering all that was happening, and something I'd want to share with Lillian as soon as I heard it. I knew I could use her as a sounding board after I followed up with this guy. She has a lot of common sense, and, Jesus, she knows everybody in the world!

As I hit the redial button and waited for his message, my first thought was *"how does he know me?"* I keep a low profile at the ACPD because I'm just there as a temporary representative of the County Coroner. But of course since I was a member of the Pittsburgh Force for over thirty years, they allow me a lot more slack. Nolan must be poking around. He must have a contact over there somewhere. He must have contacts in a lot of places. More importantly, what does he think I can do for him? People like him don't make courtesy calls.

His message was short and to the point. *"Mr Dillon, you don't know me, but I know you're involved with the Egron Murder case. My brother, Matt, is innocent. I was with him all that night. I hope we can meet and talk about this. How about tomorrow at your convenience. Give me a call back or leave a message Thanks."*

I guessed it couldn't hurt to talk with him, although I didn't want to muddy the water for the ACPD's investigation. Maybe it can even help them. At any rate, I knew I need to report it to Lt. Crosby and get his feelings about it first thing in the morning. And of course, I couldn't wait to call Lillian and see what her antenna would tell me.

Her antenna told me plenty as soon as I called her and it all boiled down to her advising me: "Do as you like, Dillon, but be careful. He has a very bad reputation around here . . . and well deserved."

In the morning, after I talked with Crosby and got his okay, I called Jack Nolan and we agreed to meet on the Boardwalk around noon. When it came to our meeting place, he asked me: "Do you know Atlantic City very well? I mean like an old timer like me would know it?" I answered: "Try me."

"There's a place across from where Woolworth's 5 and 10 used to be, " he said.. "A place with benches and a roof overhead to keep the pigeons from shitting on us. They call it a gazebo nowadays. Do you know where I'm talking about?"

I told him I knew the exact location he was talking about, and he told me I'd know him because he'd be wearing a blue suit with a white hat and eating peanuts out of a bag. And there he was at noon, looking exactly like I thought he would, with a neat blue suit and a white panama. And he was eating peanuts as promised.

I walked over to him and put out my hand. He stood up and said: "The peanuts just ain't the same. Not since Planters left the Boardwalk."

I agreed. "Do you remember when they roasted them right at the front of their store?" I said. "You could smell them a mile away." We both laughed as that long ago smell came flowing back.

Jack offered me the bag and I carefully broke the shell of one of the nuts, **very** carefully, making sure it didn't fall out on the boards where a hungry pigeon was sure to scoop it up from under my nose.

"Damn pigeons," said Jack "They still have a flock of them down here, and seagulls, too. They always had plenty to eat with people sitting right here and dropping nuts or popcorn. They didn't call it a 'gazebo' then. Just a place to sit down and watch the crowds go by."

"I ate many a peanut here, myself," I said.

Jack pointed to an ugly beige colored looking building across from us. "That's where Woolworth's was," he said, "and that's where the kazoo man used to stand."

"We were just talking about him the other day," I said, while I carefully broke open another peanut. "Somebody said he moved to Florida, a rich man. But I don't believe it."

Jack looked carefully at me, sizing me up. Then he said: "I remember hearing the same thing, and while I was waiting for you I was adding up figures in my head. I'm good at figuring.

I figure that when he started out, he bought those kazoos for about pennies apiece. Made in Japan. You know. Real cheap stuff then. He sold them for a quarter. And on a good day he might have sold at least a hundred of them. Now you figure that he made a profit of about twenty bucks a day, and he worked probably six months or about 180 days a year. You know he was here all the time during the Season, even in the evenings, and on Sundays. So that means he made a profit of . . . let's see . . . about $3600 a year. Are you followin' me?"

"Yah," I said. "That would have been about right in the 1930's. He probably did a bit better after the war."

"After he paid his personal bills" Nolan continued, "and you know, rent was real cheap back then, maybe $25 a month for a little apartment, and food was cheap — well anyway, he might have made a profit of $2500 a year. Now you multiply that by 20 years or so and you have a nest egg of about 50,000 bucks. And in the 1950's and '60's you could buy a nice little place in Lauderdale or Boynton Beach and still have money to spare. And that doesn't count any money he made in the off-months."

He paused and rattled the bag to get the last peanut. I smiled as I watched him turn it upside down and shake it, just like he and I would have done when we were kids sitting here, in the same spot, when peanuts were a dime a bag, and a big bag at that.

Then I said to him: "Jack, I'm sure you didn't get me down here to talk about the kazoo man What's on your mind?"

He laughed out loud. "It's a helluva nice thing to talk to someone who remembers the kazoo man. I'm not all that younger than you are . . . maybe seven or eight years. And yes, I do have something to talk about."

His face darkened. "It's about my brother, Matt. They're trying to screw him for all the trouble he gave them in the past couple of years. They're trying to pin the death of that girl on him and he didn't do it. I was with him all night, and I'll bet she was dead and in the ocean before midnight. But nobody is going to take my word for it."

First off, I had a couple of questions for Jack. For example, how did he know my name, and what kind of information would he want from me, an assistant to the County Coroner, and a temporary one at that? I couldn't be very important in a case like this.

"I know more about you than you think" he said, eyes narrowing. He then proceeded to give me a breakdown on the life and times of me, Tom Dillon.

"You were on the Pittsburgh Force for over thirty years. You just retired and spending some time down here on the Shore. You were well respected in Pittsburgh. Did a lot of investigative work. Very thorough, And straight as an arrow. Your college buddy's son, the Coroner down here in South Jersey, has a lot of work nowadays with bodies turning up here and there. Even among school kids. Damn shame about the kids.

The kid – the coroner I mean – lived practically next door to you in Pittsburgh, didn't he? The ACPD respects you enough to allow you to muddle in some of their affairs. Maybe because you're, what, about 75, and they figure you can't do too much harm, and your friend, the Coroner, is pretty big in the Democrat party right now and seems headed for . . . I don't know . . . whatever they want to elect him to. Am I right so far?"

I told him he knew a helluva lot about me and where did he get all that information?

"I have a lot of friends," he smiled, "and business connections."

I told him frankly that was the problem. His **business.** There wasn't much question that he dealt in drugs and probably was a supplier to big shots, either in politics or maybe in show business. I told him straight out that I didn't like dope and I didn't like people who were involved in it. As simple as that.

"As simple as that," he repeated with half a smile. "Dillon, you might be smart but you're a little behind the times if you don't mind my saying so. Now take for example the times that you were born in. Drinking liquor was a criminal act back then. And movie houses and department stores were closed in Pennsylvania because the Blue Laws made it illegal to do much of anything on the Sabbath.

Do you see those two black people who just passed by," he said, pointing to a young couple. "When you and I were kids they weren't even allowed on the Boardwalk. And look at that couple coming this way. A black man and a white woman with a kid. They would have been ***arrested*** before the war. And they would have stopped traffic while everybody stared at them and shook their heads.

Now over there . . ." he pointed to two young men in very tight pants, shirtless, and tanned, walking along with their arms around each other. "They would have been carried off the Boardwalk in handcuffs, and people would have spit on them. The police would have rapped them on the ass a couple of times, and maybe broke a bone or two along the way just to make a point. And no one would have said a damn thing."

I nodded in agreement. Yes, what he said was entirely true.

"Now why I'm telling you this, Dillon, is because everything we just saw was once illegal, but now ***legal***. Totally legal. And the biggest hypocrisy is the gambling business. I was arrested for doing numbers here in Atlantic City when I was nineteen. Numbers! Can you imagine. And now the whole business holding Atlantic City together – and making it a playground for all the beautiful people, and the common ones, too – is licensed gambling. Do you see what I'm getting at?"

"You're trying to make a case for legalized drugs, I suppose. But that's a different matter all together," I said.

"Oh is it?" he said sarcastically. "Well just wait a couple of years and you'll see 'Mary Jane' cigarettes sold over the counter . . . first in California and then eastward. Of course, you'll have to smoke them outside," he laughed. "Bad for the lungs. "

"Look Jack,' I said. " If there's something you want me to do for your brother let's get to the point."

"The point is that I want to hire you so I can *save* my brother" he said, lighting a cigarette. "And I'm willing to pay you good money to do it. I know that everyone in this town wants to see him put away. Hell, they want to see him get the chair. He hasn't made himself very popular around here, but he's not a murderer. He didn't lay a finger on that girl. I was with him until about five in the morning, and I'll bet that girl 'got it' pretty soon after she walked out that door. Maybe it was an accident. But I have my doubts."

"It wasn't an accident," I said. "Someone kept her around for a day or so before dropping her in the ocean. Maybe deciding what to do with her. Maybe in a car trunk."

I suddenly felt sorry for Jack. I knew I had no reason to. He's deeply into crime, and his brother is in deeper still. But it *is* his brother. I know how I felt about mine. When he died, a piece of my life died with him. Anyway, I have my own doubts about his brother Matt being involved at all.

After thirty years on the police force you can almost smell a liar. It's in their faces and their voices. Jack is hard, corrupt, arrogant, but he doesn't want to see his baby brother convicted of something he didn't do, and he knows everyone in this part of Jersey has a reason for wanting him behind bars, or worse. Now here I am, representing a very popular county official, knowing that this creep, Matt Nolan, is probably as innocent as a baby. Or is he? Still, my instincts tell me there's more than a reasonable doubt when it comes to convicting him and putting him away.

"I've got to think about it, Jack," I said.

He took a long drag on his cigarette. "Well think about this." he said. "Your wife has been in that Home in Pittsburgh for . . . what . . . almost ten years now? And every month you have to think about where you're gonna come up with the money to keep her there. The medicine and the tests and all that stuff. You're wondering how long *you* can last , and if you go first, what happens then?. Who's gonna be able to pay without your social security and pension checks coming in? What happens to your wife then? And what about your sister?"

He hit it right on the head. I have to admit it. Mary Catherine and I were talking about it while I was home. Without me she'll probably have to sell the house to make ends meet. She never worked in a job that allowed her to get social security. She's been a housewife all these years without being a wife. And what will she do after she passes 85? When she starts to go down hill? She probably won't stay well all that much longer.

There's no kidding about that. And she'll probably wind up in a home herself. And who'll pay for that?

"Let me make myself clear, Dillon" Nolan continued, "I want to hire you to do some investigative looking around for me because I trust you and I don't trust another damn soul around here. I don't even trust my lawyers who are the best at what they do. I have a hunch you'll give me a fair shake. I want to make sure that if anyone finds *any* piece of evidence that might help prove Matt innocent, you'll be around to see that it gets put on the table at the trial. I'm not so sure how it would go with anybody else around here. Things get lost, if you know what I mean. Or overlooked. He's my baby brother, you know. They tell me you had a brother once."

He hit my soft spot there. And then he brought out the big guns.

"Dillon," he said, "If you help me get my brother out of this, I promise you'll never pay a bill again to keep your wife. And more than that, I'll settle an annuity on your sister that will take care of her for the rest of *her* life as well. Don't worry, it can all be done legally, with no 'if, ands, or buts.' You'll report to my lawyers—Bankowitz and Banks— and get your checks signed by them. You'll have no legal connection to me whatsoever. I know you want it that way."

I sat there, numb, on the bench for a moment or two. This is the answer to my prayers. And I won't be breaking any laws working as a "consultant" to a law firm. I don't even have to come up with any proof, if there is any. If Matt's guilty, the guilt will come out one way or another. But if there's one chance in a million that he isn't involved it should be brought to light. I can't ignore the powerful feeling I've had all along that Matt isn't guilty. Well not of murder anyway, and not in this particular case.

Then I began to think of the negatives. The ACPD has a bone to pick with Matt, and I'll be on their shit list, to say the least, if I take the job. The Coroner may be in a bad position inasmuch as he "wished" me on the Atlantic City Force. How can I explain it to him? And how can I explain it to Lillian?

I told Jack I'd need a day or two to think it over, and he understood. We shook hands, and both of us looked over the railing at the ocean for a moment.

"Don't you wish we were kids again," he said., "playing in the sand like those kids over there by the lifeguards' boat. My brother is about ten years younger than me, you know.

"I used to bring him down here and dip him in the water, him hanging from my arms and screaming his head off. The water was so damn cold. But then we'd both splash in and ride the waves and it wasn't so cold after all, especially on a real hot day. The ice cream man would trudge past through the sand, but we didn't have any money for that," he said with a quiet sigh.

We shook hands and I walked away quickly. I didn't want to get too close to Jack. I didn't want old memories of mine to cloud the decision I'd have to make.

I walked up the Boardwalk and then over to St James Place toward Lillie's.place.

With every step I took I said to myself: "Lillian will help me make the decision. She'll either give me some good reason why I should do it, or some damn strong language as to why I shouldn't. Wonderful Lillie. ***What would I do without her.***

Chapter Fifteen

Lillian: *"Tom needs money, badly."*

When Tom arrived at my apartment later in the afternoon I told him right off the bat to turn Matt Nolan down cold. I reminded him that he was a notorious drug dealer, and his brother, too, and everybody in the state of New Jersey knows it. As far as I'm concerned, both the Nolans should be put in a bag and thrown in the ocean. Why in the world would Tom even consider getting mixed up with the two of them? It's a mystery to me.

Then I figure it out, quickly. It's something I never thought of before, but now it's quite clear that Tom must be nearly broke. Everything he takes in each month – pension checks, social security, whatever – goes toward keeping Evelyn in The Home. And he probably sends money home to his sister each month as well. I'm sure she's barely making it in these times, even with his financial help. It's as simple as that. Tom needs money. Badly.

So when he starts to explain what he talked about with Jack Nolan, I listen to what he has to say and I sense the conflict in his mind over money or morals. I begin to realize how difficult it is for him to pay his everyday bills, including those of his sister. As Tom always says to me: "It's hell to get old, and it's a helluva lot worse to get old if you don't have any money." But I never considered for a moment that he was in that position.

The sad part is that I'm quite able to help Tom and would be glad to do it in a minute. But I know he'll never stand for that. It would be a blow to his pride and might even open up a gap in our friendship. We've never had words up to this point. I don't want to start now, but on the other hand, I am, as the saying goes, very well heeled. I can easily pay anything he needs for Evelyn, or for anything else if he'll let me.

But I can read his mind and I feel guilty, too. Imagine my paying bills for a wife he can't support while we're both keeping a death watch on the poor soul. Not ***hoping*** she'll die, of course, but making plans in our minds for when it might happen. I used to say that all of my ethics and morals were taught me by my favorite Sunday School teacher, Mrs. Margaret Sachs. But this is something I never dreamed I'd have to cope with. And I can never take it to the Vicar at St. Andrew's. Or anyone else.

Tom went over Novak's offer again and again with me, trying to decide whether he would be serving justice in the best sense of the words: ***"everybody equal under the law."*** He agonizes over it. And the money, I'm sure, keeps interjecting itself into his argument.

Before he left his apartment, Tom told me that he called Jack Nolan again to ask what kind of information he'd be expected to uncover. Novak said first off that he wanted Tom to have a long talk with his lawyers so he could acquaint himself with the "angles" they were developing. "All Philadelphia lawyers find 'angles'", he said. "That's why they're called Philadelphia lawyers. And once you know their angles," he said, "I think you'll be smart enough to follow them up in the right directions. If I'm not able to pay you enough to do it, I'll find someone else," he said with a warning in his voice.

Jack Nolan was smart enough to know better than to get involved personally in any part of the preliminaries. In Nolan's opinion, Tom said, nothing was more stupid than an amateur trying to make his own case while he was paying big bucks to high priced Philadelphia lawyers. With angles.

Tom said that for starters, Nolan had located Rachel Egron's husband, a man named Gary Bauer, and wanted someone to pin him down to see how much he really knew about his wife. What exactly had she been up to? Why did they get a divorce? Who she was seeing? That sort of thing.

He told Tom he knows for a fact that husband Gary is "flopping" in a Salvation Army shelter somewhere in New York City. Nolan apparently has contacts up there almost everywhere, and especially in the shelters, of which there are a multitude. The shelter contacts are well aware that all kinds of people are seeking missing relatives, friends, and enemies. And they're eager to supply information. For a price.

These "watchers" make a business of keeping tabs on who's coming and going; who's a regular or a transient; an innocent or a professional. For a couple of bucks, they have a kind of "cottage industry" running as they provide names, habits, locations. Yes, of course some of the "floppers" give aliases, or no names at all. But almost 100% have some sort of identification pinned to their shorts in case they're found in the river. And the watchers find ways to check their shorts.

It's a thriving business as more "down and outers" arrive in the big city for one reason or another in these hard economic times. Nolan wants someone to find this kid, Gary Bauer, talk with him; and see how much it would take for him to "cough up some dirt" on his wife.

In my opinion as a woman, I think the first thing that Gary will want to know is how his little girl is being taken care of. That is, if he has any feelings at all. And perhaps — the thought suddenly comes to mind — it would be better for *a woman* with a softer touch to give that kind of information to him. If I could get him to talk about Melanie, he'd have to begin talking about his wife. He probably doesn't even know Rachel is dead. Or perhaps he's too far gone to think or talk coherently about anybody or anything. .

I told Tom I'd been thinking about going to an exhibit in New York called Japan Design at Javits Convention Center. It has to do with Japanese gardens, flower arrangements, textiles—all those things that I have a real penchant for. I have a friend with an apartment in the Waldorf Towers who is always begging me to stop by, and the invitation is always tempting. You have to know, of course, that there's a Waldorf-Astoria Hotel and there's the ***Towers Suites*** of the Waldorf Astoria. The Towers is where the very wealthy roost, high above Manhattan. To know that General MacArthur and the Prince of Wales and his Wally once lived there, and loved there, gives you some idea of the prestige of the place, although I have to admit that my remembering them at all rather dates me.

Tom asked me whether I'd ever been in the Towers before and I explained that my friend Susan, who invited me was one of my sorority sisters in college who managed to marry a United Nations Official. I didn't tell him how many international parties I've already gone to at the Waldorf over the past forty years or so. It isn't so much my popularity, but the fact that every one of the hundred and more countries represented in the United Nations has a national day – like our Fourth of July – to which UN types are expected to attend. Sue ticked off at least three happenings in as many days that we can go to, in addition to the exhibit at Javits. It's no fun for her, she says, unless she has me as a "buddy" with whom she can share the gossip and the general goings-on of this particular facet of the International jet set.

"Did you ever see anyone important there", Tom asked innocently.

I gave him an example: One evening in October—on October 10th, to be exact — as Sue and I were waiting for the Towers Elevator, which is extremely private and heavily secured, a group of very well dressed Chinese gentlemen came up the hallway pushing a wheelchair with a very old lady in a traditional Chinese silk dress. Very old indeed. I got the shock of my life to see none other than Madame Chiang Kai Shek. She was well into her nineties at the time, and I assumed she died many years before. And she didn't look all that bad.

Sue poked me with her arm and whispered: " Do you know who that is? It's Madame Chiang returning from a party celebrating Chinese Independence Day. But of course, no one else celebrates it in Mainland China since the Communists took over in '49 and substituted their own Independence Day. She's a real dinosaur, you know, in more ways than one. I'll tell you about it later."

By now the entourage reached the elevator and one of the older gentlemen approached us and removed his hat, bowing sharply at the waist. With great courtesy he asked us if we might wait for the next elevator. Madame was quite tired and very uncomfortable with strangers. Of course we both stepped back and smiled at the gentleman as they slipped her into the elevator and quickly disappeared.

Sue laughed and said: "Now you know why I call her a dinosaur."

"Yes,' I said, "But still alive – at least I haven't heard of her dying — after all that's happened over there, and more than that, still commanding respect after half a century out of circulation."

Tom was impressed with that, but he said just what I was thinking: "I wonder how many people still remember her or her husband, or even care anymore. When I was a kid, Mary Catherine would tell me to eat everything on my plate and think about the starving Chinese. It's a new world, and now we **owe** China about a gazillion bucks. How did that happen?"

All this talk reminded me that it would be fun to see Sue again, visit the exhibit, and share some UN stories. And of course, I'd follow-up on the whereabouts of Gary Bauer with the hope of getting some information out of him.

I told Tom this was my plan: to see the exhibit and hunt for Gary Bauer at the same time? There was certainly no risk involved, and if Gary didn't know that his wife was dead he should be told by someone, sometime. I also knew that unless his heart and brain were gone, he'd want to know more about Melanie, his daughter. I could take along a photo of her at the beach. I knew that would gain me an entrée, a privilege of admission that nobody else possessed.

Tom thought it was a good idea, but wouldn't it be like looking for a needle in a haystack?

I explained that the Salvation Army part of it makes the chances of finding him just a bit more realistic. Tom wondered if I were on the Board of the Salvation Army along with everything else. I can't claim that honor, but I do know Colonel Wechsler in the Atlantic City Branch of the Army. He and I serve together on the Committee for the Homeless in Atlantic City, and perhaps, just perhaps, he could assist in the search.

Tom knew that once I made up my mind I'd be determined to go. But I wanted his blessing on it and wouldn't have gone without it. He agreed, and a few hours later we took the same train together to Philly where he transferred to SEPTA for a ride into the city to meet his "Philadelphia lawyers" while I took Amtrak's Acela to New York City..

As I sped through Northern New Jersey I got a cell phone call from Colonel Wechsler who contacted colleagues in New York and came up with an address for me. I often complain about this "*new age and its proliferation of damned cell phones*", but in this case I give it my full blessing. Col. Wechsler told me that, in a matter of minutes, New York's computer had talked with his computer and spewed out names of "guests" currently in their fifty or so locations in the Greater New York area. Gary Neubauer's name appeared on the most current list at the W. 30th Street location. God must have guided the search – and I have no doubt He does that quite often for His Salvation Army friends. The address is a short cab ride south of Javits Center. Not a very wholesome neighborhood, and one you don't want to traverse at night, as I found from previous visits to Javits.

Thank goodness the Salvation Army is so meticulous about its records. They even have a two letter designation for various facets of their 'guests' personalities. In a very short time, Colonel Wechsler called back with a list of some of Gary's personal details. For example, their code lists him as "non aggressive" as compared with "mildly aggressive" or "extremely aggressive." Thank goodness for that. The other codes identify him as alcohol dependent rather than drug dependent. Most important for me, the code indicates regular habits as opposed to erratic ones. The "regular habits" category is most important for me because, as Wechsler explained, it means that the "guest" is generally present for breakfast, lunch, and dinner, with specific hours of 8am, 12pm, and 6pm.

I decided I'd check in with the good folks on W. 30th Street, have dinner with Mr. Bauer, and ***hope that the cuisine is to my taste.***

Chapter Sixteen

Dillon: ***"Two miracles are required before anyone can become a saint."***

I leave Lillie at the 30th Street Station and take SEPTA over to midtown. The offices of Banks and Bankowitz are on Arch Street, across from the Holiday Inn, and just around the corner from the SEPTA station.

It 's not quite Rittenhouse Square where Lillie does her investment business with one of her WASP cousins, but it's in a relatively new building, with nicely appointed offices. Jack Novak has already notified Mr. Julius Bankowitz of my coming, and he's waiting and eager to meet me. His son, Bruce Banks, is also present.

Julius is a pleasant looking man in his mid sixties, very well dressed, with a diploma from the Duquesne University Law School prominently displayed on the wall behind his desk.

"I hear you're a Pittsburgher," he says as I move to shake his hand.. "I went to school there. A long time ago when we had a great basketball team. A fine school, and a nice city. ***"Go Steelers"*** he says emphatically, grasping my hand. He introduces his son, Bruce, and adds: "As you notice by his expression, he's not quite as enthusiastic as I am about the Steelers."

Bruce shakes my hands and smiles. "Unfortunately, I never was infected with the Steeler bug. I got my diploma from Franklin and Marshal which is on ***this*** side of the mountains in Eagle's territory.

"We are what we are," I reply with a smile. I don't ask about the disparity in their names. I already figure that Julius who is a bit younger than me, and a Jew , must have had some problems breaking into the Philadelphia legal fraternity back then, and probably had a hard time establishing a practice. His son, on the other hand, went to a law school originally founded by a Protestant denomination, and with a name like Bruce is probably headed for Rittenhouse Square in not too many years. But probably not before the old man retires. I think there's some foretaste of that in the name of the firm. I suspect that Julius is already thinking ahead and recognizes that it will be easy for Bruce to separate the "Bankowitz" from the "Banks" when the time comes.

"I hear good reports about you, Tom, if I may call you Tom," he begins.

"It's my pleasure to meet you, *Julius*," I say somewhat hesitantly, but figure it's a friendly thing to do since he's younger than me by a few years. "I've heard a lot about you as well." They both laugh.

"No doubt you have," says Bruce. "We're somewhat notorious, as you know?" "But we're damned good lawyers," his father chimes in. "And they can't take that away from us, no matter what they think."

"Our Catholic friends tell us that we're the St. Jude of criminals, which I guess is a compliment," chuckles Bruce. "And what do *you* think of us?"

They both sit quite still, carefully studying my face while I search for an answer. Damn, they're good. They put me on the spot and my answer will tell them right off the bat whether they're dealing with just a cop or with an equal.

"As I understand it," I say with a rather solemn tone, "two miracles are required before anyone can become a saint. Your first miracle is finding a jury in Atlantic City where everyone doesn't hate Matt Novak's guts. The second miracle is bringing Imre back from the dead and having him write a new exit note."

"We're already planning a strategy for the first miracle," Bruce smiles. "It will take just a bit more effort to carry off the second. But don't underestimate us." He says this without a smile. The intimate preliminary small talk is over.

Julius brought the business part of our meeting to order by going into a monologue about how the selection of a "friendly" jury is something they pride themselves on. He went into great detail explaining the kind of juror they always look for, and how their line of questioning prospective witnesses gives them the clues they need to approve or disapprove them. It's quite a science, said Julius, and one which we developed over thirty years or more from common sense, not "book" sense, and based on a realistic view of the thought process of any particular prospect examined.

"I ought to write a book about it," he said. "But why give away company secrets?. It's the most important part of the trial process and determines in advance, in most cases, pretty much what the verdict will be."

Bruce interjected with the firm's contention that a good lawyer doesn't embarrass a client by having him sit through a trial. "We prefer to have a case dismissed or a settlement made which negates contending with a jury of one's peers", he said. "Think how many verdicts are tainted by the thought process of a woman who makes a quick decision on the basis of what she's paying her babysitter per hour. Or consider the man who hates blacks, but denies it, and is determined to punish the plaintiff no matter what the other jurors think. As for me," he said, "I'd prefer to throw myself on the mercy of a judge—any judge—before I'd submit myself to most of the juries I've seen in action."

"That being said," added Julius, "We try very hard to select jurors who are fair. Both Bruce and I pride ourselves on being good judges of character. I can smell a phony a mile away. "

I brought up the matter of circumstantial evidence in Matt's case, and they both agreed that with the facts they have in hand there seemed to be an excellent possibility for the case to be dismissed. If they get a good judge.

Julius interjected with the thought that Imre's note is "somewhat incriminating," but that it won't hold water if we can prove that he was an unstable character even in high school, and all the moreso after his return from Viet Nam. "Thank God he wrote: "I *think* Novak did it," rather than simply, *"Matt Novak did it."*

Bruce suggested a strategy of building up evidence impugning Rachel Egron's character. "She is the victim, of course," Bruce said, "but if we can reinforce the impression – based on as much fact as possible— that she was a rather loose character with ties to the underworld and with questionable taste in men, her death will not appear so 'shocking' to the community. It's our contention, and we hope to convey this to the jury without seeming to be cruel and unfeeling, that her death was as an inevitable misfortune predicated by her life style, and probably due to an accident rather than murder."

I thought to myself that it was so much "lawyer talk." I've heard plenty of it in my time. Boil it down and it means simply: "Let's get as much dirt on her as possible."

I interjected my opinion that, having examined the body very carefully, my experience tells me that murdered women usually show some tell-tale signs of struggle unless they're caught completely unaware. And even then their fingers usually show some sign of trauma from their struggle in the few moments before their death. But there was nothing on Rachel's body to suggest anything of the sort. And no sign of robbery. Her wallet was still zipped into her jeans. It would be a sure call for an accident except for the fact that someone seems to have held on to the body for a day or so before depositing it in the ocean.

I told them that she might have had a fall of some sort. I doubt that someone *pushed* her down steps or off a wall in an attempt to kill her. There are more certain ways. I also thought that the last line on Imre's suicide note appears simply to be an after thought: a convenient and unexpected way to pay back Matt Novak for his general bad behavior. It's doubtful that someone would have been able to plan ahead for a murder of that sort to implicate Matt No one expected the weather to be so bad, and no one at all expected him to be at the Club that night, after all.

"Let's talk honestly about Matt," suggested Julius.

Bruce volunteered immediately: "He's a son-of-a-bitch. It's as simple as that. People around here know him from way back. He has a long record: petty thievery, pimping, some perjury, assault, and unquestionable participation in the drug trade in a big way."

"Other than that," I smiled. "What don't you like about him?"

Julius entered the conversation. "He's depended on his brother, Jack, to bail him out of trouble ever since he was a kid. And besides all that, he's ungrateful and mean spirited. Which means we have to expend all our efforts to get him off the hook, not because we like him or hate him, but because we know there is definitely a reasonable doubt, in this case at least, that he's a murderer"

"More than a reasonable doubt," added Bruce. "He couldn't have pulled off an attack on that girl while Jack Nolan was with him. Jack's involved in a lot of "stuff" but not penny ante stuff. If Matt needed a girl that badly, Jack could have provided one with a cell phone call to a local hotel in less than five minutes. If there were an argument or some kind of misunderstanding that led to pushing or shoving, Jack would have put an end to it quickly , maybe by slapping Matt around, rather than the girl, for acting so stupid. He certainly wouldn't risk his whole operation on a girl like Rachel. She was a nothing. Nada, as my Hispanic friends say. "

"Then we agree that he's innocent," I said.

"Absolutely," said Bruce, "and it means we have to start by getting in touch with people who knew her— people she worked with, or her former husband as an example — and try to get something to pin on the girl."

"As matter of fact," I said with a straight face, I already have one of my agents working on the husband part of it. She's in New York City right now checking out a lead." I didn't add that I had only **one** agent, but a damned good one at that. They smiled and nodded their approval.

The business part of our conversation is over. We get intimate again. Julius decides that we'll go to lunch at the "Goose Quill", a restaurant that caters exclusively to the legal trade, and carry on our conversation there. He says that lunch is on the firm, of course, and that it's his understanding that I'll be paid directly from Banks and Bankowitz rather than from Jack Nolan.

I guess I realize at this point that I 'm an active participant with Nolan whether it's on paper or not. I feel better knowing that I'm on the side of the law in this matter. I suppose I should rest easier knowing that in the opinion of professionals like Julius and Bruce, we'll all working together to keep an innocent man from going to prison, even though we all agree that prison is where he ought to be. The older I get, the funnier life gets to be.

Well I need the money, but I won't ever tell Lillic that. She doesn't need to know how I've been scraping along for the last couple of months. And knowing her, she won't ask.

I wonder what she's up to in New York?

Chapter Seventeen

Lillian: ***"Major Williams is a woman. Why am I surprised?"***

I love New York. I know that every kid who goes there on vacation comes back with a jersey that says the same thing, but I do really love the city. I've spent lots of time there and I know every corner in Manhattan.

When I got off the train on 34th Street, I walked up the escalator and on to the little plaza separating the station from Madison Square Garden. I know it sounds kitchy, but in that particular spot I can feel the throb of the city right up through my shoes. Possibly because the Long Island Railroad rumbles directly beneath it. Ha!

I gave Sue a call on my cell phone and asked her to meet me at a little Belgian Restaurant on a corner between the Garden and Macy's. She said she'd be down in fifteen minutes.

I know I can amuse myself for that length of time. There's always someone in that area selling things from under their coat, if you know what I mean. Today a young black man with a bright red coat is selling watches. Both arms are laced with watches, and he's holding a string of them. Once as I passed MacDonald's just across the street, a young man was selling basketballs . . . . believe it or not . . . . basketballs. He was very, very tall and had special pockets in a long, loose "garment" he was wearing. I can't describe it and you'd have to see it to believe me.

I venture into a jewelry store that has been there as long as I can remember: an odd little place that specializes in thing-a-mabobs from the Middle East. Rings and necklaces and pill boxes. Things like that.

All of their stuff is genuine and unique. There's a musty smell about the place and much of the jewelry has a green patina. Once when I returned from a fast trip to Dubai with my husband, I had forgotten to buy a few trinkets for my nieces. So I dropped by this place and bought some little things that I "passed off" to them as Dubai-made, and they were thrilled with them. Ironically, the jewelry from this little shop is probably a lot more authentic, and much less expensive, than anything I would have bought over there.

I walk a few more blocks and take a table in the Café Antwerp where Sue arrives minutes later. We have a happy reunion as you can imagine, and I remark on her new hairdo which makes her look at least fifteen years younger. She laughs and says "*maybe ten.*" The nice thing about having a friend as old as yourself is that you don't have to lie about your age and you can let all your prejudices hang out. We order the large platter of mussels, garnished with sea weed, Belgian style, and the chicken cooked in pea soup. You have to taste both of these to understand how wonderful they are. I don't cook much, but I love good food. And some of the best food at reasonable cost is in New York's ethnic restaurants just like this one.

I wonder if anyone at the UN has begun pushing her husband to retire. He's a few years younger than Sue, but not by much. She says that he's greatly respected and has very good "connections." He'll retire when he wishes to, and he doesn't wish to do so just yet. Besides all that, when he finally decides to retire there are a number of African nations who want to retain him as their special representative, i.e. lobbyist.

I tell Sue about Tom and his special relationship with the coroner in New Jersey. Of course she has a lot of other questions about him. I answer some, but let her linger on others, telling her that when I meet her next time I might have more to tell. "Maybe the two of us, Tom and I, can come," I said coyly. She reminds me that the spare bedroom in her apartment is always available, and that she is extremely liberal for being a conservative Republican. We both laugh. How 1950ish!

While we linger over a small aperitif after lunch I call the Salvation Army Office at its West Side location and talk with the director, Major Williams, who, it turns out, is a woman. Why am I surprised? The Salvation Army broke the "glass ceiling" eons ago. She tells me that Gary has not materialized for lunch, which means he will almost certainly be there for supper at 6:00. She's already aware of my request to meet him and grants me permission, if he's willing. When I explain that his wife's death is a matter he should be aware of, and that he needs to know the whereabouts of his daughter, she agrees immediately that he needs to talk with me whether he wants to or not.

Sue and I finish lunch and take a cab down to Javits Center which is at the Hudson River end of 34th Street at 11th Avenue. It's a brute of a building, extending for many blocks in what was once, and in many ways still, a blighted area. As we stare up at the huge glass expanse of the place, I remind her of the evening in July of 1955 –just after our graduation— when she was leaving on the Andrea Doria for Italy. The ship was docked just south of here, and her father arranged a bon voyage party in her cabin on the night before she sailed. It was much easier to do that sort of thing in those benign days.

What a lovely party, and what a beautiful ship. It's heard to believe she was struck by another ship just off Nantucket a few years later and now lies on the bottom of the sea. "Imagine all that furniture and the beautiful paintings," Sue sighs.

I thought of the forty or more people who went down with her.

All the great Atlantic Liners docked on this lower side of Manhattan facing the Hudson: QE2, Ile de France, Queen Mary . . . all the great ones. I remember my father bringing me down here as a child in 1942 and pointing out the once-beautiful Normandie lying on her side after burning at the dock. I suppose that's the sad part of living in the past. Remembering beautiful things that can never be replaced. But I live for today and when I find the time I have a notion to book a Queen Mary II cruise.

Sue and I go into Javits Center and are soon immersed in Japan Design.

We even attend a lecture conducted by a Japanese gentleman who is an expert in his field. Fabulous. The hours fly by and I tell Sue I'll have to be on my way to the Salvation Army establishment. "Take a cab," she commands, knowing how I love to walk in the city, even in the worst areas. "We'll catch up later at the Waldorf" she says cheerfully. "Buzz me up when you get back and we'll meet in the Main Lobby next to Peacock Alley."

Now the real purpose of my journey to New York commences. Here's where I go to work.

I arrived at the Salvation Army "Settlement" at a quarter to six, and Major Williams was waiting and eager to greet me.

"Gary arrived back here about ten minutes ago and went downstairs to wash up", she said.. "We have showers down there and our rule is that no one eats dinner until they're clean. Gary's very good about that. A very pleasant young man, all in all. But quite frankly, he has no ambition. No 'get up and go' as we used to say. He's an habitual drunk, and it's getting worse."

"You know the circumstances that bring me here, don't you? " I reminded her.. "That his wife is dead, and his child is being taken care of by his mother-in-law in Trenton. Well it's a bit worse than that. His wife was murdered. They found her in the ocean a few weeks ago. There's a suspect, but all of it is circumstantial evidence. Gary may not take it too well. I don't want you to be shocked ."

Major Williams looked at me with knowing eyes. "You'd be surprised, Ms Moore, how *well* I'm insulated against shock. In the ten years I've been here I've encountered every kind of shocking situation you can imagine. Most of the crime and depravity in the past was brought on our "guests" by themselves, by their own stupidity or heedlessness. But with the recession," she said sadly, "we've had an influx of what I call 'innocents abroad' who've simply been run over by the economy and have no way of getting back on their feet. They don't like being here," she continued, "but they see us as their last resort. Most of them never dreamed they'd be living like this and never prepared themselves for it. They have no reserves in terms of money or resources or caretakers, and they see no hope for themselves in the future. And quite frankly, neither do I."

"What about Gary?" I said. "Does he have any redeeming features at all?"

"You'll understand when you meet him," she said. "He's basically a farm boy. He came to Atlantic City, so he tells me, to work in a casino, but he's simply not 'sharp' enough for positions on the gaming floor. They had him doing manual work but he said he might as well have stayed on the farm for that. That's why he left Iowa, he told me. And of course, he regrets it all. Here he comes now," she said, turning toward the staircase." I tidied up the conference room and I think you'll be comfortable, and private over there."

She pointed to a small room in the corner of the building, and gestured to him as he moved closer to us. "This is Ms Moore . . . from Atlantic City. She wants to talk to you about Melanie, your daughter."

Gary seemed surprised, but couldn't suppress a smile when he heard the word '*Melanie.*' "You've seen her recently?" he asked with his voice rising with the question. "Is she okay?" he said, as the smile faded and he realized I might be here on a more serious matter.

We walked into the conference room and I closed the door. I asked him to sit next to me on the couch rather than around the other side of the table. Then I broke the news about Rachel to him as gently as I could.

"Your wife, Rachel. I can't make it easy for you. She's dead."

He gasped, and tears came to his eyes. He repeated the word "dead" as if it were more than he could comprehend. He repeated it again: "Dead? But she was only twenty-five. She'd have been twenty-six next month. How could it possibly have happened?"

I let him cry as long as he needed to. I had a large handkerchief in the ready and gave it to him. He pulled it over his eyes and wept unashamedly. "I really loved her, you know. She was the one who wanted to end our marriage. I left because I thought it was the only way to make her happy. I really loved her. I still do."

I put my arms around him. He was so . . . skinny . . . skin and bones . . . like a fourteen year old. He leaned against me, still sobbing. Full of hurt. As I brushed his forehead, I could see Melanie in his face. And I cried a little, too. And I knew that he had no part in what happened to Rachel. Now came the hard part.

"It might have been an accident," I said. "But they found her on the beach, and it's more likely foul play."

"On the beach?" he said with surprise.

"Washed up on the beach, " I explained.

I watched his face pale. Tears stopped. He was angry as he spit out the words: "Who did it? Did they find out who did it?"

I told him that there was at least one serious suspect. I explained who he was, and where he was on the night of her death. I told him everything we knew to date and how I was involved indirectly . . . that I was not a police woman, and only remotely connected to the case by circumstances. I emphasized that he had nothing to fear from me and that I chose to come only because of Melanie. He was immediately energized by the name.

"She's okay, isn't she? "he asked with a tremor in his voice, as though there might be something even more unspeakable to report.

I explained that she was with her grandmother, away from the beach, up in Trenton in a big house with Ruth's niece and her two little boys. Perfectly safe. He was more than relieved to hear that. "I always got along with Ruth," he said. "She never got involved in our arguments, and never took sides against me. She was okay. She'll be okay with Melanie, "he added with a sigh of relief.

"Now I want you to think hard, Gary. Think about anyone you know who might have wanted to do Rachel harm. I know it's a long a shot, but is there anyone in this world who had any reason at all to get her out of the way? Now mind you, I don't know that murder was involved. It could have been an accident. But if not, what's your take on all of this?"

Gary looked me full in the face. "There are **plenty** of suspects" he said. "We just don't know them, that's all. She was in the drug business. Used to pick the stuff up and deliver it to her contacts. She picked up money sometimes , too, and passed it along. I didn't know her contacts. She'd never tell me that. I just know she did it. That's what mostly caused the trouble between us. There I was working at a casino," he said angrily "doing handy man jobs while she was making thousands of dollars. Thousands. And I told her again and again and again that one day she'd get caught. She got tired of listening. She got tired of my drinking as well, which I admit had gotten out of control. One evening she told me to get my things together and leave. She told me that I was simply a hindrance and that I should leave. And she said some other things as well which you wouldn't understand."

He paused for a moment to catch his breath.

"And so I did what she asked. I came up here to New York because I thought there'd be more opportunities. I thought I could get a good job, sober up, and go back with some money in my pockets with a good reason for us to get back together again. What a laugh. It's hell up here when you've got nothing. And now I'm trapped. "

I told him that no one is trapped unless they want to be, and I asked him what he was doing to meet ends meet. I knew that even the Salvation Army wouldn't go on providing for him if he simply drank himself into the gutter and refused to get out of it. I wondered why he didn't make some effort to see Melanie from time to time. New York City is just a short bus drive from Atlantic City. .

He told me that he never, ever wanted Melanie to see him as a drunk or in shabby clothes and that's why he stayed away .He couldn't stay sober. It was as simple as that. As far as how he made a few bucks here and there, he told me it was so unspeakable that he couldn't talk to me about it. I pushed him on that by telling him that I had lived a long time and heard about everything that anybody ever did to get quick money. He told me: "Not the way I do it."

I decided to shock him. I can change from "Lillian the motherly" to "Lillian the realist" in about half a second if I need to. And I did. I looked him squarely in the face. "You sell yourself. Your body. Don't you? To women and men? I suspect to men, because that's why you're so ashamed of it. Men usually aren't all that ashamed about what they do to women. Am I right about it? About what you do?"

He cringed. Didn't say a word.

"Now let's stop talking about what you do and why you do it, and get down to facts. First, do you know anything at all that can help us find out more about who killed your wife? And secondly, when are you going to get some iron in your spine and get out of here so you can help Melanie and be around for her while she's growing up? I don't want to hear about the rest. You can change all that. And I can help you, if you let me. I have the resources and the contacts to do it, I can assure you. Now for God's sake, buck up. Be a man!"

I don't suppose anyone ever talked to him quite like that, or gave him some alternatives to consider. He saw the fire in my eyes. He knew that I intended to give him one last chance, and if he didn't take it . . . well, that was his problem. He knew I had money and, shall we say, power behind my words. So he listened up.

"What did you say about the name of the band at the Rendezvous Club that night?" he asked.

"I didn't say much. I don't know anything about modern music. Anyway it was just a bunch of young fellows, about your age."

"Well, you ask the bartender who was on duty that night. Ask him for the name of the band. Ask him if Tony Spada was in that band. If he was, you got yourself a lead and I'll tell you why. Whenever Spada's band plays there, Rachel's sure to turns up two or three times a week. Around 10:00 or so when the band does its last set."

He gritted his teeth.

I was in one of his bands for a couple of months", he continued. "Guitar. Couple of years before I got married. I got to know him pretty well. Enough to realize he wanted to make out with Rachel, and it ticked me off, because he knew I had my eye on her. I left the band after a short time and, of course, I married Rachel. After I left her I have an idea Spada might have tried to link up with her. Now if Spada was in that band that night—the night she died— there might be a connection."

I told Gary that I didn't think anyone had even suspected anyone in the band because they left as soon as the lights in the club went out, and I assume the whole bunch of them went out as a group . . . which is what everyone else assumes.

"I can only tell you, Ms Moore, to ask the bartender and he'll know how many times Spada and his group have played that club and whether they've been regulars for the past couple months. You can't go by the name of rock bands. They change names and personnel fairly often, but Spada is always the leader, no matter what they call themselves. Check it out. It might do some good. Now as for turning my life around, that's something I can't do. You see, Ms Moore, I'm HIV Positive. I haven't even told the people around here. They'll probably kick me out. So you'll be dong me a favor just by letting me alone. When I'm drunk I don't think about it. So let me stay drunk. It's easier that way for everybody."

He touched my hand gently. "Just leave me alone. Okay? Maybe you can tell them in Atlantic City that I died or something. I don't want my parents to know. Not in a hundred years. It's better that I just disappear. And as far as Melanie goes, it's better she doesn't know me at all than know what I turned out to be. Maybe someday when she's older and when you can talk with her, you can make up a lie about what a great fellow I was, and how much I loved her. You'll do that for me, Ms Moore, won't you? Promise me you'll do that."

I'm a realist. I know he can't change. From the looks of him, he won't last too much longer on the street. And I know how lies make life worthwhile sometimes. So I told him I would do just that. *Lie.* And I'd make it a big lie so that Melanie will see him in the best kind of light. I looked him in the eye and promised: "If that's the way you want it, I'll tell the others that I found you and then lost you again. And you can be sure I'll have someone follow up on Tony Spada."

"One more thing," he said to me as I was getting up from my chair, ready to leave.

"What's that? " I asked.

"I haven't wanted to tell you, but I think you love Melanie as much as I do, and you ought to know the whole story." He hesitated, took a big breath and went on.

"You ought to know that Melanie's *not my child*. Don't get me wrong. I love her as dearly as I would love my own, but she's not my child. Tony Spada got Melanie pregnant while *we were engaged*. Imagine that. He denied it and skipped town for a while. Rachel told me the whole story just before we got married because she knew the months wouldn't add up right. I was angry and disappointed. Rachel said that it wasn't my fault and she couldn't understand why I would want to go through with the wedding. I told her: Because I love you, that's why."

I was stunned by Gary's admission. I just couldn't take it all in.

Gary continued: "I told Rachel that whatever child she brought into the world would be *my* child. That would be my revenge on Spada. A lot he cared. But then, after Melanie came and I was having trouble with my job, Rachel started seeing Spada again on the sly. I didn't know at first, but pretty soon I figured it out, and I was going to kill him. That's when she told me to leave. She said our marriage was wrong from the start and that she shouldn't have tried to make it work She said she did me a terrible wrong, but now she was going to fix it. I told her that Melanie was as much mine as her's, but she came back with the idea that it would be best for Melanie not to know *any* of this. She said she was going to legally change her last name to her own: Egron. Do you see the position that put me in, Mrs. Moore? She just wanted to erase me from their lives."

"You didn't . . . . kill her, did you?" I asked with a lump in my throat.

"Of course not," he answered. "I just started to kill **myself**, with booze and other things. And I guess I succeeded with this Aids stuff. Can you understand why I just want to step out of everybody's way? Can you understand?"

I thought I might be able to talk with him and give him some hope, but I was too stunned by what he told me that I simply said I'd need to go back to my hotel and think about it. I suggested we meet in the morning. I said I'd come by for breakfast and we could work something out. There was no reason for him to carry all the guilt. There was plenty to go around. And I kept thinking that if I could get him back to Iowa, back to his parents for awhile, he might have a chance. We left with a mutual hug. Once again, I could feel his frail, boney frame as I embraced him.

I left without dinner that evening. I couldn't have eaten a bite. I left, but not before giving Major Williams a large check to help in her work. I told her that I'd be back in the morning. That I had many things to think about. Major Williams said she'd make sure Gary was up and about in the morning and ready for some more discussion. She asked if she could "sit in", and I agreed. I told her that I was hoping he'd agree to go back home for a few months anyway. Mornings were getting cold in New York, and the fall had only just begun to set in. I thought his Mother would certainly give him loving care and put a few pounds on him before he made any further decisions.

"We'll have a doctor look him over tomorrow afternoon as part of our regular check-up procedures," Major Williams promised, as I left the Settlement house.

When I got back to the Waldorf that evening, I met Sue in the lobby, next to Peacock Alley Restaurant. She insisted we have a drink, and frankly, I needed one badly. I told her what happened and how I was trying to help that young man.

"No use giving *me* a sermon about it," said Sue, sipping her martini and looking over the crowd for possible celebrity sightings. "There's nothing you can do to help someone who doesn't want to accept it."

"I think he wants help, but I also see him slipping away," I said, as I somewhat shamefully finished my drink.

"Working with the UN," Sue reflected, "We see millions slipping away, and there's nothing *anybody* wants to do about it. So let's have another drink and talk about how wonderful times were in the 50's."

"They weren't all that wonderful," I said. "But one joy in getting old is *thinking* that they were and thanking God that we made it through the raindrops so far."

"So far", said Sue. "At age 75, let's drink to that!"

I called Major Williams at about 7:00 in the morning and told her I was coming down shortly, and that hopefully we could make some plans for Gary together.

Major Williams listened for a moment and then gave me the bad news.

"He left us sometime during the night," she said. "And he took the few things he had here with him. I can almost assure you, Mrs. Moore, that he won't be coming back. Like so many others," she explained, "he probably decided that he simply wants to disappear and so he walked away and probably got drunk to ease the pain. He'll wind up in a gutter somewhere with pneumonia. A dead man walking, as they say. Not unusual at all," she concluded, "just typical in Year 2009. And nothing you nor I can do about it. ***He's chosen his own fate.***"

I couldn't help wondering what was happening to our young men. Where was their "get up and go?" Or more likely, where were the opportunities? What changed?

My father was well off, but ***his*** father worked in a hardware store in Scranton. He made sure his two sons were encouraged to "give it all they could" and both left home with a suitcase and a few bucks in their pocket. My uncle Pete, played the clarinet. Grandad laid out a few dollars each week for his music lessons and he became very good at it. He joined a small orchestra made up of young men about his own age. They played at proms and weddings and in pit orchestras at theatres here and there. In 1928 they had a week's engagement at the Dennis Hotel in Atlantic City and were "discovered" by a music agent. Many of the men in that orchestra led by a man named Henry Thies went on to be "stars" in the Big Band Era of the 1930's.

As for my father, he found his way from Scranton to Philadelphia and worked hard — very hard—in an oil refinery. Fifteen years later, ***he owned it.***

Chapter Eighteen

Dillon: *"Conn went twelve rounds and was winning on points."*

I called Lillie on her cell phone and she answered from the Waldorf Towers.

I was excited to hear that she uncovered another suspect. I knew Julius Bankowitz and Jack Nolan would be, too.

Then I broke the news to her that Matt was sitting on his backside in jail this evening because he did a very stupid thing. He tried to make a run for Mexico. A friend had a private plane parked at Teeterboro, but he got a speeding ticket on the Jersey Turnpike and never made it out of South Jersey. Now he'll stay in jail until the trial. He's something more than a person of interest.

Lilllian offered that a Nolan in jail, any Nolan, was a good thing in itself.

I told her that the lawyers were furious. An attempt to leave the country was a sure sign of guilt – or appeared to be. They scheduled a meeting tomorrow and suggested that both me and "my agent" be present. At 3:00pm. At their office. Lillian said she had no problem taking Acela from New York to Philly in the morning and getting over to Arch Street by cab in plenty of time. I told her I'd meet her there. Her news about Tony Spada would be the best of the day, considering the new complexities of the case of the State of New Jersey against Matthew Nolan.

We all met at 3:00 pm and the atmosphere was less than pleasant. The whole case seemed to go down the drain with Matt's attempted flight. As usual, Matt Nolan was using his own half-brain to sort out his problems rather than relying on professional help, and well paid ones at that. His brother, Jack, was too stressed to be with us. Julius called him while I was there and I heard his high pitched voice from the other side of the room.

"Just do your best in a real shitty situation" he screamed to Julius over the phone. "I don't care what it costs, or what you have to do. Just get him out of this, damn him."

The four of us: Julius, Bruce, Lillian, and myself sat at the conference table trying to work out a strategy. Julius made it plain that he didn't care so much about Matt getting thirty years or life, as he did about the reputation of his firm.

" Maybe we could reduce it to manslaughter and five years", he said. " If he were indeed, guilty. Our plea would be that it was an accident rather than outright murder. Young Bruce agreed. We all seemed to be of one mind on this issue at least.

Lillian ventured that she felt unqualified to speak but had two pieces of information which might make an impact on the case. I could see that it was difficult for her to put ***anything*** on the table which might make it easier for Matt Nolan, who she, and almost everyone else in the State of New Jersey, detested. But I knew she wanted to help me and at the same time make sure that justice was done in the case, whether it was for Nolan's benefit or anybody else's.

First, she said, it was becoming more and more obvious that Rachel was not the sweet innocent the papers made her out to be. According to Gary, Rachel was heavily involved in the drug trade, and he had become more and more concerned about her 'occupation' as a bag lady placing the whole family in harm's way. They'd had a terrible argument over it, and she forced him out of the house so she could continue her trade.

But there was more than just that. Her child, Melanie, is not Gary's daughter. Somehow she got messed up with a musician in the band that played at the Club that night. ."In other words," said Lillian "Considering the little I know about the law, I think it wouldn't take much to convince a jury that Rachel practically condemned herself to death, leading the life she did. That's my take on it anyway."

"You got it right," said Julius. That's one of our main talking points. That's what our witnesses will emphasize when they're called up."

"You don't tell them what to say, do you?" asked Lillian warily.

"Of course not,"interjected Bruce. "But we certainly ask them to be honest and tell everything, whether it's good or bad. Sometimes jurists hesitate to say anything bad about the dead. You know the old saying."

Lillie continued by asking that we leave the little girl's name out of it. "There's no proof at all that Rachel ever used her as a feint. None whatsoever," she said strongly. "And no reason to put that child on the public record. I want your promise on that or I won't go any further,"she said most emphatically. .

Both Bruce and Julius nodded their heads in agreement. Julius said that bringing in pieces of information of that sort involving a child were more injurious than helpful. "When you give the jury a picture of a little innocent child and then tell them that the kid was part of the crime, they have contempt for you right off the bat. I've seen it time and again, and we never resort to dirt like that. ***Never!***"he emphasized.

Lillie continued her story about Rachel having an affair with a musician named Tony Spada. She also explained that Rachel's husband, Gary, once played in the same band as Spada and," as she explained further, "after their marriage, Gary became suspicious of something going on between the two of them, despite the fact that Rachel denied it."

Lillian paused: "I have an idea the whole band knew what was going on. I called a contact I have in Atlantic City just as a hunch this morning before I left New York. She was able to get me Marty the bartender's home phone number, so I called him. Got him out of bed, and talked with him for about ten minutes, warning him that Rachel's husband told me *everything* about Spada and the rest of the band, as well as the *bartender* at the club – all of them withholding evidence, and that I had a duty to notify the police as well as Jack Nolan and his lawyers. I scared the bejizzus out of him."

She went on to say that the bartender was shook up at this and confirmed that Tony Spada and his band *were* playing the evening Rachel died. "In fact," he said, "Rachel made it a point to visit the Rendezvous Club a couple of times a week. I suppose just to keep in contact with Spada. I guess she didn't want to do it by phone."

Lillian continued her story by adding that Marty the bartender told her that he didn't say anything before about this because he got paid by the Club to listen to his customers but not to talk and tell. It was a code of honor among bartenders. Almost like a priest at confession. It was no surprise for him to see Rachel there that night or any night in the week, and he decided it was none of his business one way or the other."

Julius interrupted. "To hell with his code of honor. He should have told this to the cops. Why didn't he?"

Lillian said she asked him the same question and he said that he didn't tell the police anything about Spada because they didn't ask. He said he didn't want to get the band in trouble.

"But after talking with me," Lillie continued, "he realized it was time to get it off his chest. Especially when people like Jack Nolan and his Philadelphia lawyers were hovering around. He didn't want to become a suspect himself. He agreed that Tony Spada would have to explain things himself, for better or worse."

"Our reputation precedes us," laughed Bruce, "and that's a damned good thing."

Bruce and Julius congratulated Lillian for the information and said they'd follow it up immediately. And of course they'd pass it along to the AC Police. "We want to cement good relations with those guys," said Julius. "They want this case settled as much as we do. The only difference is that they want to pin it on our client, and we want to convince them otherwise. Spada may be the connection – the missing link — that all of us missed thus far," he said, "and we can't discount the husband, Gary what's-his-name. It could have been a crime of passion."

Lillie said she couldn't offer any additional information and certainly didn't feel qualified to participate in any strategic planning affecting the case, so she excused herself and told us she was going over to the Philadelphia Museum to check out the new Egyptian art exhibition. She told me she'd keep in touch with her cell phone, and maybe we could eat somewhere later in the city and then go home together on the late Atlantic City train. I agreed, and gave her a peck on the cheek as she left the office.

Julius and Bruce were ecstatic about the new possibilities that Tony Spada and the husband presented for the case. They made some telephone calls while I was there to some of their contacts in AC and immediately "put a tail" on the young musician. "What makes it "sweet"," said Bruce, "is the fact that Spada and his orchestra are doing their best to advertise themselves and their schedule of appearances. It won't be hard to plant some contacts at their gigs and talk around while they're there," he said. "As a matter of fact, they're pretty good. I've heard them play in places a lot better than the Rendezvous Club. I have to wonder what they're doing in a dive like that."

Julius looked at me and said: "Too bad you and I would 'stand out', to say the least, at one of their concerts. My taste in music is more in the Beatles mode. What about you, Tom?"

"The other day I was talking to a young man about music," I said, "and asked him if he ever heard of musicians like Glenn Miller,

Artie Shaw and Kay Keyser. The kid said he knew about Miller and Show, but who was the lady? That tells it all," I laughed.

Julius looked at me blankly. "Who *was* she?" he asked.

I spent a while longer with Bruce and Julius and watched them develop a plan of action that opened my eyes to the legal world. No use going into details. They thanked me for my help and especially my "agent's" help, and gave me a fat check.

"There'll be more coming," chuckled Julius. "There might even be a bonus when Jack hears about Spada and the husband. It could be a big break in the case."

Julius was of the opinion that Jack would be willing to spend every nickel he had to spare his brother. Bruce smiled: "And we'll be happy to assist him in doing it."

I left the office and called Lillie and she suggested meeting me at the best seafood restaurant in the world. Or so she said. She amazed me by what she knew about food, and flowers, and art, and books and everything else that was fine and elegant in the world. I knew, now, that she had money, but she didn't push it in my face. Of course she didn't know anything about scraping along in a place like Lawrenceville. When she mentioned coming to Pittsburgh in the past, it was always places in Sewickley or in the East End. We live in different worlds, and yet there's always a connection between us over one thing or another.

I told her once that my family knew the Conn family who lived over in the East Liberty part of town. She immediately said: "Do you mean Billie Conn, the boxer?"

"You bet," I said, "The Pittsburgh Kid! But how do you know anything about boxing? And besides that, it happened a *long* time ago."

"You have to understand," she said, "that my husband, Rodger, was a Golden Gloves boxer in his teen years. My father was into boxing as well. He and my mother went to the Louis-Schmeling fight at Yankee Stadium in the summer of 1938. I don't remember that, of course, but he said he had to talk my mother into going in the first place. She still had a lot of that old Quaker blood that I told you about. She was a Coates after all. Well the funny part of it all was that they arrived a bit late at the Stadium. The first round had already begun as they were heading for their seats. When they got to them, Mother turned around to dust off her seat with her handkerchief and the fight was over! *Just like that.* Louis knocked him out in two minutes and forty seconds."

"Now to take it a step further," she said, "My husband, Rodger, was at the Louis-Conn fight at the Polo Grounds in the summer of '41. He was sixteen at the time, and both he and his father were great fans of "The Brown Bomber," because his father had worked with GM for several years in Detroit."

I told Lillie that, as just a little squirt, I remember listening to it on KDKA Radio, and not just me, but everybody in Lawrenceville."Hell, everyone in Pittsburgh was sitting on their porches and doorsteps listening to it," I told her. "All the girls said he was more handsome than a movie star. And of course he was white. You have to remember the times. And you have to know the neighborhood at that time. Not too far from us, in what was called the Hill District, there were just as many blacks listening to the fight and rooting for their own. Nothing wrong in that. But people make it sound bad today. Well anyway," I continued, "Conn went twelve rounds, and was winning on points."

"Rodger said he should have stayed out of Joe's way", Lillie interrupted. "Apparently Louis hooked him in the thirteenth. Rodger said that he and his Dad went wild with excitement."

"So did the Hill District," I added woefully. "But then, they didn't have much to celebrate about up there."

Lillie and I wound up at the restaurant she mentioned. One of the oldest in Philly, but I can't remember the name off hand. And everything was delicious. Little portions – a bit of this and that – but delicious.

When we were on the train that evening heading back to Atlantic City, I told her how much I appreciated what she'd done for me. I knew she had no love for Matt Nolan and that it grieved her to know that she might be setting him free.

She said I didn't know her very well if I thought she'd withhold evidence that might set someone free. If they deserved to be free. But on the other hand she added that she doesn't enjoy "playing God" either. "I think I could have done more to help Gary Bauer," she said remorsefully. "I really feel bad about that. But you can't go too far interfering with someone else's life."

"You seem to want to be involved in every good cause in the world," I said.

"From afar," she reminded me. "I made up my mind to work for good causes from afar, but not up too close. Otherwise, I get personally involved, and that saps my time and energy."

Lillian said that she was worried that my work with the lawyers and with Jack Nolan might be detrimental in my relations with the AC Police Force and with the coroner. I reminded her that it was practically volunteer work. "Just a few bucks here and there. Nothing on any contract. Only temporary. Everyone will understand. No one is trying to hang Nolan unless there's evidence to prove it. Then, they'll be happy to do so. The case will probably drag on after I'm long gone."

On the train home, Lillie fell asleep against my shoulder right after we passed Lindenwold , the half-way mark. It felt good. I was so very lucky to have a lady like that on my arm. But of course the picture of Evelyn in the Home moved into my mind, clouding the good feeling I had. God help us," I thought. "It isn't Evelyn's fault."

This part of the trip between Philly and Atlantic City was always the longest.

Chapter Nineteen

Lillian: *"There were a lot of reasons to think we might be wasting our time."*

Tom and I met on the Boardwalk at about 7:00 am after I finished my daily "chore" with the cats. We sat on a bench in the bright morning sunlight eating donuts and drinking good strong coffee from paper cups that we moved from hand to hand because it was so hot. We watched the gulls, as we had a hundred or perhaps a thousand times over the years, screaming and quarreling over a bit of pizza left on the bench beside us. Yes, the pizza restaurant behind us was open at this ungodly hour and there were patrons already bellying up to the open window — somewhat like a drive-in restaurant, except this was a "walk-by."

The bench was a good place to avoid the bicyclers who chose that hour of the morning to begin their three hours of opportunity to ride uninhibited to either end of the Boardwalk until the police, driving by in a very visible white car very leisurely and courteously, provided the signal to return their rentals to Longo and Sons up by Resorts Hotel.

As we roused ourselves, we looked over the railing toward the beach for a moment and speculated on how frigid the water must be this morning. The surfers in their black body suits didn't seem to mind the cold a bit. They just plunged into the sea and cavorted about as the porpoises often do.

The murder case was never far from either of our minds.

"You know, Lilllie," Tom said, "I have an idea about another person who could provide us with some personal information about Matt Nolan, and maybe Imre, too, but it's a long shot"

"And who might that be, Tom?" I asked. Tom told me it was *a very* long shot, about as long as you can get, but asked me to hear him out.

"Remember when we talked to Imre he told us he'd been bullied in high school by Matt Nolan. I think he said they graduated together. That would have been in 1967 or so. Now if the bullying was really severe — if he hurt Igor physically or mentally, Imre might have had a good reason to keep it stored up until he could get some revenge. Settle the score! Does that make sense? What do you think? Maybe even set Jack Nolan up."

"That's along stretch," I said. "But I'd like to know more about Imre's mental state at that time. Was he *imagining* that Matt was bullying him more than, say, any other kid he came in contact with? Was he considered a "weirdo" even back then? Was he a congenital liar, or strictly honest?" Or is he a high functioning autistic, as I suspect?"

"The only person who can answer that would be someone who saw both those kids in action together on a regular basis", Tom said. "Maybe one of their mutual friends, if they *had* any mutual friends, which I doubt, because they were such different types of kids. And the kids at school — who would be in their late fifties now — would probably be biased, or more likely, forgetful of what happened back then. Kids don't think a lot about bullying unless it happens to them. And then later in life— like at their fortieth high school reunion — a lot of them even become good friends with the "bully" despite their past differences."

"That would be true of *kids*," I said thoughtfully, "but what about teachers? Do you suppose there are any teachers left in this area who'd remember either one of them? Let me add up the years. Teachers in 1967 might have been born anywhere between 1917 and the late '40's. Agewise they could be anywhere between their late sixties or early eighties up until . . . well . . . most of them could be gone by now. I mean, dead."

I wondered how we could find out? Atlantic City High School has been relocated several times in the past fifty years or so. The school that Imre and Matt attended was over on Albany Avenue across from the World War monument. Now it's just a vacant lot, and a new school building's located somewhere out of downtown. I don't even have a clue where it is.

I had a long shot thought. "There's a woman at our church about ten years older than we are who doesn't get around much anymore," I said, "but she's lived here all her life and probably went to the school in the late '30's or early '40's. Her kids might have gone in the sixties. She's on my list of shut-in's and due for a call from me this month. Why don't I ring her up right now?"

"It's worth a try," Tom said, thinking all the while, I suppose, that it was sure to end at a blank wall. "Why don't you get on the other line, but don't breathe too hard," I laughed.

I dialed the number and was soon in conversation with church friend, Mary Stoessel, who began by telling me all about her ailments and problems. I looked at Tom and shook my head in frustration while the negative attitudes flowed from Mary.

I listened to her litany of sorrows for a few moments and then said: "Alright, Mary, I know you've been having a hard time, but do you think you could give me some information which might be very helpful." Mary indicated a stir of interest in the word "information" which might be of a gossipy nature.

I continued. "Now put on your thinking cap, Mary. You went to high school here in Atlantic City, didn't you?

Mary brightened up immediately. "Yes, of course. Class of '40! I keep all my year books right here in the cabinet at the side of my chair.

"I was thinking of something a bit later . . . like '67."

"Oh I'm sorry, Lillian, I'm afraid I can't help you there. Even my two boys were out of school by then."

I thought for a moment and said that I was interested in teachers rather than students. I asked Mary if she could remember any of the teachers who spanned the years at ACHS? Perhaps she could look them up in her children's yearbooks. Mary thought about it for a moment. Then she said brightly, "I can give you the name of one of my children's *favorite* teachers, Miss Clara Parker. She was there forever. And she's still living after all these years."

"Bingo." Tom said in a whisper. "But what years did she cover?"

I anticipated his question. "How long did she teach at the high school? Do you remember, Mary?"

"Miss Parker", she reflected. "Let's see. She came to the school just before the war started. I remember how active she was with the war effort. She started a little victory garden with the school kids in a plot of ground not too far from our house, and she was still at the high school when my kids went there in the 1950's. They really loved her. I think one of my boys told me that she taught English at the high school for about thirty years. I suppose she must have retired in the late 60's. Maybe the early 70's."

"Tell me, Mary, have you any idea where she might be now?"

"Oh I know exactly where she is. At that fancy Assisted Living Home out on Black Horse Pike. I know, because that's where they wanted to put *me* after I fell. But I made it through rehab and I can get around just fine in my own place. Sorry I can't make it to church, Lillian, but you know how it is."

I continued cautiously. "Is she . . . can she still talk . . . ?"

"Well she could when I saw her up there a couple of months ago. In fact I thought she was quite spry for her age. Now tell me, Lillian, why do you want to talk to **her**, if you don't mind telling me?"

"It's a long story, Mary," I said, "but after I talk with her I promise to share the whole story with you."

"Oh that'll be nice," said Mary with thoughts of a juicy story brightening her day.

We said our goodbyes, and Tom and I planned our strategy. We certainly didn't want to make Miss Parker uncomfortable with our questions. We'd have to tell her about Imre's death, but we wouldn't go into details about Matt Nolan. Of course, the "kicker" in this whole thing was whether Miss Parker remembered them at all, or whether she remembered **anything** at all, for that matter. She might have retired before they graduated. There were a lot of reasons to think we might be wasting our time.

I volunteered to have a personal visit with her. "I think I'll be able to tell in about twenty seconds whether she can provide us with anything we can use, " I said.

"You know what! ", Tom said, as if a thunderbolt idea suddenly struck him. "As long as you're looking for one of the ACHS teachers, why don't I hunt up their football coach? I remember Jack Nolan telling me something about Matt being on the team back in the sixties. I wonder if I could locate a coach or an assistant coach, or maybe the Director of Athletics?"

Tom said that most coaches can't remember all their team members over the years unless they had a real championship year, and then they can rattle them off, one by one, by name, nickname, and position. And whether he had a good team or not, any coach can certainly remember players who were very good, or very bad. Nolan might fall into his memory bank somewhere. "I'm not sure about Imre," he said,"but he was a big bruiser and I'd be surprised if he weren't on the football team."

I suggested that we stop over at the new high school and using Tom's semi-official title as the coroner's investigator, ask whether we could see their collection of yearbooks which I'm sure they keep as a matter of record. We could check three or four of them covering 1964-1968, and I maybe we could come up with something.

Within the hour we were standing in the Supervising Principal's office at the "new" Atlantic City High School and reviewing yearbooks together. We explained our reason for coming and quickly located Miss Parker's photo in all four of the books. In the 1967 book we hit paydirt. Matt Nolan was the quarterback of the '66 team. Imre was not listed as being on the team but he was identified on the team photo. Curious!

Then I realized that the team photo might have been taken in September, 1966, at the beginning of the season. The games were played *after* that picture was taken, and the player listings were printed in the spring of 1967, just before the yearbook was published. I know all about yearbooks. I was the editor of one. Something must have happened to Imre's position on the team between September and June when the yearbook came out. The coach was noted as Steve Shupka.

We went back to the 1966 yearbook which had information on the '65 team. Matt was quarterback and Imre was a guard. Back further then to the 1965 yearbook when they were both sophomores on the '64 team. Matt played end, and Imre, guard. Shupka was coach in all three years.

Tom asked the principal if he knew what happed to Steve Shupka.

"Of course I do, "he smiled. "I heard about him as soon as I arrived here as Supervising Principal. He coached several great teams over the years. After he left ACHS he went on to a large consolidated school district in Bucks County, and in the mid '80's I was surprised to read in the newspapers that he'd been hired by the Eagles—not as a coach — but as a consultant on methods of exercising to help toughen up the body, increase flexibility, reduce injuries, and that sort of thing.

"I guess you might say he taught the players how better to roll with the punches," the principal continued: "Apparently he was quite successful, and went on to write a popular book about it called, "Shupka's Rules for Rolling". That surprised me more than anything. He was a very good coach, but between the two of us, although I've met him a few times at various affairs over the years, I heard from those who knew him better than I that he was not exactly a 'scholar.' But all agreed that he was a very pleasant man and good with the kids. His players always loved him.

"Dumb," Tom said, "But very rich by now, don't you think?"

"Positively," said the principal. "He lives over on the Main Line. We use his book here at the school incidentally, and he's been over to speak at some of our athletic banquets from time to time. Nwver takes a dime. I can give you his name, address and telephone number if you'd like. He's a very open person. Easy to talk with. Give him a call. You can tell him that I suggested you come over to see him."

We thanked the principal very much, and Tom and I talked about our next steps as we drove back to my apartment. We agreed that tomorrow morning we'd go our separate ways: me to see Miss Parker, and Tom to interview Coach Shupka.

"Suppose we meet at Kornfeld's for dinner at about 6:00, no, make it 7:00. " Tom suggested. "I might get caught in traffic on the Jersey Turnpike." Tom always thought 6:00pm was the proper time for dinner, but I preferred seven or even eight. So 7:00pm was a good compromise. .

We had our work cut out for us.

Chapter Twenty

Dillon: *"I drove away from Coach Shupka's house knowing that I met a great man"*

I phoned Coach Shupka and he said he'd be happy to talk with me. Invited me for breakfast. I drove over to his house in Paoli in the morning and he turned out to be a very pleasant man, indeed. He had ten years on me, but was well tanned and obviously in really good shape. Better shape than me.

Breakfast was hearty, with plenty of what you'd expect an old athlete to eat: a heaping bowl of rolled oats with honey and skim milk. Plenty of fruit: orange slices for Vitamin D, he said, and bananas for potassium. Dates and raisins, just because he likes them. The muffins were hot and filled with dried cranberries. Plenty of green tea to wash things down. I thought he might prefer coffee.

We began to talk as soon as we sat down at the table.

He knew both boys, Matt and Imre, he said. Not because they were among his top athletes during his career, but because they stood out from the hundreds of faces and names he recognized from good teams and bad. .

"Of the two, I knew Matt Nolan the best", he said. "He was arrogant and obnoxious most of the time, but he was a helluva good quarterback. Unfortunately, we didn't have a team that year that could back him up. Otherwise he would have taken us to the All-State Championship game. Off the field he wouldn't listen to anyone except his brother. I don't know about his mother and dad. They never seemed to come into the picture. All I know is that twice he got into trouble with me and came damn near being kicked off the team. The first time was when I caught him smoking. He knew it was against team rules. I called up his brother, Jack, and Matt stopped then and there. Cold turkey.

"And what was the second time?" I asked.

"It was in the game with Egg Harbor. I remember it well because I sent in a play to him in the fourth quarter of a game we were losing by three points and instead of using my play, he made up his own. I was so damn mad I could have choked him, right there on the field.

As it turned out, he threw for a touchdown and we won the game, but that didn't make any difference. It's the worst thing you can do on the field. Ignore the coach. I never forgave him. Just before graduation I told him that if he did that to an officer over in Viet Nam –where a lot of the kids were headed in '67—he was in for some real big trouble.

"He told me he wasn't planning to go to Viet Nam. His brother had arranged for him to go to CCNY and he wasn't going to spend any time in any damned jungle. Arrogant little s.o.b., that's what he was."

"And what about Imre," I asked. "He seemed to be on the team, and then off. Can you tell me the reason for that?"

"I can give you a couple of reasons," Coach said. "For one thing, he was kind of a strange kid. Don't ask me to explain it. He just kept more to himself than the other boys and seemed to have different ideas. You know kids. They can spot a kid who's out of place in a minute .Lucky for Imre, he was a brute of a kid. Stood shoulders above most of the other boys. I suspect he might have been older than the others, but his uncle said, no, he was only fifteen when he came out for the team in his sophomore year."

I interrupted him. "He seemed to have dropped out sometime early in the 66/67 season. His senior year. Am I right?"

"Yep, " said Coach. That's why I remember him so well and always connected him with Nolan when I thought about him. Nolan always gave him a hard time; made fun of him to the other kids; even spread rumors that made Imre seem like he was nuts or something. I didn't hear all of it. Just pieces here and there. I called Nolan on it once and he said that Imre wasn't doing his best on the line. He let a couple of players punch through and catch him in the backfield a couple of times. But I knew better. I knew Nolan took too long to pick out his receivers .He was a kind of prima donna out there, holding his arm in the air, and waiting , waiting for the best catch, and sometimes waiting to catch the eye of a cheerleader. He got smeared once too often and he blamed Imre rather than himself.

"They had it out in the locker room, before I got there, after the second game of the season. Nolan sucker punched him and Imre got so mad he just pushed Matt against the wall. Just held him there, pushing against Nolan's chest until he choked. He actually threw up. The whole team watched it. Nolan was humiliated, and after that he avoided physical contact but had other ways to torment the kid.

From that time on, all kinds of lies flew around school. People laughed at Imre at lunch time and he quit coming to lunch. Walked home instead, which was all the way at the other end of the city. He turned in his uniform one afternoon and I tried to talk him out of it, but he wouldn't have it. I begged him to stay on the team. told him we needed him. But it was no go. After that, he just faded into the background. Never took part in any school activities. Never dated anyone that I know of. Joined the army right out of school and went right to Viet Nam. That's the last I heard of him. But you know what I think? I think the kid didn't know his own strength until he had Nolan up against that wall, and I think he could easily have killed him then and there. That's what he was afraid of. Not of the other kids, but of **his own** strength and rage."

"Coach," I said. "I think you've hit on something that we hadn't thought about before." I explained Imre's tour of duty in Viet Nam; his captivity in a bamboo cage; the injuries to his head and body. I told him I thought Imre was like a volcano when he came back. Ready to go off, and yet afraid to go off. It explained a lot of things.

I told Coach about his suicide note saying that **maybe** Matt Nolan murdered a girl that we found in the ocean. It must have made him feel good, at the end of his life, to put Nolan on the spot with an ugly rumor. And yet, he didn't go all the way and say outright that Nolan murdered the girl.

"I didn't often get involved in all my players' private lives," he said. "If I did I wouldn't have a minute's rest worrying about them and wondering if they were getting into trouble. I just felt my job was on the field, teaching them to play the game and play it with good sportsmanship. That's as far as I could go. The families and the school had to do the rest. And mostly, they did, without my help.

But every once in a while if I felt I **really** could make a change in a kid's life, or point him to something better, I'd jump in and do it. Some guys tell me today that if I hadn't interfered they'd be on the streets or in prison. I don't know about that, but I know that I always handed out what they call 'tough love.' I told them not to make any excuses with me because I wasn't buying them. 'Just do what's right,' I told them. And never put another guy in a corner so he can't get out. Always leave some space. Don't humiliate anybody. Ignore the bumps and just do the job. That's common sense, isn't it?

Coach's Golden Retriever, Honey, came running over to us and put her head in my lap.

"She's such a baby," Coach said. "Not a dog that a big tough guy like me ought to have. When I was growing up in Scranton," he said, "I had a mutt that lived in a doghouse out back of the house." He rubbed Honey's neck affectionately and slipped a slice of banana to her. "Look at that," he said. "She eats everything, don't you, Honey," he said, holding the dog's face in his two big hands.

"My dog in Scranton ate what we ate from the table. And it wasn't bananas. Just a couple of bones. I come from the coal country," he said. "Times were tough then.. And now I have it so good, I can hardly believe it."

I told him that I understood that he had written a book. About exercising.

"It was what they call 'ghost written', but I supplied all the details. You see, as the professional game gets rougher and rougher a lot of the guys are suffering some pretty bad injuries. I recognized that it was due to a lack of information on how best to roll with the punches. And some yoga stuff, and some Jap stuff about falling back when pressure's applied, and then shifting the energy and bouncing back. Most of it I learned at Sokol."

I asked what 'Sokol' was and he explained that it was an athletic association which most Czechs and Slovaks belonged to in towns where there was a heavy Slavic population. Like Scranton. He told me that you start out as kids and do all kinds of exercises with barbells and that sort of thing. Then, he explained, you work up to gymnastics like you see in the Olympics. The rings, the somersaults, the horse – all those things. You learn to exercise more relaxed, with more flexibility, he said. And when you can roll with the punches, he continued, you avoid a lot of injuries you get when you go head on. "I thought about it a lot while I watched the pro games on television, " he said. "And I got a friend who could write and he took down what I told him. Then I took it over to the Eagles and they bought into it. And I made a good life doing it, "he added, "teaching the techniques to the players. A damned good life. And I saved many a guy from multiple concussions. They get a lot of them in the pros today, if you notice."

I knew at that moment that Coach Shupka was anything but "dumb as a post." I suppose it was his foreign-sounding name that set some people off. And when I thought about it, the same thing was true of Imre. His name was different and therefore, he must be different, too. Well, he fought for his country in Viet Nam. He was a real American, and moreso than a helluva lot of us who were back home in those days.

I thanked Coach, as he handed me a copy of his book and wished me well.

"I hope I helped with your investigation," he said. "I don't know how it'll turn out. I just know that Matt Nolan was never up to anything good and I suppose he'll have to pay for it. But you can bet his brother, Jack, will move heaven and hell to get him off."

"He's already started to," I said.

"One thing more," he said. "You might want to get in touch with a kid that used to hang out with Imre. He was a black kid. There weren't many in that high school at that time. That's why I remember him so well. The two of them were kind of on the edge of school life, if you know what I mean. He might be able to give you some information that would be more helpful than what I told you. After all, I only saw it from a coach's point of view. The black kid saw it a lot more up close. I don't remember his name but he won't be hard to find in the yearbook. Let me dig out my '67 edition. Do you have a minute?

"Yes, of course, " I said, as Honey brought me a well worn rubber ball and "suggested" by her eyes and her movements that I toss it for her. She even moved back to the spot where she wanted it thrown. Honey and I passed the time until Coach came back with the book spread open.

"Here he is," he said, "Henry Martin. You can check around in Atlantic City if he still lives there. It's worth a try."

I thanked Coach again and drove away from his house knowing that I had met a great man. Maybe not so important in the scheme of things as some men or women on Wall Street or in Washington DC, and all of that,. but a good man who looked after his kids and pointed them in the right direction. And for once, it was paying off. He was living pretty good in Paoli. Imagine that!

I was soon across the Delaware Bridge and headed toward Atlantic City. I looked forward to a good, heavy, unhealthy dinner with Lillie at Kornbfeld's. But first thing I did when I got home was check out the telephone book and see if Henry Martin was still in town after all these years.

Sure enough, there was his name with an address on Mediterranean Avenue. I called him immediately but got an older man who either didn't know who I was talking about or didn't want to know. I decided to walk up and scope the neighborhood —it wasn't all that far away — since I had a lot of time before my 7:00 o'clock "date" with Lillian.

I found the address easily enough. It was a project-type apartment, and there was an old black man sitting on the steps who I greeted with a smile. I told him I was looking for Henry Martin, and did he know him?

The man sized me up and said: "There ain't no Henry Martin living in *this* apartment house."

"Are you sure?," I asked. "He's listed in the telephone book."

"I don't know what book you're lookin' at, but Henry Martin don't live here. I never heard of any Henry Martin in this neighborhood, and I've lived here a long time. A *long* time.

I knew the game and so did he.

"If you think I'm a policeman, I'm not," I said emphatically.

"How do I know *who* you are? "he said, "and what do I care? I'm just tellin' you that Henry Martin don't live here. Now you go find him yourself. I can't help you."

Just at this moment, Henry Martin appeared at the top of the steps. I recognized his face from the picture in the yearbook. He looked very much as he did in the sixties. He was a natty little man, well-dressed and carrying a briefcase and he began laughing.

"You are a very lucky man, whoever you are. You know why? Because Henry Martin is on his way to the Amtrak Station, and

Acela leaves in about thirty-five minutes for New York. So you better tell me what you want so I can tell you whether I'm really Henry , or just someone you *think* is Henry Martin. Around here, when Somebody white comes poking around, the word on the street is: 'Don't give your right name.' You ought to know that because you look like some kind of investigator or a process server. It's written all over your face. Am I right?

The old man grinned from ear to ear and held his hand flat in the air to match Henry's.

"You're right," I said, "but it has nothing to do with you. It has to do with a young man you knew long ago and who hung himself earlier this week."

"You're talking about Imre Nagy, aren't you?" he said, dropping his voice and his tone. "What do you want to know from me? Listen," he continued, "Why don't you tell me all about it while we walk over to the Amtrak Station. My train for New York really *does* leave in about half an hour, and I have to be on it. So what do you want to know about Imre?"

We started toward the station in almost a jog, and I quickly compressed my thoughts to match the pace. I told him I knew that the two of them were high school buddies a long time ago and maybe he knew something about Imre's character that I didn't, because I wanted to prove that he wasn't involved in the murder of the girl they found in the ocean last week. I told him that he'd do his old pal a real favor if I could make a few good points for him.

I gave him my name and my connection to the Coroner, not the police department.

His feelings about Imre began pouring out as he slowed down and gave me a brief history of their friendship.

"I came to that school as an intelligent, well brought up little black boy, seventeen years old, and not looking for trouble, but for an education. But they all treated me pretty badly. You know how times were back then. Even some of the few other black kids who attended the high school at that time considered me "uppity" and shunned me.

On one particular afternoon I was having one of my regular "let's push the black kid around" moments. Only it got too rough, and someone knocked me down on the sidewalk and I cut my lip and it started to bleed. They just laughed. But Imre, this big, broad-shouldered football player, came running over and laid into them. Pushed them aside and knocked one of them down to my level. He gave them hell, and they started to call him names as they carefully backed away, and then ran away. Like the hyenas at the zoo.

Imre told me not to be afraid of them as he pulled me out of the gutter. "Those guys rag me as bad as they rag you but you're just a little squirt so they think they can kick you around and nobody will help"

"I think they made their point," I said to Imre, putting his handkerchief up to my lip.

"Almost!" said Imre. "They ***almost*** made their point, but I've been watching you and I've decided to be your bodyguard."

"My bodyguard?", I said in surprise.

"I've been watching you." he said again. "You're a smart kid and I need some help in my school work. Maybe we can get together. Besides that, they hate you as much as they hate me. Some of your black friends don't even like you, so the two of us don't have much of a choice so far as making friends with any of them. It's hopeless. I'm even thinking about dropping off the team," he told me. "Why should I use my muscles to make ***them*** look good when they hardly talk to me off the field."

He walked me home, making sure nobody was hiding in the bushes or anywhere else. But my tormentors had long since exited the spot. They knew how angry Imre could get. Just between you and me, looking back I think he had seizures when he was angry or confused. But I'm no doctor, just a television producer."

I asked Henry about Matt Nolan, and he practically spit out his name. He told me that Matt was the instigator of many of his problems. Always jabbing away at kids around him who were younger or weaker or different like me. He liked to show off in front of the girls. That was his biggest problem. And not many of them would give him the time of day. So he spread stories about some of them as well. How he had made out with them, and all that kind of stuff. "A big bragging lout., that's what he was."

I asked Henry whether he was following the story about Imre's suicide and the girl they found in the ocean. He said his work in New York kept him busy, and just every once in a while he stops by in Atlantic City to see his father who is also Henry Martin. Henry Martin, Sr., who was sitting on the steps. We both laughed about how he ragged me.

Henry went on to say that he and Imre had a good relationship for the rest of their Senior year, and he thought that Henry's helping him with his studies helped him graduate. "When the other kids knew that Imre was standing behind me, they ceased their tormenting pretty quickly. I always called him 'the Big Guy'", he laughed.

"We'd study at my house after school", Henry explained. "My mother got to like him a lot, but my father – who you met – was always awkward about having a white boy in the house. It was how he was brought up."

We never met at Imre's house. He lived with his Uncle Istvan and I don't know the details of where his mother and Dad fit into the picture. Anyway, old Unc *didn't want no black kids in his house at no time.* Imre didn't make any excuses about it. That's just the way it was. Although he did say once that in middle European countries like Hungary and Germany, the devil was always depicted as being black rather than red. I guess that makes as much sense as why white people in Atlantic City didn't want us in their houses either."

We were nearly at the station and Henry said he really had to run to make the train. He explained that after high school, he and Imre just drifted apart from each other like high school friends so often do." Occasionally, " he said "we'd meet on the street and say we'd have to get together for a drink, or something like that, but of course we never did." Henry said he hadn't seen Imre for at least five years.

As he was about to hightail it up the steps that led into the station, I shook his hand and left him with the fact that Imre implicated Matt Nolan with the murder. Henry got a broad smile on his face.

"Best news I've heard in a long time. I hope they get Nolan . . . **good.** He wounded a lot of kids along the way. It's time he paid up for some of it. In fact, I hope he's innocent and they pin it on him anyway. That would really make my day."

He was suddenly gone, and I walked to the cab stand and took a taxi back to my apartment. I couldn't wait to tell Lillian about this dapper little black man who seemed to have "made it." No thanks to Matt Nolan or anyone else who threw him in the gutter – or tried to – forty years before.

Chapter Twenty One

Lillian: *"I watched a little child futilely trying to catch a pigeon: something that hasn't been done in a hundred or more years of Atlantic City history"*

When I called LeHavre Residences and asked the Director to speak to Miss Parker about my proposed visit, he told me that she had received my earlier call on her answering machine and that she was always open to having guests and, indeed, would be especially glad because she heard a lot of good things about me. Where she heard this I didn't quite know, but apparently she explained to the people at Le Havre that I was very active in charity work and all sorts of 'city things'.

They are very careful about visitors at LeHavre.

"Just ask her to come after lunch . . . on Tuesday if she can make it.," she told them. "I'm pretty well booked for the morning, but I have a bit of time before my scrabble at 2:00."

I borrowed Tom's car and made the short drive to a spot on the Black Horse Pike.. I arrived at a gate house "guarded" by a pleasant young man in a tailored gray uniform who opened the gate and directed me to the "Commons" area where I could call Miss Parker directly. The grass was emerald green and immaculately trimmed, and I passed a beautiful little pond with a fountain gushing in the middle. Much like Versailles, if you've ever been there, but on a much smaller scale, of course. There were lovely cottages along the route, and parklets here and there with the most beautiful hydrangeas fully in bloom. Blues, purples, pure whites. I was never "lucky" with hydrangea. Could never get them to bloom. I thought I might ask somebody while I'm here.

The main building – the "Commons" – reminded me of a chalet near Mont Blanc in the French Alps which I visited in '77 or '78. There were windows , floor to ceiling, all around, and a huge fireplace with fine leather chairs and lovely sofas with floral patterns.. "Good material", I thought as I walked toward the registration desk.

The receptionist welcomed me quite warmly by name. "We're waiting for you, Mrs. Moore," she said, handing me a telephone and asking me to dial 9-212. Ms. Parker answered and told me to turn to the right as I left the building and look directly toward the putting green. Her cottage, #212, was on the path that lay above and behind the green. "Just follow the numbers", she said, "and you can't get lost."

As I walked up the manicured path and around the green, the residents passing me on the way greeted me very pleasantly. Everybody was well-dressed and smelled good, even from a distance. How often I visited "senior citizen homes" where there was a distinct smell of —what shall I call it — decay! No amount of disinfectant ever removed it entirely. But it was different here.

The men were all ruddy and clean-shaven and the women wore cashmere sweaters.

I don't know exactly what I expected when I came to her cottage number. I knocked gently on her door and ventured a "good afternoon."

"Come right in:" she called out sprightly. The living room was clean as a pin, as my Mother would have said, and I thought about that because this woman was about the same age as my Mother was when she passed away at 88. Miss Parker might have been a few years older. I promised I would stay only until she decided to kick me out, and we both laughed.

Miss Parker was dressed in a fashionable light green summer dress. She had a very small face and a large twinkle in her eyes. Large deep green earrings matched her necklace. Her hair had just been set, probably earlier that morning. She was reading a book and placed it carefully on an end table as I moved closer to her chair. "Our Saturday evening Bible class has decided to study Thomas a Kempis," she said as she rose from the chair and extended her hand, " and I'm trying to get a jump ahead on it."

I asked her how many attended the class. "About twenty," she said. "And it's growing very nicely since we started to serve wine and cheese – but only *after* the lesson, and not before. That was my idea, "she said brightly. "I've seen your name in the papers every once in a while, Mrs. Moore, and I'm very glad to meet you."

"And I've heard only good things about you, Miss Parker," I responded.

"Thank goodness we all address each other in civilized terms around here," she smiled. "Some of those youngsters at the hospital I visited recently— and some older ones who should know better— insisted on calling me "Clara" the first time they laid eyes on me. I was an English teacher for over forty years, you know, and thousands of children passed through my schoolroom, and I never had any of them ever call me by my first name. Not even after they were all grown up and met me on the street. Moreover," she said, "Their parents wouldn't have done so either. Particularly since I had so many of them in my class twenty or thirty years before."

I told her that the same "sudden familiarity" annoyed me as well, as did the impertinence of telemarketers who begin with: "Good morning, Lillian," as though I've known them for years when, in fact, I've never set eyes on them and don't intend to buy anything they're trying to sell."

"I'm glad we're of one accord with that," she laughed. "But I always temper it with the fact that they haven't been taught any better and probably think that we like to be reminded of our youth. But do you know, "she added quietly, "that many of the telemarketers are blind, and it's the only way they can learn a living? We must be tolerant of that, don't you think?"

I hadn't thought of that, and it was one of those of life-changing remarks. I realized I had a lot to learn from this old teacher.

"I'm eighty-nine," she volunteered. "Going to be ninety next month, and to answer your question, unspoken: *Yes*, I do like it here. Everyone is very kind and civilized and we try to make newcomers as comfortable as possible. There are a lot of activities here, and I participate in all of them. Well, almost all," she said.

"I can walk perfectly well," she said, "but they insist I use that three-legged cane over there until I recuperate completely from my hip operation." She pointed to the corner of the room. "Besides my very slight limp, I feel very good. Of course I'd love to be back in my little apartment and get in my car and drive wherever I wished, whenever I wanted. And have all my books close at hand. But they have a very fine library here, and exceptionally good internet arrangements. I've never been a "complainer" and don't intend to start now. Life comes one day at a time for me and LeHavre has become my home in every sense of the word. I'm here for the duration, as we used to say during the war. The Second World War. There've been so many since.

I told her that I have a little apartment of my own and enjoy more than anything else picking a well-worn book off my shelf and reading it as long as I please without a thought about the clock.

"Well, Mrs. Moore," she said, "I think we'll get along just fine. Now tell me, please, how may I help you with your inquiry about some of my former students? I remember almost all of them, " she said. "Every once in a long while when I'm walking on the Boardwalk — when I *could* walk on the Boardwalk— I'd see one of them from way back when and stop them and call them by name. They were always amazed and flattered.

She smiled as she thought of it.

"I always try to remember some little detail about my former students and surprise them by saying, for example: 'I remember your being elected Prom Queen,' or 'You always read beautifully in my class.' With the boys I recall events such as helping me dig up the victory garden each year during World War II, or shoveling the snow off my car during the Big Blizzard of 1950. Things like that."

"I wish I had as good a memory," I said. "Sometimes I can't remember what I had for dinner the night before."

Miss Parker frowned slightly: "I only hope I can recall something about the students you have in mind. What were their names and what years did they attend high school?"

I told her that there were two of them. One was Matt Nolan, and the other, Imre Nagy. Both Class of 1967. I supposed that she'd remember the Nolan boy, but possibly not Imre. But she said it was the other way around. She remembered Imre very clearly, but what she remembered about Matt Nolan was not very much and mostly disagreeable.

"He wasn't in my home room and he took his English Class from another teacher. Thank goodness."

She leaned toward me in a confidential way and said: "You know he got a little girl in the family way while he was still a Junior. I knew her Mother and Dad, and it was a crime. Just a crime. A sweet thing like her. They moved out of town before the baby came. You remember how things were back then. But he just went on his way as if nothing had happened. I couldn't stand the sight of him. Most people didn't know about it, but I heard it from a family friend. Anyway, I had no use for him after that and really didn't care much about his football achievements or anything else."

I told her that his reputation followed him, and that I'd never heard a good word about him or his brother, Jack.

Her eyes narrowed and she said penetratingly," You're here because of his mixup in that murder case aren't you? I've been reading about it in the papers and I see his name mentioned. I'm not surprised, although I'm sorry for his brother. I had Jack in school in the 50's. He's about ten years older than Matt. He wasn't the smartest student I ever had, but he was courteous and honest. You could always believe what he said. He did a lot for his little brother and was always paid back with trouble. He practically raised him, you know. Their father was a drunkard. What else can you say. A common drunkard who didn't work a day in his life and died in the gutter. A sad case. That's why I always had a soft spot for Jack."

"My concern is not so much with Matt," I said, "as it is with Imre. Can you tell me anything about Imre that might be helpful in piecing together this whole mystery?

You're aware that he was a suicide."

"Yes, I saw it in the papers when it happened. Now that's the saddest case of all. Poor boy. I think he was a high functioning autistic, although we didn't call it that in those days. He was in my home room. Always super-punctual and overly fastidious in everything he did. Compulsive even in the way he ate his food – one very small portion at a time. And hygienic – always cleaning off his desk or arranging his books just so before he sat down. I should have been a psychologist, Mrs. Moore, because I noticed a similar pattern of behavior among a lot of children over the years, but couldn't quite put a finger on it. We didn't know much about autism in those days, but their habits made them stand out from the rest of the children. They were the kids who were sure to be bullied. And Imre certainly was, even though he was quite a big fellow."

"Did you ever see him resist – fight back?" I asked?.

"No," she said, "that was the strange thing. He could have snapped most of them in two, the little snipes. But he showed great restraint. I didn't follow football, but I was told that when he was on the field facing others his own size and strength he did quite well. I suppose that was because he knew it was just a game"

I agreed with Miss Parker and told her that I, too, recognized signs of autism. I asked her if she thought Matt Nolan in particular taunted him a lot. She said there was no question about that, but then, he taunted just about everyone, and everyone respected his strength if not his character.

"There was just one incident that frightened me about Imre," she said. "It happened one afternoon after school. Imre was cleaning up a mess I'd made when I spilled my thermos bottle in the *"flight"* of everyone leaving the room when the bell rang. The coffee squirted all over the place, sprinkling my desk, the blackboard, everywhere. I left to wipe off my blouse when Matt Nolan must have been passing by and looking into the room.

He must have caught Imre off guard and next thing you know he managed to push him into the janitor's closet at the back of the room and close the door on him. He was holding the door tightly shut when I came back into the room. I could hear Imre pounding on it from the inside. I told Matt in no uncertain terms to open the door but he defied me, laughing. I suppose he thought he'd have a bit more fun before obeying.

The next thing I remember was Imre breaking the hinges and the door flying open. He, pushed Matt violently to the ground. He was red in the face and looked as if he were about to stomp the life out of him. He lifted his foot into the air directly over Matt's chest and I know he could have killed him. Easily. I grabbed his arm and said something calming. I don't even remember what I said. But Imre looked at me, and put his foot down . . . . gently . . . on Matt's chest, and then just stood there, sweating profusely, totally enraged."

"Luckily they both respected me, and I pulled them apart. I had to be as sharp with Imre as with the other one. I made them shake hands and promise never to do anything so foolish again. By now the janitor –who heard the crash – came running into the room. I made up a lie and told the janitor I was having trouble opening the door and asked the boys to help me. *'And look what happened'*, I said shamelessly. The Janitor gave me a sharp look and then glanced over to Matt Nolan. *'Funny we haven't had any trouble with that door before.*' Then looking back at me: '*I'll see that we get new hinges on it, and ready for tomorrow, but you need to talk to Nolan.*'

Miss Parker said that there was nothing more she could do. The two boys left the room, and the worst seemed over. I told her that it gave me a very clear insight into Imre's character. But sadly, now it was too late for me, or her, to help him.

"About forty years too late," she agreed.

She went on to say that so many children suffered from psychological problems in the past that were never dealt with. She told me about a child in one of her classes who just couldn't sit still. He kept poking his neighbors and annoying them until most teachers lost complete patience with him. He came to the public school from a parochial school where the nuns were none too gentle. He once had a ruler broken over his back, he told me. But it didn't deter him one bit.

She paused for a moment. "When that lad came into my class," she said, "I knew I had more than a behavioral problem. It was deeper than that. I called his parents and had a long talk with them. I suggested a psychologist and they took my suggestion because they were nearly beside themselves trying to cope with the child. They had a little money and were able to pay for special treatment. Then they placed him in a special school near the University where he wasn't cured, but certainly modified, if you know what I mean.

"He's in the insurance business today," she told me, "and doing well. Imagine," she frowned, "if that family were poor, and this child would have struggled through high school under that burden? Imagine how many other children over the years suffered corporal punishment and mental anguish during their growing up years?"

"Miss Parker," I said, "There are a lot of good things that have happened, and are happening, in education today. I have a friend from Pittsburgh who told me that when he went to school in a "mill town" near the city, no child up through fifth grade wore glasses. Many of them couldn't hear either, but were forced to sit alphabetically whether in the front or in the back of the room."

She nodded her head in agreement. "Discipline was the word of that day. And discipline in moderation is a good thing. But a little compassion is also in order. Now before you go," she said, "I need to tell you that I knew Rachel Egron as well . . . the girl who this is all about. But only after I retired from school teaching. For several years I taught Sunday School at the Presbyterian Church just behind the Madison Hotel. It's gone now. When it closed they turned it into a bar and restaurant. The bar was where the altar used to be. I said it was a sacrilege and that it wouldn't last long. And it didn't."

She paused for a moment and excused herself as she went to her kitchen and brought me a plate of cookies and lemonade. Then she began her thoughts about Rachel again.

"There was a lovely little girl named Lisa Shaulis in one of my classes. Always prettily dressed and well mannered. It was a pleasure to teach her because she could already read pre-kindergarten. Well anyway, she brought a little friend to Sunday School at Christmas time back around the early seventies. Her name was Rachel, and I told her that was a Biblical name and she should be very proud of it.

She sipped from her lemonade as though to gain some additional strength to continue.

"She was a thin little thing, and from the looks of her clothes, a very poor child. Her family lived in those untidy houses clustered around the Light House at that time. Not such a nice neighborhood then, but as you can see when you go down that way, it's improved considerably. I never met her parents, but I understand her father was just "no good". At least that's how he was described to me. Apparently he just worked here and there, never more than a full week at a time. I heard he was a small time racketeer, but I doubt he was very successful at it. Rachel's mother did cleaning work for people and some sewing at home. A hard working woman, but weak as water."

She took another sip of lemonade and continued her story: "Apparently they lived from hand to mouth, as the old saying goes, and I suppose it was pretty much the same kind of life that the Nolan boys lived with *their* good-for-nothing father. Those three kids—Jack, Matt and Rachel – really had to scratch for themselves growing up. The two Nolans were older than Rachel. I doubt they knew each other growing up. But I see the same picture of home life in both cases."

"Rachel came to my Sunday School Class with her friend ,Lisa, just a few times. She was so quiet that I hardly knew she was there. But when I asked her questions or told her Bible stories she was attentive enough and seemed to have a hidden intelligence which no one had yet stimulated – certainly not at home."

Miss Parker picked up a napkin, paused for a moment and offered me more cookies. They were delicious, and I asked if she made them herself. "From scratch," she said. "You'll have to look at my kitchen before you leave. A marvel of miniaturization."

Obviously, she had never seen anything like mine!

She continued her story. " The last Sunday Rachel came to class, I asked her to take the offering. It was a task I assigned each of my dozen or so students at one time or another. They simply passed a little wicker basket among the other children , but they all took the job very seriously. After all, as I pointed out, they were doing work for Jesus. After she collected the coins, Rachel stared at them intently before giving the basket back to me. It was probably the largest number of coins she'd ever seen at one time in her young life. I also noticed a bruise mark on her wrist as she extended her arm. I asked her how she got it and she was very evasive. After class, she left, and I never saw her again."

She paused to reflect on the rest of her story, and particularly the part about Rachel's father.

"Rachel's little friend, Lisa, told me that she thought Rachel's father hit her every once in a while. Of course in those days people didn't involve themselves as much in other people's business. I wish to God *I had*. Lisa said the family was moving to an apartment in the Project near Baltic Avenue. That was the last I saw her."

Miss Parker pulled her hands together, as if in prayer. "Rachel just moved off my radar screen, so to speak. But I never forgot her. I never forget any of my students. When I heard about her death on tv, my heart sank. I thought to myself that her murder had begun a little piece at a time, beginning with the first time her father hit her. Her little friend, Lisa, left her way behind a long time ago. She's a Psychologist at Pennsylvania General Hospital and doing very well for herself. What else can you expect from a child whose parents read to her every night before she went to sleep and introduced books to her even before she could read them. And what else could you expect from little Rachel trying to make it in life all by herself?"

Miss Parker agreed with me that the world had come a long way since the two of us were young, but that somewhere along the line we lost our sense of community. In her opinion, the school was no longer the center of the community, and there weren't very many churches in the city still open. That was a great shame. In fact, she said that she felt no sense of community at all anymore outside of LeHavre. At LeHavre, she said, she had more friends and knew more people who cared about her than she ever had before. She hoped that I'd be a new friend as well and come back every once in a while to just sit and talk.

I agreed at once. It really *was* a pleasure to spend time with her. She was not a bit depressing or complaining as many people her age – and my age – are. I didn't have to wonder why so many people called Miss Clara Parker *their favorite teacher.*

The clock was heading toward 2:00, but we continued to talk longer about our remembrances of our own school days. Things were different back then, but not always as wonderful as we remembered them to be. We both agreed on that. When I told her that I'd worked for a short time after college at Wanamaker's, her eyes lit up.

"How I loved going over to Philadelphia on Saturday mornings and spending a day at Wanamaker's," she said. "Especially at Christmas time when they put on their big light display. I'd have lunch in the Crystal Tea Room and then go over to the main lobby and listen to Christmas Carols on that huge organ they had. If I planned to meet a friend, we'd simply say: "I'll see you under the Eagle."

I knew exactly what she meant, and I knew exactly where the golden eagle was. Every Philadelphian did. "It's a Macy's now, "I said rather sadly.

"So I've heard," she answered, her eyes dimming just a bit. "Was there ever a store like Wanamaker's? Then in summing up: "Well there'll never be another like that one."

I reminded her that she had an appointment for scrabble in a few minutes, and she asked if I would walk with her down to the Commons. Her leg was healing well, but just a bit "iffy". Of course I agreed and we left her cottage ("no locks on doors around here," she laughed) and headed down the path past the putting green. I asked if I could visit her on holidays. I could remember that rather than a definite schedule. She thought that would be fine, and I thought it would be a good way to bring her a small gift of some kind without making too much fuss about it. What a lovely visit we had.

When we got to the "Commons" she wished me goodbye. Then she got very solemn. "There's just one thing that troubles me here," she said. "My mother had money, and my Father as well. I sense that you're well off, too. "

"Yes," I admitted. "Very well off indeed."

"Did you notice," she said, "that everyone here has enough money to enjoy a wonderful life, with all the amenities and all the activities they can possibly participate in. The men have billiards and golf at the Country Club up the road. The women have bridge clubs and painting classes, and can even go shopping at the mall on any morning they choose. The swimming pool – Piscine Aquitania – is heated and open throughout the day. The Normandie Dining Room offers four entrees plus specialty plates. Café Provence is as decorative as a small French bistro and just as charming, and certainly more hygienic than anything you'd find in France. Some of the men even maintain boats at the Inlet in Atlantic City."

She grasped my hand. "It's all a fantasy in French. We can eat outdoors in the summer at the Restaurant Jardin. And we have a little jewel of a movie theatre called, appropriately enough, the Bijou. Because we *all* have money here, we enjoy and revel in it. Nothing wrong in that. But think of all the teachers *you and I knew* who are living out their seventies and eighties in "nursing homes" or "assisted living" arrangements where the only excitement is the notice on the activities board that reads "the next holiday is Flag Day." I've walked through so many corridors in places like that, smelling antiseptics, or worse. Places where residents are lined up in wheel chairs along the wall and stare up with vacant eyes. Some of them even tug at my dress as I go by and say softly: *"will you take me home?"* What's to become of them, these teachers who were so bright and dedicated and full of hope for their students not so many years ago. Baseball and football players are rewarded with pensions in the millions of dollars. What are their accomplishments in comparison with a teacher's? This LeHavre is truly a safe harbor for us. But what about them?"

"I can't answer that, Miss Parker. I can't even give you an answer as to why anyone –teacher or not — outside these walls who's over seventy, and heaven forbid, seventy-five or older, is regarded as out of touch, and therefore, out of mind."

She embraced me, and then waved me "goodbye" as I headed toward my car.

When I got back to my apartment the sun was still bright and warm and there were plenty of strollers on the Boardwalk. So I walked down St. James and into the stream of people, stopping near the Taj for an ice cream cone. I sat down on one of the benches and observed the people and the pigeons. There was plenty of time for me to meet Tom at 7:00pm at Kornfeld's.

I thought about the richness of my life, and the poverty of so many others. Here I am giving myself sermons about how people neglect senior citizens and forgetting that somehow I might have paid more attention to Imre before he took his life. Would it have helped? If I had asked him to dinner with Tom and I on that evening, would it have changed his mind?

Some things are unobtainable. Some things depend on fate and luck and karma – whatever you want to call it. Some things are reachable, and some aren't, no matter how hard you try.

I reflected on my own good health and good life – and yes, good luck — as I watched a little child futilely trying to lure one of the pigeons near the gazebo on New York Avenue with a piece of popcorn, and perhaps catching it in her hands . . . something that hasn't been done by any child on the Boardwalk in the hundred or more years of Atlantic City history.

I thought of all the good times I had with my wonderful family. How we enjoyed swimming in the ocean no matter how frigid the water was . A big thermometer on the side of Central Pier looked down on the beach and "told" the temperature of the water each day. It seemed always to register "65 degrees". We knew that was a lie just to lure the tourists onto the beach, and we'd shiver with delight and jump in anyway.

Deep sea fishing, as I said before, was a favorite attraction for the hale and hardy, until they felt the little fishing boat roll and heave as we hit "heavy" weather or rough waves. We caught sea bass and mackerel, and occasionally a small shark which made all of us "ooh and aw" until the captain unhooked it and threw it back into the sea.

Grandma loved the beach as much as we did, and went into the coldest water more quickly and bravely than anyone of us. As usual, she was setting the example which, of course, Grandmas are expected to do. A good example for me to observe during my playtime with Melanie.

And, oh yes, Miss Parker told me that I didn't have luck with hydrangeas because I cut them down in the fall. "Hydrangea flowers only come out on old wood.*"There's a lesson in there for people who think 'they're too old'"*, she said with a twinkle in her eye.

Chapter Twenty Two

Dillon: ***"We could quietly fold our tents and silently steal away"***

When I arrived at Kornfeld's's at 7:00, Lillie was already seated at our regular table in a quiet corner of the restaurant. I leaned over and kissed her gently on the cheek while she pointed to a beautiful crystal carafe which Mrs. Kornfeld had already graciously set on the table.

"From the old country", she said nostalgically, as she placed two fine stemmed glasses in front of us, all the while looking at Lillie with a smile, as if she alone recognized the beauty and quality of them. Mr. Kornfeld was his usual pleasant-grumpy self, enthroned on his well-worn cushion on the chair by the cash register, and waved to us when he noticed I had arrived.

The restaurant was in its usual chaotic mode as two waitresses scooted through tables with steaming plates of Hungarian specialties. And of course, Mrs. Kornfeld continued barking her enduring cry while escorting newcomers to their tables: "Not too much sour cream on the blintzes!" In all the times we've eaten here, someone in the kitchen apparently has never quite gotten the message about the sour cream.

Lillie couldn't wait to hear about Coach Shupka and his "take" on Nolan and Imre. I was wondering about her experience with Miss Parker. We went over details together and by the time we finished, we knew quite a bit more about both Imre and Matt Nolan than we had before. It was a given that Nolan would come out on the bitter end, while Imre was granted more sympathy based on memories of those who knew him when he was young.

I tried to sum things up:

We both agreed that based on both past and present history, Matt Nolan was a bad egg right from the beginning and continued to be one. If anyone deserved to sit in jail –as he did now—it was him. It was clear that he made life miserable for everyone he touched, and especially for Imre in their school days and beyond. And it was clear to us that Imre had deep psychological problems long before we met him. His terrible experiences in Viet Nam compounded his problems.

As Lillie told me more than once, if he hadn't commit suicide a few weeks ago he probably would have done it *eventually,* depending upon stress and circumstances. At first glance, he didn't seem to be involved in the murder, while Nolan proceeded to incriminate himself without much outside help.

The Spada connection was still an open question. Lt..Crosby at Police Headquarters told me that Spada had alibis from three of his band members who said that all four of them waited the storm out at another night spot further down the beach later that evening and into the morning. Spada went there is his own car with the instruments while the other three followed shortly thereafter. But for one reason or another, he arrived about half an hour later than the other car. He said he had to stop and fill his gas tank. Crosby said that would take some looking into and maybe some twisting of arms to get the full story.

I told Lillie that when I give Crosby the info about Spada's direct connection to Rachel, he'll certainly have a lot of questions to ask him." As far as Gary Bauer is concerned," I said, " It seems like a long shot, but who's to say that he might have come down here not for Rachel but for Spada. But then he saw Rachel again. Maybe they had an argument and there was an accident. The problem was locating Gary again." Lillian disagreed with me about Gary. "Just a poor, sick boy", she said.

We discounted Marty the bartender as a suspect as well as the other two patrons who were in the bar late that evening. And we had to consider the possibility that a total stranger might have killed her for a drug-related reason, or perhaps a hired hit man got the wrong girl. In any case, the motive was always missing, or tantalizingly just out of our reach.

I drained my glass and questioned, with a shade of frustration in my voice, why we ever got involved personally with this case. I told her that in the past six weeks or so while I was in Atlantic City and working on behalf of the county coroner, I dealt with at least ten homicides of one kind or another. I made my initial investigation; advised the local police; sent my report along to the county coroner; and then forgot about it. If I felt there'd been a murder, the case went to the local police, the city's medical examiner, and on to the District Attorney.

I told Lillie that I'd been on the Force in Pittsburgh long enough to know that it wasn't very professional for me to pursue a case like this which is clearly beyond my pay grade and outside the local police parameters. But to tell the truth, I need the money badly. And keeping in touch with the case kept me in touch with Lillie. These are the most important reasons I've stayed with a case which I should have long since passed along to others, or avoided altogether. I told Lillie about my growing frustration with the whole affair.

Lillie smiled at me. She was thinking what I was thinking. "For all the trouble it's caused us, there's a good side to it. After all, this case was the reason for our getting together in the first place. If it hadn't happened, ask yourself what you'd be doing this evening, or what I'd be doing .There's a bit of 'kismet" in all of it."

"Sorry," I said, "I didn't see that movie."

Lillie said I knew very well what she meant, and since we had already voluntarily involved ourselves, it was a reasonable to try to resolve it or at least pass along our "clues" to the lawyers, or to

Lt. Crosby, or the DA, or to whomever else was taking the case seriously.

Or, I emphasized, as I drained my glass, "we could quietly fold our tents and silently steal away."

"So you know about Kismet, do you? "smiled Lillie.

I told her that I just thought we had gotten into more deeply than we should have and now we ought to step back and let justice takes its course. We didn't know any of these people at all until a few weeks ago — as I pointed out to her — and now we have sleepless nights trying to fit all the pieces together. At least I do.

I explained to her that in police matters —and extending that to courts of law — there are always a lot of loose ends. A lot of unclosed cases and unsolved mysteries. It's not like the tv shows where everything is tied up in a pretty knot in half an hour and where somebody always confesses and outlines the whole event in full detail. It just doesn't happen that way very often. Almost never.

I asked her: " Do we have any obligation to make sure Matt Nolan suffers for this crime, or for his past crimes? Do we have any real evidence to do that? It all seems very circumstantial to me. Even his attempted flight to Mexico is circumstantial. Considering his record, don't you think the DA is doing everything he can to throw the book at him? And when it comes to throwing things, don't you think Matt's lawyers are going to do everything *they* can to have the whole case thrown out of court, if it ever gets near to court.

Lillie agreed with me 100% .But she said emphatically that if we were able to find even a little something that no one else had uncovered, and if it meant that justice could be done when we exposed it, doesn't it seem as if it would be the right thing to do? "

I asked her what we had uncovered of consequence? Just some hearsay remembrances of how kids acted forty years ago.

Lillie looked straight at me, with a frown on her forehead; somewhat hurt, I thought, by what I said.

"I have a real problem," she said. "after what I heard today, and what you told me.

I'm not entirely convinced that Matt Nolan is guilty, but much as I hate to think about it, I'm concerned that Imre *may* be. The ball keeps bouncing back to Imre. Now why do I think that? Let me lay out what I think might have happened that night."

I guess my eyes must have rolled back on that comment. I've heard a gazillion amateurs explain crime scenes to me and they invariably get them wrong. But it was only fair to let her unravel her theory. And anyway, I always enjoy hearing her talk – no matter what she says, and 99% of the time she makes sense. I hoped this wasn't the other 1%.

She took the last sip of Tokay and began laying it out for me. "Now here's what I think happened," she said, "Right off the top of my head, of course. I think Rachel was at the Club to meet a contact, either to exchange money or drugs. I think the contact could have been Matt Nolan. But then it could have been Imre. After all, we know that his uncle is into drugs and perhaps pulled in Imre as well. Willingly, or unwillingly. Rachel stayed late, probably to wait until most of the other customers left. Her contact would know to wait as well."

Lillli paused to put some more "pieces" together for me. I pretended rapt attention, and thought how pretty she was. I wouldn't have dared to say "at her age". But she was damn pretty and I was lucky to be with her.

"Then the lights went out!" she said, jumping back in her chair. "That changed everything. Now just suppose that Imre – who, you remember, told us he always carried a small flashlight with him – just suppose that he suggested she follow him to the back of the Club through the corridor that led to the door that, in turn, opened into the exhibit building."

Lillie was obviously making it up as she went along. She even apologized for making her story sound so complicated, but went on with it anyway.

"There are a couple of good reasons why she followed without question and without fear. She probably did business with him many times before and had no fear whatsoever of his "persona" as Igor. Secondly, she knew that rain was coming down in buckets and she must have heard something of the commotion as the others leaving the Club discovered one or two feet of ocean way that far up into Kentucky Avenue. She realized that she could hand over the package to Imre and that he, in turn, could lead her to the front of the building so that she could exit right on the Boardwalk which, of course, was high and comparatively dry. As a woman, I can't help thinking that she might have had some concern for those very pretty – and very expensive shoes she was wearing. In her eyes, Imre might not have been threatening at all."

Lillie paused for a second, rubbing her hands together, as if she were close to the solution. I couldn't help think that only a woman would consider the "shoe" issue, and it was an interesting deduction as to her location at the time of the crime. I thought that maybe I'd better listen more closely. She went on.

"And then something went terribly wrong. Maybe she didn't have the money that she was supposed to hand over to him. Or the dope. Or not enough of either. Maybe they had an argument over it. Maybe she decided to leave but couldn't find her way out. He grabbed her. She screamed, and that might have set him off. Remember he was a powerful man. A wrestler in high school. Perhaps he just very quickly snapped her neck."

She demonstrated the snap with her hands. She'd have made a damn good prosecuting attorney!

"Maybe, in his state of mind he was back in Vietnam again. It's a small neck, as we know .It wouldn't have taken much pressure. But I don't think he meant for a moment to harm her. Not for a moment. So she fell to the floor and he got scared when he realized she was not breathing, so he carried her over to the side door – the one we left from – where the ocean would have been several feet deep by this time and moving quickly with the surge because of the wind and tide. He dropped her in the surge. Maybe by accident, or maybe because he knew she was dead. No one would have seen him do it. It was pitch black, and the door faces an empty parking lot, as we know."

Lillie thought she had it all put together and went for the "finishing touch."

"Now we know Imre isn't by nature a murderer and no doubt he agonized about what he did. And then later, when he learned that the police wanted to see him again, and possibly implicate him – maybe put him in prison — it might have prompted him to escape "the voices" and "the cage" by taking his own life. If that makes any sense. Apparently he thought that Lt. Crosby had uncovered some new evidence . Maybe he thought someone saw him drop the body in the ocean. In any case we know he had a conscience and a penchant for "correcting things" because of his autism. Perhaps he felt his death was the only way to atone for Rachel's, or more likely he couldn't face the possibility of being imprisoned again. What do you think, Tom?"

She sounded very pleased with her theory. My head was reeling, trying to follow the route she described and the sequence of Imre's mental gymnastics. But I quickly recognized a flaw in her tale.

"You got it all wrong," I said almost apologetically. "I'm sorry, Lillie, but you're dead wrong. It might have happened the way you said it did if we'd have found the body not more than 24 hours after the storm. But as it turned out, we found it two days later. And I can assure you that the body we found had only been in the water much less than a full day. So It laid around a while somewhere else. Maybe in someone's car trunk. Maybe in Spada's car trunk, or in some stranger's car trunk. Maybe Rachel wasn't murdered on the night she left the Club. And to confuse matters even more, there's the little matter of why a dress manikin showed up at the about the right time and the right place *where she should have showed up* . . . on the morning following the storm. How could we connect Imre with that? Are you with me, Lillie?"

I really hated to burst her bubble.

"Oh my gosh," she said. "I forgot about Miss Pengo. I forgot all about her. But then again, maybe the manikin was just a coincidence and we shouldn't include it in our scenario at all. What do you think?" she repeated.

I told her that there were a lot of "maybes" in her story. All of it possible but highly improbable. Nothing in her story could be proved . Not a thing. And so complicated. "Yes," I agreed "The manikin could have been a coincidence. All kinds of debris float onto the beach after a storm like that. And it wasn't the first time an oddity washed ashore. It happens all the time up and down the beach .And didn't we all talk about it being a kid's joke? That internet stuff involving the Pengo character. What would that have to do with Imre? I doubt he was "up" on that kind of stuff. Didn't he tell us that he didn't own a computer at all, and didn't want to?"

"Maybe Our Miss Pengo could tell us something," Lillie said, shaking her head. "But she ain't talkin'".

"She doesn't even exist anymore," I said. "When the Captain of the Lifeguards came in later that morning, I understand he threw the manikin into the garbage and told them not to play tricks like that again. Right now, Ms. Pengo, or what's left of her, is buried in a garbage dump somewhere near Seacaucus."

Then I took both her hands, looked her straight in the face and said: "If you want to continue to play detective, it's okay with me, Lillie. Anything you do is okay with me. But all we have right now is some second-hand heresay evidence and some guesses as to why Rachel may not have wanted to get her shoes wet. It doesn't mean anything unless we can actually produce a viable piece of evidence that would connect and incriminate either Matt, Jack, Imre, Spada,

Gary, the bartender, a 'hit man' or a complete stranger, or even the garbageman for that matter. That's the way it works with the law. When I consider that a stranger might have done it, I think about that guy up in Washington State who picked up and murdered girls along the road who just happened to be in the wrong places at the wrong time. No rhyme or reason to it at all. No motive. For all we know, Matt or Jack could have hired somebody to do it and were sitting in the Rendezvous Club to make sure it was done right."

"Well that would have been stupid," countered Lillie. "They would have wanted to be at least fifty miles away from the spot where she was murdered if they knew she was gong to be murdered. And they'd have an airtight alilbi . . . like maybe having coffee at the time with the police department in Hoboken."

Lillie was about to continue the scenario when a very nice plate of chicken paprikash appeared on our table, accompanied by a wooden board heaped with thick pieces of rye bread and goat cheese. Our arguments paled in comparison. So we ate, and enjoyed every bite of it. I even managed a piece of Linzer Tort with whipped cream.

We continued our conversation over coffee, and Lillie was beginning to unwind a "new theory" that implicated Tony Spada when my cell phone rang. I quickly pulled it out of my coat pocket. It was Mary Catherine. She told me that Evelyn was in a very bad way and it seemed to her that she wouldn't last the night..

She asked me to come home but cautioned me not to "speed up." She didn't want to lose both of us. I told her that I'd get back to my apartment and pack a few things and be on my way in about half an hour. I should be in Pittsburgh in about six hours. I told her I'd go straight to the Home. She told me that she'd be there, regardless of the time.

Lillie understood immediately. She told me to leave as quickly as possible and we'd talk about anything else later.

I kissed her goodbye, and was on the Atlantic City Freeway about fifteen minutes later heading toward Pittsburgh. I expected this to happen for many weeks, but even now as it *was* happening, I drove in a daze.

When I pulled off the Turnpike and picked up Route 28 in Acmetonia in the morning, the sun had already started to rise. I soon pulled into the parking lot at the Home and found Mary Catherine waiting for me in the lobby.

"She's gone Tommy," she said, as she pulled me close to her and kissed me, just as she did so often when I was a little boy .

"She died about an hour ago, and they said they'd not do anything until you arrived. Thank God you made it safely. I was worried the whole time, thinking you might speed and have an accident."

She did all the talking while I listened numbly. "There's nothing we can do for Evelyn now. I was holding her hands the whole time. Her eyes were closed and she never opened them. I didn't know whether she was alive or dead. It went so quiet and gentle. Just like her.I brushed her hair with my hand and when I felt her face it was already cold, and I knew she was gone. I said a prayer for her soul, although God knows she didn't need one after all she suffered."

I simply stood there and listened without saying a word. Mary Catherine said it all. I just needed some time with Evelyn to say goodbye. And I did. No use in gong into that. It's a personal thing. It doesn't need telling. There are no words to say about a marriage like ours where she never gave me a bad word or a reason to be angry. Not once in over forty years.

I walked out of her room with a heavy feeling in my heart, like it was broke. I know people say that all the time. I know. But you have to go through something like that to understand what it means. There were some details that Mary Catherine and I had to clear at the front desk, where everyone was very thoughtful and helpful. ***Then we went home to Carnegie Street.***

Chapter Twenty Three

"Lillian: *"I would have stayed in Antarctica and lived on an iceberg if he wanted it that way"*

It was two weeks since Evelyn died and Tom called me every day from Pittsburgh, sometimes twice. I told him he didn't have to worry about me when he had so many other worries on his mind.

The funeral was a very bad experience for him. He didn't want to talk about it and I didn't push him. There were a lot of things to settle with the Home where Evelyn stayed. And all kinds of forms to fill out. Changes in Social Security check addresses and joint bank accounts. It's not easy to die. Not for those who remain after us at any rate.

Tom decided to move Mary Catherine as soon as possible to the "Assisted Living High Rise" called the David L.Towers, not far from the family residence on Carnegie Street. The Towers are just a few blocks further up the hill from where she's lived all her life. She resisted at first, and then , realizing the strain she was putting on Tom and herself, decided to "give up the only home I ever knew" as she put it. Well, she lived there for over seventy years. I can understand why she hesitated.

I can understand why *I've* hesitated to do just exactly the same thing. Of course moving to a beautiful condominium on a top floor facing the ocean is one thing. An assisted living residence with reduced space and a communal dining room — after living in an eight room house with high ceilings and plenty of closet space — is quite another. Even the best of what's out there can never match a house like that.

"You can't imagine how much junk we accumulated over the years," Tom told me in one of our telephone conversations. And of course it's up to him to get rid of almost all of it. He told me that when he and his sister went through some of the things, especially the boxes of pictures and what-not's, Mary Catherine couldn't imagine getting rid of *any* of "her stuff." It was just too precious to her. Too many memories.

Tom told me plaintively, "I'd hold up an old plate or a souvenir of one kind or another and Mary Catherine always had a long story about who gave it to her, or to our mother; as well as what the occasion was; how long ago it was; and on and on. As we "redd up" as we say in Pittsbugh when we mean "cleaning house", our whole family experience for the space of well over three quarters of a century, compressed into eight rooms in that old house, on that familiar corner in Lawrenceville, unfolded before me.

In another phone call he told me that he started making some minor repairs at the house and then realized that what looked "minor" sometimes turned out to be "major."

"I started to scrape and peel wallpaper off the kitchen walls which were really spotty," he explained. "Then I found that there were not just two or three layers which I expected, but more like seven and eight, and some of the layers were glued rather than pasted to the others. I had to rent a 'steamer'" he said, "and it was really messy. I got the kid next door to help me and we had a helluva time cleaning up afterwards. Then I had to put a base coat on, and then a final coat of paint. But even Mary Catherine said it looked good and that we probably should have done it years ago."

We had many conversations that opened my eyes to how "ordinary" people deal with everyday problems. I have to say I've been spared most of that sort of thing in my life. My father had money and my husband was well-fixed. When we needed something done around the house, or wanted some new thing , we just ordered it, and it was paid for. I'm not apologizing for my life. I'm just comparing how people with money do things, and how those without, don't.

There were many experiences and problems in those weeks that I could have helped him with. But I knew that it was the one thing that would destroy our relationship. So I listened and kept my mouth shut. And sometimes I had to smile, despite myself.

I'm not an electrician," he told me,"but you have to realize that Mary Catherine has been living with just a few wall plugs all these years, and that 'modern' people need a lot more. A whole lot more. That was a job that required an electrician, and luckily one of my friend's sons works for the light company and was able to do some work for me in the evenings at reduced cost. Mary Catherine can't understand why people don't just make use of extension cords as she does. My God, Lillie," he told me, "It's a wonder she didn't burn the house down years ago."

Then there was the problem of what to do with all the excess furniture: lamps, curtains, rugs, and all the rest of things she wouldn't be able to take to the high rise. Tom said she had a very hard time picking out a few things she'd need in her new apartment and reluctantly – very reluctantly –told him to get rid of the rest in the best way he could. Tom called Goodwill and they sent along a truck to pick the stuff up. "I helped them a bit," he said solemnly. "There were just two middle-aged guys who came along with the truck and needed all the help they could get."

I almost reminded him that he was a middle aged man – no, an **old** man – himself.

Tom was upset about the fact that our government can build roads in Afghanistan but can't lend a few soldiers here and there to help organizations like Goodwill, the Salvation Army, St. Vincent de Sales and all those other groups doing their best to assist people struggling in **this** country. I have to admit that I wonder about it myself. Does anybody have an answer to that?

In another phone call he told me how difficult it was to sell the house on his own, so he hired an agent and the agent was doing a good job lining people up to see the place and hopefully place bids. It would probably take a bit longer to get a firm buyer.

I told him to take his time and not to worry about how long things took. After all, he owed it to Mary Catherine to make sure she was "settled" in her new apartment, and that it would take a reasonable length of time which only she could determine. I knew her well enough to know that she would make the best of it, no matter what, and try to spare Tom as much as she could. She had already made the move, although Tom said she walked down the few blocks every morning to Carnegie Street to make breakfast for him, and back again for supper.

And as far as fixing things around the house, there was only so much Tom could do by himself. I kept reminding him that he was "no kid," and he laughingly agreed. I told him to tell the agent to "sell it as is." From my own experience I told him that there are a lot of buyers out there looking for Victorian houses in that area of Pittsburgh referred to in the papers as "Up and Coming Lawrenceville. Even once in the New York Times. When they get their hands on a good Victorian," I said, "they invariably turn the place inside out and make their own special changes, no matter how many minor repairs were made prior to the sale. I know I'd have my own ideas about the difference between renovation and restoration.

And it turned out just that way. A professional couple involved with the Carnegie Museum fell in love with the place. They made an offer, and Tom accepted it. Tom said he'd be winding things up fairly soon and that I could expect him to return within a week, or two at the very most.

Before we hung up that evening after he gave me the good news, I made a very "modest proposal" and waited with some apprehension as to how he'd react to it. Here's how it went: I told Tom I was thinking seriously about buying a condominium in one of those new high rise apartment buildings just a little ways up the beach. A spot just a street off the Boardwalk between Hackney's Restaurant and

Captain Starn's boat rentals. Of course, both of these enterprises are long gone, but he pinpointed it without any problem.

I told him that the condominium I looked at the previous week was about thirty stories high and that the views from the highest floors were spectacular.

"Each apartment has a fairly large reception area, " I explained, " plus a spacious living room; a beautiful kitchen that has a nice sized dining area next to huge French doors that lead to a balcony that looks out on the ocean; two bedrooms; a small reading room— or you could turn it into an office— and plenty of closet space. There's a beautiful bathroom as well as a smaller one in the master bedroom."

I was nearly breathless after explaining the layout. He seemed interested but said to me rather anxiously: "Can you afford it?"

Now I made "my pitch". I told him that I thought I could swing it by myself, *but if he could chip in with part of the monthly rent*, I'm sure I could handle it. In fact, I said I wouldn't bother him with details, but both my father and husband left me with a modest sum – well invested with cousin Jake – that was to be used exclusively for any future living accommodations. I told him I was sure Jake would take pains to make sure I was getting a "good deal" since his company was helping finance the construction costs for the building. Which was true! Of course Tom wasn't aware of how much and how well my funds were invested.

Tom hesitated a moment before answering. Then he asked me to allow him to think it over and give me an answer in our next phone conversation.

The next phone call was not long in coming. Just after dinner on the following evening he called me from Pittsburgh to give me the glad news that Mary Catherine seemed to be happily resettled. In fact she said she was sorry she hadn't made the move years ago. She loved her little apartment and the fact that so many of her

Lawrenceville friends were just a few rooms away, but far enough to preserve her privacy.

Tom also told me that the house had been sold and that settlement was scheduled for the next afternoon. After that he would take a few days to work out final financial matters with the Home and finalize the funeral expenses and other little chores. He would be on the Turnpike on Friday morning, he said, and we could eat at Kornfeld's that evening.

He finished the conversation by saying that he considered what I told him about the condo and wanted us to be together, but couldn't we stay at the little apartment on St James Place for a while longer? It seemed so much more homey, and with both of us paying their share of rent it would be much more economical. But most importantly, he really liked the little place. He even started liking Mexican food, or so he said.

Now I knew why I loved him. Yes, I loved him And I would have stayed in Antarctica and lived on an iceberg if he wanted it that way. I told him that it sounded good to me and that if he wanted to take the tour of the new condominium when he arrived back in Atlantic City on Friday– just to see it – it would be fine with me. Or it would be fine if we stayed just where we were, where things were more cozy and familiar. That would be okay, too.

I meant every word of it. I was filled with yearning and excitement for the next two days. I even broke my rule about communicating with the cats as I fed them each morning down on the beach. I told them about the wonderful things that were happening to me, because . . . because I just had to tell someone that life doesn't have to be over when you're seventy-five, or eighty-five or anytime you're still able and willing to make plans for the future. That's the secret. Plans for the future.

The cats were non-committal.

Chapter Twenty Four

Dillon: *You know you love someone when every time you see her, it's the first time*

I was on the turnpike heading east at exactly 6:03am, Friday morning. The radio was giving me the weather: Clear and sunny. No clouds in sight. And that's exactly how I felt.

The house was settled and the people who bought it asked me to have a final walk-through the night before I left. With all the furniture gone and bare walls all around there was a curious *empty* sound — if that makes any sense — as we made our way from room to room. I always hated the dark brown wainscoting in the dining room. So old fashioned. But they seemed to think it was one of the best features of the room and they chattered away about how they'd take it down to the original wood – a fine grade of oak – then stain and lacquer it. The wife questioned the lacquer, but I guess they'll work it out. They have no idea how many kids have chipped, bumped and scratched that wainscoting for over a hundred years and more, and how many times it must have been repainted.

They oohed and awed over a real honest-to-God Tiffany lamp that hung in the little upstairs spare room –not much bigger than a closet— that my mother called her sewing room. I never saw the beauty in that lamp and still don't. Of course I never told Lilllie about it because I knew she'd ask me to bring it back to Atlantic City. Mary Catherine didn't particularly like the lamp either and when I asked her if she wanted to take it to her new apartment in the high rise she said simply: "where would I put it?" The new buyers added a couple of big bucks to the asking price and everybody came away happy.

The attic smelled dusty, as it always did, even though Mary Catherine and my mother before her always kept it clean and orderly. We always used it as a storage room, and one half of it had a couple of cedar chests and wardrobes where our winter clothes were stored – heavy coats, sweaters, boots, ice skates and such. The new buyers were ecstatic about the possibility of turning it into their *atelier*, as they called it, where they'd have ample room – and excellent light — to set up easels and paint and whatnot. I told you they were connected with the Carnegie Art Museum. They're the ones who put on the big International Show every couple of years, so I guess that tells the story.

Our house sits fairly high on a hillside above another row of houses on a lower street level. You'd have to know something about Pittsburgh topography to understand it without seeing it. But anyway, the new buyers especially liked the view of the river and the green hills that lay beyond the river in the Millvale and Troy Hill sections of town.

If they'd looked out those windows while I was growing up, they'd be looking at an ugly gray foundry that stretched about three city blocks in either direction, blocking the view of the river and the hills and everything else in the neighborhood. When steel left Pittsburgh in the '70's, the foundry was leveled and now it's a flat grassy field used mostly as a parking lot.

They say that apartment buildings are planned down there but nothing's happened so far. The Lawrenceville area where I live has become very *"environmentally conscious"* in the past few years because people recognize that clean rivers and blue skies and good views are worth money. Butler Street, our main drag, now has a series of art galleries, boutiques, interior design shops and some really good new restaurants stretching all the way from around 16th Street out to 62nd Street. They don't call it "up and coming Lawrenceville" for nothing.

The couple that bought the house told me that they'd done some deed checking and found that the builder of the house back in the 1880's was a musician who was a personal friend of Stephen Foster. I never knew that. But I did know that Foster was a native of Lawrenceville. In fact, his father founded the town back in 1814. For patriotic reasons he named it after the famous Captain Lawrence who said those famous words as he lay dying during a naval battle fought during the War of 1812: *"Don't give up the Ship"*

Young Stephen grew up not too far from our house. He and his bride, Jeannie, travelled down to New Orleans from Pittsburgh by steamboat in 1852 and that's where he got inspiration for his folk music from a lot of what he saw along the way and especially from the colored folks who were slaves at that time. They have a statute of him over on the Pitt campus. An old black man with a banjo is seated at his feet. Maybe it was meant to portray "Old Black Joe," a character in one of his most famous songs. There was some ruckus about it during the 60's, but people on the whole, both black and white, recognize that Foster wasn't putting the black man down with his music, but raising him up.

Foster died young and neglected in New York City. It wouldn't be the first time a Pittsburgh boy was led astray in the big city. He had no business sense and toward the end sold his songs for pennies. They were, and are still, sung by millions of people throughout the world. The man who built our house turned out to be a German immigrant who was an accomplished violinist and who became a major influence on Pittsburgh musical life. He founded a music store in Pittsburgh and made quite a lot of money composing some music of his own. Foster was one of his protégés and later they wrote some music together. Both he and Stephen are buried near each other in Allegheny Cemetery, just a few blocks away from our house on Carnegie Street.

When we finished the tour I gave them my spare house keys and told them I was on my way up to my sister's to spend the evening. As they got into their car and pulled away, I took one last look at the house. How I wished that every light in the house would have been burning and I could have passed through the front door one more time to find everyone in their place as I remembered them when I was a kid.

Mother in the kitchen making a "good smell" as I used to tell her as I came running through the door. And Mary Catherine busy setting the supper table, laying out silverware and smoothing the table cloth. My father in his chair by the radio listening to Gabriel Heater's "war news" in the living room. My little sister sitting quietly on the piano bench next to Dad with our cat "Boots" in her lap, and my brother, with a furrowed brow, doing his homework on the desk in the corner of the dining room. I'd ask him how he liked being in Ms. Brennan's home room — a math teacher who'd been at Arsenal for maybe a hundred years! He'd laugh and say that she was always comparing him with our sister, Mary Catherine, who, though not an honor student, was one of her favorites a decade earlier.

We'd talk about the basketball team and the big game coming up with Schenley, our arch rival. Then Mother would call us and we'd go to the table for a wartime meal consisting of thick slices of spam baked with crushed pineapples while Mary Catherine furiously hand beat a large metal pan of creamy mashed potatoes. "No lumps!" I'd yell at her, with my elbows on the table, holding my knife in one hand and fork in another. "I'll give you lumps" she'd yell back as she passed the big spoon to Dad first and then slid the potatoes deftly into a large porcelain bowl on the table in front of him. There was always a bowl of stewed tomatoes or green beans made from victory garden produce. And my how we "gabbed" while we ate. Every body talking at once, but listening in to what the others said. Then afterwards, Mother and Mary Catherine did the dishes. My little sister helped. Dad took his seat next to the radio again and dialed to Fibber McGee, and my brother and I off to see a Flash Gordon serial at the Arsenal Theatre down the street.

Maybe that's what heaven will be like.

Mary Catherine had a nice supper waiting for me in her apartment in the high rise and after we talked a bit into the night I slept for a while in the recliner. I was up early, but not earlier than Mary Catherine who managed to have some eggs and bacon on my plate so I wouldn't leave on an empty stomach. With a hug and a pat on the head she sent me off, but not before looking me straight in the eyes and telling me that "I had done my part" and that she was proud of me and hoped I would be happy because she prayed for that *more than anything else* these last months.

I told her that I'd be okay and that I'd be back, and this time with Lillian, to make sure the two of them would get to know each other and like each other as much as I knew they would. Then I was on my way.

I like driving in the morning while it's still dark, and I was never more anxious to reach Atlantic City and see Lillian again. I'll tell you what Dad once told me long ago about how you know when you're in love. He said: *"You know you love someone when everytime you see her it's the first time."*

I drove throughout the morning and crossed the Walt Whitman Bridge into New Jersey in the early afternoon after leaving the damnable Schuylkill Drive behind me.

When I reached Absecon I pulled over to rest for a minute and called Lillian on the cell phone. She'd been waiting by the phone all day, she said, even though she knew I probably wouldn't be getting in until early evening. It was so good to hear her voice again.

I asked her how the case against Nolan was going, and she told me that it seemed to be at a standstill. Nothing in the newspapers or on the tv. No one seemed interested in it except Matt Nolan's lawyers, of course. She hadn't heard a word about it from anyone and didn't expect to.

But she had a theory, she said, and she couldn't wait to try it out on me .I told her I could hardly wait. But as I matter of fact,

I couldn't care less. It was time to put all that behind us. It really didn't have anything to do with us in the first place, and to tell the truth I never felt right about taking money to get a guy like Matt Nolan off the hook.

As I drove over the little bridge that separates Atlantic City from the mainland and then past the Convention Center, all my thoughts were about Lillian and the wonderful life that stretched ahead of us. What a lucky guy I was and what a great feeling it would be to see her *"for the first time."*

Chapter Twenty Five

Lillian: *"We will hang on like barnacles"*

Tom called me on my cell phone as he made the turn around the War Memorial heading down Atlantic Avenue toward St. James. Yes, I know that using a cell phone while driving is against the law. I met him at the curb. I guess we acted like two kids who hadn't seen each other for years when really it was just a few weeks. But long enough. Long enough.

He had his arm around me as we entered Kornfeld's, and Mrs. Kornfeld greeted us with: *"Well look who's here!"* as she escorted us to our quiet corner table.

"We have home made chicken soup with liver dumplings. And the special tonight is stuffed cabbage with mandels"— they're almonds, she explained—" and raisins. This is what we eat at home," she said, pointing to her husband at the register who waved his hand in reply. As we settled in and began talking about the trip, she deposited a bottle of wine and two fine crystal goblets in front of us. "A little white wine will go good," she smiled down at me. "It's Katzenkeller Riesling. It means 'cat cellar'and I know how you love cats."Then she looked straight at Tom and said: "Ms. Moore hasn't looked so good while you were gone. A little pale. So there's no check for tonight. And drink it all. It'll do you both good."

Now Tom is a good talker. Born with the gift of gab, he always says .And he just couldn't *stop* talking as we sat there and enjoyed the wine and the ambience and the warm glow of total contentment. How else can I sum it up? It was all there. Everything he'd done in the past weeks and everything he wanted to do in the weeks ahead.

He told me all about how much he had accomplished with the house repairs, and how glad he was to have such nice people buy it. And artistic, too. "They're going to turn our old attic into an atelier," he laughed. Then he added, "That's an artist's studio, isn't it?"

"Yes it is, my dear", I said, and he shook his head in amazement. "Imagine that", he said, taking a sip of wine, "Just imagine that! An atelier in the old homestead."

He told me how well Mary Catherine accepted her new home in the high rise. "I really think she likes it. I don't think she's kidding me. She showed me the schedule of events for the week, including, among other things, bingo on Thursday evenings, of course, and line dancing on Friday's. As a joke I told her that she might meet some nice old fellow who likes to dance and if he wasn't too old, he might whirl her around the room. She just laughed me off. *'Just let some old duffer try!'* , she said, as if dancing with a man at her age was unthinkable."

Tom paused for a moment and grasped my hand rather tenderly, if you know what I mean. He told me that the moment Mary Catherine laughed about the "old duffer", he realized that even though he and his sister were born just ten years apart, they lived in two entirely different generations.

"Do you know what I mean, Lillian?" he said. "I guess I told you once before that my grandfather died at 75—*my age now* — and he was a very old 75 back in '44. He looked old, dressed old, and acted old. Dad was just 67 when he died in 1972, and he looked and acted just like *his* Dad. When I think about the two of us," he continued, "I know you agree with me that something happened somewhere along the line – maybe in the '60's when everything changed .Whatever it was and whenever it was, it seems to have changed the concept of just exactly what' old age' is. '

I told him I totally agreed, and that it was more than just an assumption on his part. It was fact! I told him that when I read the death notices back in the '70's and '80's it seems to me that most of the people dying were in their "70's and early '80's . But when I read them today, the deceased are more likely to be in their late '80' and '90's, not to mention a goodly number past 100!

"Exactly," said Tom. "I'm sure young people *"don't get it"* and probably wish we'd act our age . . . or whatever age they think we're in. Poor things," he said. "It's a pity that we *"don't get them"* either. "

We both laughed as we clinked our glasses together in total understanding.

That brought me to the subject of the condominium that I'd been looking at. I asked Tom if he'd like to take a look at it on Monday morning. He said he wouldn't mind at all if it pleased me but that the little apartment on St. James was totally okay so far as he was concerned. And a lot less expensive. Of course, as he quickly pointed out, there was one thing we needed to do as soon as possible if we stayed on St. James.

What's that?" I asked.

"We'll need a bigger bed!"

I gave him a long sultry smile. *"I've already ordered one!"*

After a very delicious and very filling dinner — and an empty bottle of Riesling — we asked for the check, but Mrs. Kornfeld yelled over the usual roar of discordant restaurant sounds to her husband, "No check for Ms. Moore this evening. Did you hear me?"

As we passed by the register he looked at his wife and said with a laugh: "How can we stay in business if we don't make any pengos tonight?" I was almost out the door, but turned back. "What did you say, Mr. Kornfeld? He told me that he reminded his wife that they wouldn't be able to stay in business if he didn't make any money tonight.

I corrected him. *"You didn't say money, Mr. Kornfeld, you said 'pengos'."*

Mrs. Kornfeld interrupted with a smile. "A pengo is like a dollar in Hungary where we came from. Or at least it used to be when we were young. Pengos is what they called their money before the war. I don't know what they call it now. Maybe Euros?" she asked questioningly, turning to her husband.

"How should I know?" he answered gruffly.

I turned to Mrs. Kornfeld. "Let me ask you this. If I found something – a package maybe – with the word 'pengo' stamped on it, why wouldn't it have a number in front of it if it meant money?"

She said that was an easy question because the pengo started out being worth almost a dollar in American money, but when the Inflation began just before the war you might start the day with 100 pengos and it might be worth only $25 that night. It got so much worse that you finally needed a wheelbarrow full of pengos to buy a loaf of bread."

Mr. Kornbfeld re-entered the conversation by saying that nobody ever put a number in front of pengos during the Inflation until they were ready to sell it. "You could ask old Mr. Nagy about that. You know . . . Imre Nagy's Uncle Istvan who owns the exhibit building up on the Boardwalk. He's very old now but very rich," he said. "He was in the importing business and told me that when they shipped things to him from Hungary in those days, the value of the stuff changed several times while it was still on the boat."

"Old Istvan could tell you a lot of stories like that", added Mrs. Kornfeld, "but he's very old now and not doing well. He belongs to the Magyar Club with us but he hasn't been out for a long time now. It's too bad his nephew Imre died because he could have told you about all the things that his uncle imported from the old country and keeps in storage at his building on the Boardwalk. Imre often said that his uncle bought many things in his lifetime but never threw a single thing away. Of course, the old fellow had a head for business and sold a lot of it at good prices or he wouldn't have been able to buy so much property and live so well."

"He was a bootlegger, too", added Mr. Kornblau gratuitously. "But the honest stuff he imported from the old country was all first class. Real luxury items like furniture, dishes. silverware, jewelry and lots of beautiful furs and clothes. They sold a lot of it at the auction houses on the Boardwalk. Do you remember them.?"

"And the Globe Threatre, when it *was* a theatre, bought a lot of his stuff for props and for costumes, so I'm told," added Mrs. Kornfeld. "The wardrobe mistress at the Globe, when it went into Burlesque, was a member of the Magyar Club years ago and we knew her well. She helped "fit" the girls and did a lot of the sewing and alterations for them. She said that Mr. Nagy's costumes and dress goods were all of the finest quality material and that even the dress manikins were imported. I always laughed because she made such a big thing out of it, and when you think about it, how much material would you need for burlesque costumes?"

Mr.Kornfeld chuckled heartily, as if reviewing in his memory some of those scantly clad burlesque ladies of the past.

As Tom and I walked out of the restaurant, I poked him gently in the ribs. "You see, I had it right. *There is a connection* between "Miss Pengo" and Imre."

I began to spin out what I had told Tom previously about my version of what happened on the night Rachel was about to leave the Rendezvous Bar, but I added a new twist:

"Suppose Rachel followed Imre from the Rendezvous Club into the Exhibit Hall instead of leaving the Club with the rest of the crowd. She might have gone with Imre simply to keep from ruining her new shoes. I told you that before. Remember, the water was over the curb on Kentucky Avenue. Now suppose she accidently fell in the dark and broke her neck. No murder involved. A total accident. Unexpected. With no warning.. It was pitch black in that building. I don't remember any windows when we were there, do you?"

I paused for a moment to recreate the scene, and Tom remarked: "Haven't we gone through this scenario before?" "Yes, I answered," but I have a new twist." He groaned at the thought.

"Imre is in the dark — probably dropped his flashlight — and frantically feeling around the rubbish in the back of the building where the door to the Club is located. He might have picked up one of the dress manikins that Mrs. Kornfeld talked about from all that stuff stored back there, and maybe he *thought* it was Rachel. Remember how realistic little Miss Pengo was?. Completely articulated. Her legs and arms flopping about, just like when the lifeguard carried her from the boat. " I continued my little tale, but Tom's face told me that he wasn't buying it. Too complicated. Nevertheless . . .

"Thinking *'she'* was Rachel, suppose Imre carried her to the side door and hoped to give her some air but never expected ocean waves outside. And then, just suppose he was suddenly hit by a heavy wave as he opened the door —remember the pictures of that tsunami in the Far East— and the manikin slipped from his arms and suddenly floated away with the surge into the darkness. Dress manikins in Europe at that time were often life size with legs and all. Not just a metal base like American ones. How was he to know it wasn't Rachel?"

Tom threw up his arms with that. "Maybe you ought to give *me* some air before you finish that yarn!" But I continued.

"What about the old Russian exhibit that Imre said was still stored there? The one I saw on the Million Dollar Pier as a child. Wasn't there a red-headed Russian girl lying beside the sleigh where the peasant was fighting with the wolf? Perhaps that was little Miss Pengo, and perhaps that's the manikin Imre picked up while he was feeling around in the pitch black. At any rate, he picked up *something in the dark* that he imagined to be Rachel and lost it to the waves. He might have jumped in after it for all we know. But the current was much too strong. And remember that it was pitch black" Tom smiled and said softly: "One chance in ten million of that sequence of events. Especially the part about the gypsy girl. Imagine winning at any table in any casino in Atlantic City with those kinds of odds."

I carried on with my theory even though I began to feel a bit "shaky" as I drew my conclusion.

"In the morning when he woke up and found Rachel still lying in the spot where she fell the night before, he must have gone mad. He quickly hid her body among some of the junk at the back of the building until he could decide what to do next. After a day or so, after his mind cleared, he decided to get rid of the body just as he had the mannikin — on another dark night with the tide running in. No wonder he commit suicide when he came to his senses. He knew that no one would believe his explanation when they considered him as Igor, the wild Cossack. As I said before , when the police called and wanted to speak to him again he must have had visions of his interrogations in Vietnam, the beatings, the cage, Poor man, Poor wretched man. He was totally innocent. And so is Matt Nolan."

Tom took my hand. "Let it go, Lillian. Let it go. We've been over that scenario before. Please don't get involved again. Let's move on and leave the detective work to the detectives."

"Well they seem to be doing a very poor job of it, " I said. "The mark on Little Miss Pengo's bum connects the dots, don't you see! It wasn't a coincidence that she floated up when and where she did. Even the small bits of information that we've uncovered can probably rule out Matt Nolan and save Imre's reputation and end the story just where it should be ended — without a murder at all."

"Let it go," Tom repeated with the slightest hint of frustration in his voice — something I didn't want to hear. "It just drags us down into the whole mess again," he said. "Nobody cares. And take it from me, Jack Nolan's attorneys are probably already prepared to spring Matt." Tom shook his head. "I just can't take the stress, Lillian. I've had too much stress in the past couple weeks and after what I've been through I think just a little bit more would kill me. I mean it.

Honestly, I mean it. And to be honest, I don't want to take another nickel from Jack Nolan or his lawyers. It just isn't right and I don't know why I started in the first place."

That was enough. He didn't need to say more. Tom was more important to me than anyone else in the world. I couldn't risk losing him. I stopped right where I was, threw my arms around him, put both hands on his cheeks and kissed him. I mean **really** kissed him. "You'll hear no more from me," I said. "**Case closed**. Let's go home. "

He put his arm around my waist and we walked the few blocks to our beautiful little apartment atop the Mexican Restaurant with the magnificent view of the ocean where we would live happily for the rest of our lives. End of story.

But it was **not** the end of the story. The end worked itself out with just a bit more help from us, and here's how it happened.

About three months later, after Tom and I were well settled in at our apartment on St. James, and had already made several trips to Pittsburgh to check on Mary Catherine, as well as taking a week's vacation in Florida and another in New York where we stayed with Sue Roberts and her husband and had a marvelous time – and promised to stay with them again and maybe accompany them on a trip to Paris — and now were preparing for Christmas 2010 together— **that's when it happened.**

It began with a late evening call from Jake. He sounded agitated and eliminating the small talk, came right to the point. "You'll see it in the papers tomorrow, " he began, "So I thought I should alert you before you read it for yourself or watch it unfold on "Today in Philly' on Station 11."

He paused to clear his throat.

"It seems that one of my account executives was caught with his hand in the pie. There was one of those unannounced visits from the State Auditor and by mid morning he discovered some figures that didn't add up."

His voice was shaking as he told me, and I expressed shock without my usual banter. I knew this was a very serious matter, possibly shaking the foundation of the company. I've always recognized that Jake is a bit of a snob, but after all, he is a Coates and has a solid Quaker core of honesty and fair dealing. He prides himself on being able to select employees of the highest caliber, and must surely feel betrayed.

"I trusted him," he said. "He was one of my up-and-coming young account executives and headed for bigger things. But he let me down personally, and the company, too. The auditor laid out all the details on my desk. He was kiting!"

"I think I know what you mean, Jake, but explain exactly what happened. I needn't ask whether you were personally involved. I know better."

Jake gave me the full details. "Kiting", he explained, "is creating lines of credit under fictitious names and then transferring the funds into accounts controlled by fellow conspirators, or perhaps to friends or relatives. It was a tricky business in the past, requiring the total and undivided attention of the "kiter". It was like juggling balls in the air, catching one and transferring another without dropping them. And hoping the state or federal auditor wouldn't make an unannounced call at an inappropriate moment. That's about as simple an explanation as I can give you, Lillian. But today, with e-commerce it becomes much easier to control the process if you have enough electronic savvy and hold a position of trust. Really, Lillian, it's a simple matter of programming the system and pushing the right buttons. But very difficult to observe. And it makes the boss –that's me – look like a real chump."

"Can you tell me who it was, Jake. Would I know him, or her?"

"That's why I'm calling you. It was Raymond Balcer, the young man I introduced you to when you brought Mrs.Egron to the office last summer. You remember him, of course."

"Of course," I answered. "How could I forget.?"

I paused for a moment and then said, with some hesitation, "Did he play with Ruth's accounts?"

Jake said right out what I was thinking. "Mrs .Egron had **exactly** the type of accounts he was targeting. Yes, Mrs.Egron's accounts are involved as well as the accounts of a good many more of those widows he mentioned during our conversation. The type of women who pay little or no attention to the "mechanics" of their finances in exchange for a friendly voice at the other end of the phone and the prompt receipt of their monthly checks."

I gasped at the thought of how much damage he could have inflicted on poor Ruth. And what about Melanie? Her name was on the accounts as well and her future depended upon them. "How much did she lose?" I asked with a lump in my throat, and not the proverbial kind.

Jake was very reassuring. "Mr.Balcer is bonded, of course, and we have adequate insurance covering such matters. It happens in the banking business and in financial planning firms such as our own. To be honest, I don't know the full extent of the damage at this point. Just the broadest details of how Balcer was caught in the act. Electronic transactions also leave a trail, after all, and maybe a more traceable and permanent trail than when everything was all done on paper, if you know what you're looking for "

"What will you tell Ruth?" I asked.

"Here's where I need a big favor from you, Lillian" he said. "We pride ourselves on working with clients on a more personal basis than some other firms. I think we both recognize immediately the character and educational level of Mrs. Egron. A lovely lady, but one who could lean either way in a matter like this: either pure panic when she hears the news or complete trust when she believes the reassurances of a friendly party,"

"Jake, if you tell me honestly that her investments are safe, I'll call her personally and even make a trip up to Trenton to explain it to her, face to face. Can you promise me that from the bottom of your Quaker heart?" "Yes, I can," he answered. "But she needs to know that there'll be a lot of ugly publicity and innuendos in the press. It will all pass, but her money remains safe. Every penny of it. Of course I don't need to tell you that the Board of Directors might have my head. But whether that happens or not, her checks will continue to come to her under the same conditions as in the past. *I promise*."

Jake paused for a moment and I could almost feel his shame flowing through the wires. "You know the sad thing, Lillian, is that I really liked the young man. I brought him up from nothing. He comes from a poor family and he went to a small state college in northern New Jersey near Newark. He wanted to be a math teacher but he told me that after he spent his year-in-training – his student teaching – in a large center city school he became completely disillusioned. He staked everything he owned – plus most of what his parents owned — on an enrollment at Wharton. He was a super student and when we read his resume and his.excellent references, I insisted that we take him on. And for the past six years we haven't been disappointed. He was headed for big things until this came along. I'm ashamed of him, but most of all, of myself. But I promise you that all our clients' accounts are perfectly safe, no matter how the media reports it.

I told Jake that his word was good enough for me. After all, I have a chunk of money over there, too. Another word needn't be said. I promised I'd make a call to Ruth in the morning and be with her by the afternoon to explain what was happening. The chance to see Melanie again would be well worth the trip in any case.

After I hung up, I told Tom all the details I knew. He understood completely that I had to go. He always understands. That's the kind of man he is. That's why I love him and will continue to love him until one or the other of us . . . . no, let me put it another way.

I'll love him day by day, and one day at a time. We'll hang on together like barnacles, and no storm will part us. **Well said, don't you think?** And so, off to Trenton.

Chapter Twenty Six

Dillon: *"She lived a long and very active life".*

Summer passed and the fall as well, and this morning we had a sprinkle or two of snow on the Boardwalk Lillie wondered if it was okay for her to telephone Melanie and wish her a Merry Christmas. I told her to "go ahead". It was time.

Lillie told me that Ruth was delighted to hear from her and more than willing to have her come up to Trenton for a visit after the New Year, and that she could hear Melanie's squeals of excitement before Ruth put her on the phone. Lillie promised a gift and I knew that just seeing Melanie again was a gift of her own beyond comparison.

That's why I didn't discourage her from going. It gave her a good reason to connect with the Egron case again which I knew was still a shadow in the back of her mind. She never speaks about it with me because she knows how I feel about it. For me, it's over. Finished. The press, the police, and himself, Tom Dillon – as the Irish would say — have passed on to other things.

I'm back working with the coroner's office again and doing a good job if I have to say so. Mary Catherine is happy in her new digs and we see her at least once a month, plus holidays. I fit nicely into the little apartment on St. James and enjoy our mini-vacations, especially going up to New York from time to time and staying with the Roberts. Sue is something else! Sharp as a tack. And funny in a nice way. And her husband has become a good friend. It's always nice to have your hosts beg you to stay a little longer.

When Lillie returned, she was ecstatic about the qualty time she was able to spend with Melanie. And to make it better, Ruth suggested that Melanie spend a week or two with us in the summer. You can imagine how well that idea went over. Lillie is already making plans.

Lillie has a secret. I know her well enough to sense when she's holding something back from me. She has such an open, totally transparent personality that the strain of not sharing a thought or an idea with me is almost like telling me a lie. Which is something I've never known her to do. So I go with the flow and don't ask any questions because sooner or later I know she'll share it with me in her own good time when she's sure it won't upset me.

It didn't take long.

She told me early one morning as we sipped coffee on our little veranda watching a pale-looking sun rise over the ocean. There were red clouds tinged with orange on the horizon, and she said very quietly, "sailor take warning," Then she rose from the chair and gathered together her "cat rations" as I called them, for her trip down to the beach.

"Look", I said, "I know something's bothering you, so why don't you come out with it and we'll talk it over. I know you want to tell me. You're just busting to tell me. So ***whatsup***, as we say in Lawrenceville? Does it have something to do with Jake? Is he in big trouble with the bank examiners?

She told me that Jake was fine and that Ruth and Melanie were fine, and that all the depositors, including herself, have been reassured about their accounts. It had nothing to do with that, she said. " But there ***is*** something troubling me", she admitted..

"While I talked with Ruth," she said, "A big bright light suddenly went on in my brain and as I added two and two. I think I have the answer to what happened to Rachel. In fact, I think I know ***exactly*** who killed her, and yes, I think it was definitely a murder and not an accident. And I think I know ***why*** she was murdered."

"That's a mouthful," I said. "So what's it all about?" She told me that she hadn't discussed it with Ruth because she didn't have quite enough evidence to do that yet, but she was sure. *Totally sure*. It couldn't have been anyone else, because no one else would have had such a strong motive.

I was dumbfounded and maybe a bit angry about her going back to this thing that we tried so hard to forget. On the other hand, I knew she had it right this time or she wouldn't have said another word about it to me. I proved her wrong so many times before. And she knew how strongly I felt about dropping the matter.

Lillie looked at me for a clue as to whether she should continue. I nodded and said I wanted to hear more because she seemed so certain.

"I *am* certain," she said, and you will be, too, when you put all the pieces together like I have. And then she came out with her story. All of it. And this time, very convincing.

"I was having a very pleasant visit with Ruth," she said."Melanie was reading quietly from the book I brought her. Actually she was looking at the pictures more than reading, but doing very well. I bought it in the bookshop in the 30th Street Station. It's very large and beautifully illustrated, with all the fairy tales and little stories that I remember so well. She especially liked the one about the little ducklings who wore rubber shoes and carried umbrellas. "

"Well anyway," she continued, "Ruth started reminiscing about Rachel. Her daughter was still very much on her mind and she talked about how bright Rachel was at Melanie's age, and how she, too, could read before she went into First Grade. Tears came to her eyes, of course, as she continued telling me about Rachel's school years."

"She told me that Rachel would have celebrated her tenth Atlantic City High School reunion this year," Lillian added with a sigh. "She said that Rachel was always so pleased that she graduated with the Class of '00. It was such a big joke with her and all her other friends and classmates."

Lillie said that after Ruth wiped her eyes, she picked up a high school year book which lay in a small bookcase next to her chair.

"Here's her senior yearbook," Ruth said as she opened it and pointed to photos showing Rachel as a student librarian and as a member of the high school band. "She was very talented," Ruth said, "but also very smart. Especially in math and bookkeeping, She got straight A's in both. And a whiz at the computer. Way ahead of the other kids with the computer. She didn't date then, unlike some of the other girls her age. But from what her friends told me, she had a crush on one of her teachers. Who didn't experience things like at seventeen. I didn't pry. I knew she would have been embarrassed about something like that. And it was just a school girl crush."

Lillie told me that as they moved through the pages of the yearbook very slowly, Ruth would stop here and there to point out some activity or another where Rachel was involved, pausing to remember what a beautiful and talented child she was, just ten years before. Lillie said that no mother should live long enough to see her child die before she did, and of course, Lillie knew that from her own experience. I guess that's why they were able to hit it off so well together.

"Then," Lillie continued, "Ruth replaced the yearbook into the bookshelf and pulled out another.

"This is the '99 yearbook," Ruth said. "You'll see how much younger she looked. Only sixteen at that time but still pretty as a picture. Do you want to look through it while I make some coffee for us and put some cookies on a pretty plate for Melanie? There aren't many pictures of Rachel in this yearbook. She was so shy then."

Lillie admits that she's a kind of connoisseur of yearbooks, having been the editor of her own high school's edition in 1951 and a member of the staff that produced the Bryn Mawr annual in 1955. She told me that she leafed through Rachel's book looking more for production features than students. How did they cover the faculty, for example?

She explained that this was always a sore point for yearbook editors. In college yearbooks, of course, it's impossible to show all of the faculty photos and even if they were able to allot enough space, there would have been questions about "who should be in and who should be left out." College professors are very touchy about status and positioning and things like that. But in high school books, the photo of every teacher has to be featured and there's always the question of how much space to reserve for them . . . big pictures or little pictures; in groups or separate? After all, as we all know, teachers aren't *nearly* as important as the Seniors who deserve very large pictures and long write ups in prime space.. Lillie says there's a lot more involved with yearbook production than most people realize.

At this point I asked Lillie to get to the point, which she did. And what a shocker.

She told me that as she skimmed over the faculty pages *she suddenly stopped dead* – a good choice of words in light of what happened – as she recognized a familiar face and verified it with the caption below it: *Student Teacher: Bookkeeping; Computer Science; Assistant Wrestling Coach: Raymond C. Balcer.*

"There he was," said Lilllie. "Raymond Balcer! A ten-year younger Raymond Balcer, soon to leave teaching forever and move on to the Wharton School of Business, and then on to the distinguished financial investment firm of Emory, Drexel and Coates, Rittenhouse Square, Philadelphia."

As a student teacher, Lillie said, he would certainly have met pretty Rachel Egron, an A+ honor student in both math, accounting and bookkeeping, and a computer whiz no less. Wouldn't they have attended classes together as teacher and student for at least nine months during the period 1998-99? And wouldn't they have made an immediate connection – this very pretty sixteen year old girl and this handsome teacher not more than 6 or 7 years older than herself? Of course she had a crush on him. And of course she wouldn't have mentioned him to her mother.

I suddenly remembered that Balcer expressing complete surprise when Jake Coates mentioned that Rachel had worked in one of the casinos? And now that I think of it, he said he supposed that she was one of those **well-to-do society types** when she first started doing business with the company. And he made a broad accusation that perhaps she was involved in the drug trade because it would be difficult to account for her money any other way in such a short span of time.

Lillie nodded her head in agreement as I started to put the pieces together. She suggested that Mr. Balcer's presence at the company was without a doubt the very reason Rachel picked Jake's firm for her financial transactions. Perhaps Mr. Balcer suggested it. "And I suppose" Lillian went on, "they renewed their relationship as they conducted business transactions together at least once and or twice a week for five years or more. And here's a thought. Maybe Rachel revealed her drug dealing to him. Maybe she involved him in some extra curricular activities such as delivering drugs to 'larger personalities' — if you know what I mean. Apparently he already had serious cash problems before he met her. That's only conjecture, but we know from the facts of his arrest that he desperately needed money. Maybe he gambled too much. There's another avenue to pursue."

I had to chime in myself. It was all very convincing as I began to make sense of it. Regardless of the details of their relationship, I pointed out to Lillie that the key to the whole picture, it seems to me, is the fact that when she and Ruth met him for the first time at Jake's office in Philly, he never mentioned his prior relationship with Rachel back in high school, did he? Not even as a good conversation opener. For some reason he never mentioned a word of it. He gave the impression that he knew her only from his brief financial transactions with her a few moments each week. Undoubtedly there was a closer relationship that he didn't want to share. He was married after all.

"Exactly," said Lillian. "When Rachel caught him with his hands in the money drawer he had to silence her, didn't he? And it angers me to think that he even suggested that her mother might be involved in the drug trade as well. Don't you remember when he mentioned that in Jake's office?"

When you put it all together, I said, Rachel knew where every penny of her money was invested and she was savvy enough to be able to track it on her personal computer, probably on a day-to-day basis . . . which I'm sure she did. Now let's imagine that she caught Mr.Balcer with an incorrect balance or a strange movement of the money in or out of her mother's accounts . . . something of that sort. It's called "kiting". But Rachel would have caught on. She didn't work in a casino as a pit boss without having her eyes open for the slightest glitch where money was concerned.

Lillian picked up on that. "No, of course she would have caught on. And when she agreed to meet him, and finally confronted him – let's say outside the Rendezvous Club on the evening of the storm –well, figure out the rest of the story yourself. Didn't the bartender tell us there was a suspicious visitor to the club who walked in, looked around, and walked back out again? Was it Balcer, and might he have decided to wait in his car until he saw her coming out? "

Like a guy when he breaks up with his girl, I theorized, Balcer knew that if he arranged to meet her in a public place — in a bar — she'd be less likely to scream at him or make a scene. But then maybe he caught a glimpse of Matt Nolan, who of course he remembered from high school. Or, because of the storm, he decided to wait outside."

"And what happened when she got into the car?" surmised Lillian. "Some strong words from Rachel? Threats to expose him? We can only imagine. But it must have ended badly. He had a wrestler's 'moves', as we know. She was fragile. She struggled. He gave her neck a bad twist. It was an accident. *Maybe* it was an accident. But we know he drove around with her in the trunk for a day or so before he dumped her in the ocean."

Lillian suggested that I pass this information directly to the Coroner. She's right. He can order an inspection of Balcer's car – front seat and trunk. If there are fibers that match the clothes we looked at on the day she washed up on the beach, it'll be enough to indict him. The best part is that he's "contained" already on the embezzlement charges.

He'll do four or five years for that, and in the meantime the police, the DA, the Coroner – every one of them will have time to dust off their files and start again. There'll be other clues from the car. With the forensic techniques they have today, they can pick up the trace of a something that Balcer overlooked. He might even confess. White collar felons sometimes do that if they can claim it was an accident and can make a plea bargain. And if the Coroner makes a few political points with his conclusions . . . who knows . . . he might even give me a raise! Or put me on the job permanently.

"I was hoping it might get him elected Governor," Lillie said. "But just one more thing," she said with a long sigh. "It's what always complicates this case. Who was Miss Pengo, our little mannikin? I mean, what was she doing in the ocean on that particular day after the storm and the day before Rachel washed up on the beach?"

"That, my dear, we shall probably never know," I said, squeezing both her hands in mine very gently, as if to keep them from getting any further involved in this highly complicated case.

"The only thing we know for sure from all of this," I said, " is that Miss Pengo, our little mannikin, is not a penguin, but a Hungarian lady of indeterminate age and questionable reputation with painted lips and red hair, and that she's had a long and very active life and died, as she might have wished to, in a very flamboyant and theatrical style. A Zsa Zsa, if you will. I think she must have been well over eighty years old – possibly much older— and she would have loved the way she left the scene, carried off in the arms of a handsome young lifeguard."

Lillian chuckled very softly and sweetly. "It just goes to show that in Year2011, seventy-seven is really just the youth of old age. There's still plenty of life ahead and even the ending can be exciting. Don't you agree?" Then she added with a smile:

"And I think the cats down on the beach are unanimous in that."

Chapter Twenty Seven

Lillian: *"Didn't I tell you I'd have the last word"*

Even in this unisex age one must admit that women always have the last word. So I don't mind adding a few short paragraphs about what's happened in the two years since Tom and I met on the beach that summer morning in 2009. Life goes on just as the tides ebb and wane, and we two old barnacles hang on quite contentedly in our little apartment that overlooks the sea.

We haven't married –yet – and it's not because we don't love each other but simply because we both come from a generation that respects a decent and extended period of waiting/ mourning — call it what you will— following the death of a spouse.

Mary Catherine has been watching the calendar, however, and held a reception for Tom and I at St. Lawrence O'Toole's parish hall in Pittsburgh to celebrate our "engagement" last year. She invited all their friends and neighbors from the old neighborhood, as well as her new friends at the "Home." It was her way of saying: "I've been watching the clock. *It's time. Now it's okay to do it whenever you please and be happy.*" The Irish respect death but love life more.

Yes, I still feed the cats, and Tom continues his part-time work with the Force here in Atlantic City. There was a new tv series which debuted last year and Tom was asked to appear in some of the shots. He even had a few lines of dialogue. It's all about Atlantic City in the 1920's, and they made him dress like a cop of that era. They even consulted me with respect to a set which looked like the entrance to the Traymore. Imagine that. Then as a courtesy, they included me in the crowd shots taken in the Nereus Ballroom – or at least as they imagined it to be. Tom says they picked me out right away because

233

I was "haughty" enough to represent a rich dame in the gilded 20's. Quite a compliment. I think? Perhaps I should look up "haughty" in my Oxford Dictionary. The English know best about how to express those things.

Matt Nolan is free, of course. Jack continues to looks out after him. It's his brother, after all: warts and all. With all his faults, I find something decent in Jack, although Tom doesn't quite see it that way. Mr. Balcer's life hangs in the balance, particularly since the police found a very small semi-precious stone from Rachel's lovely shoes in his trunk. I leave him to his fate. Jake's company has been cleared of any misdoings. The Kornfelds still make the best stuffed cabbage in the world, and the Sanmartino's haven't raised my rent. They need to replace the kitchen appliances in their restaurant to meet new city sanitary standards. I suggested extending them a personal loan at a 1.5% rate. It's about what I get on my checkbook interest. In a moment they moved from being desperate to ecstatic as Mrs. Sanmartino smothered me with kisses and multiple Spanish blessings. They don't know that I'm putting the 1.5 away as a graduation gift for their oldest son who plans to go to Rutgers next fall. I continue to have much to be thankful for.

Miss Parker passed away, very quietly and gently a few weeks ago, just after she passed her ninetieth birthday. With a book of poetry in her hands. All of Atlantic City mourned.

Mr.Bankowitz made some changes in his operations and is now the "Junior Partner" of the firm, while his son, Mr.Banks, is the "Senior Partner." Bankowitz is a very wise man.

And now the best of it: Rachel's mother has decided to return to Atlantic City and take a small apartment in the controlled rent area near the Lighthouse. She wonders if I still would be interested in registering Melanie at the Friend's School. Would I ever! I can hardly contain myself. So she'll be going to Bryn Mawr after all. Will I live to see her graduate? I'm certainly going to try.

Gary Bauer turned up at the farm in Garden City, Kansas. Very thin, very pale and very sick. His mother and father welcomed him with open arms, somewhat like the story of the Prodigal Son. I doubt he'll last much longer , but at least he'll die between clean sheets and holding loving hands. I weep to think about it.

Tom and I are both 77 now. But we still find life sweet. And we seem to have all our wits about us. At least that's what we keep telling ourselves. I had a gall bladder operation last summer but was home the same day, eating ice cream on the veranda. Not so long ago I'd have been recuperating for weeks.

Tom volunteers for medical projects involving "old people" at the hospital. The latest one is a balance study where they place him in a harness before he does his walking exercises just in case he stumbles. Fat chance of that! He's always proud to be in "the control group", and they pay him a bit of spending money for his efforts.

Susan and her husband have scheduled us for a cruise with them to Fiji in February. Tom says that's a long ways from Lawrenceville, in more ways than one.

I asked Tom if he had anything to add, and he told me that I've undoubtedly told you everything he would have said.

By the way, I looked up the word "haughty" in Webster's and it's defined as *"disdainfully proud; arrogant."* But my Oxford Dictionary, on the other hand, describes haughty as: *"of exalted character, style, or rank; eminent; high-minded; aspiring."* The British got it right. That's exactly what I am. Or what I think I am. Didn't I tell you I'd have the last word!"

The End